A Brain. A Heart. The Nerve.
by
Ann S. Epstein

Alternative Book Press
2 Timber Lane
Suite 301
Marlboro, NJ 07746

www.alternativebookpress.com

A Brain. A Heart. The Nerve.

Publication Data
Ann S Epstein [2018]
A Brain. A Heart. The Nerve/ by Ann S. Epstein—1st
ed. Ask Publisher for Further Publication Information

ISBN 978-1-940122-43-4 Printed in the United States
of America 10 9 8 7 6 5 4 3 2 1

To little people with big dreams

TABLE OF CONTENTS

PART ONE
Most Sincerely Dead
Culver City, 1938
Chapters 1-4
PART TWO
And Your Mangy Little Dog Too
Berlin, 1935
Chapters 5-8
PART THREE
A Place Where There Isn't Any Trouble
London, 1936
Chapters 9-12
PART FOUR
Feed Those Hogs Before They Worry Themselves into Anemia
New York City, 1937
Chapters 13-16
PART FIVE
There's a Storm Blowing Up, A Whopper
Hollywood, 1942
Chapters 17-23
PART SIX
I Think I'll Miss You Most of All
New York City, 1955
Chapters 24-31
PART SEVEN
And, Oh, What Happened Then Was Rich
Liberty, 1964
Chapters 32-40
PART EIGHT
Now Which Way Do We Go?
Los Angeles, 1970
Chapters 41-45
PART NINE
Looking for My Heart's Desire
Dornum, 1980
Chapters 46-50

PART ONE
Most Sincerely Dead
Culver City, 1938

Chapter 1

Meinhardt Raabe didn't want to be one of 122 nameless Munchkins in *The Wizard of Oz*. He was after a one-of-a-kind role. Not that it would pay more money. Everyone in the singing midget troupe got $125 a week, less than Toto the dog, and their manager, Baron Leopold Van Singer, stole most of that. What he craved was the dignity of a distinct part to stand out above the others.

A movie grip had hung the script high on a chain beside the audition list to prevent the midgets from stealing or defacing it. The crew called them runty pimps, whores, and gamblers, ready to proposition studio electricians for a few extra bucks. Judy Garland told *Variety* that the "little people" got smashed every night until police scooped them up in butterfly nets and dumped them back in their hotel rooms. The press believed a pampered 17-year-old girl, as if she had a right to pass judgment on adults who'd fled a Nazi force bent on sterilizing or killing them.

Meinhardt's neck ached from looking up to read the script. He was searching for a crate to stand on when Charles Becker came up beside him. Both had escaped Berlin as young men and met two years later in New York, busking on the corner of Broadway and 45th. Meinhardt had been ready to fight for the coveted spot when the easy-going Charles readily conceded it to him. If they occasionally found themselves vying for customers on a busy corner after that, they'd sing a duet and Charles let Meinhardt keep the take before moving on. Crowds got a kick out of watching a midget duo with faint German accents sing and soft-shoe to "Tea for Two."

"What are you thinking of auditioning for?" Charles asked.

"Mayor or coroner," Meinhardt answered.

"Not a member of the Lollipop Guild trio. Certainly not one of the Lullaby League ladies."

Charles chuckled. "I'll be happy with anything, even the Lullaby League, but I'm too flat-footed to stand on tippy-toe and warble."

The fact that Meinhardt was seeking a role at all still surprised him. Until a few months ago, his dream was to open a high-end clothing store for men and women. Owning a business meant he could hold up his head with pride, and make his Oma Gretel, the grandmother who'd raised him, proud too. She was a seamstress who'd taught him her craft as he played with fabric scraps and spools of thread at her feet. If he could bring her to America, Meinhardt would guarantee her the same dignity in old age that she'd tried to instill in him as a child. But the Depression and looming war had stranded her in Germany, while propelling him across an ocean. It was she who'd urged him to flee three years ago, soon after his twentieth birthday.

Motivated by the memory of his Oma, Meinhardt ignored the crimp in his neck as he turned the script's pages. The mayor's part sounded obsequious, a tiny man ingratiating himself with Oz's full-sized residents. The coroner, by contrast, broadcast authority when he pronounced the Witch of the East "not merely dead, but really most sincerely dead." That line clinched it. "My baritone seems better suited for the coroner," he told Charles.

"In that case," his friend said, "I'll try out for the mayor."

The costume sketches beside the script confirmed Meinhardt's choice. The mayor's plaid vest and olive green cutaway coat looked foolish compared to the dignified coroner's outfit, a deep-blue frock with emerald sleeves over a light blue cassock. The wide-brimmed hat would partly hide the big spit curls the makeup department painted on the bald-capped heads of all the Munchkin males.

Even Tommy Cottonaro, the bearded man, had to suffer those babyish locks.

Meinhardt resolved to talk with the head of makeup. Just because midgets were short was no reason to treat them like children. If he got the part, he'd also tell Adrian Greenberg, the costume designer, to pad his shoulders. Adrian had introduced that look in women's fashions to make them appear more powerful. It would add stature to a small man's image too.

Charles and Meinhardt walked to the film set where the midgets sometimes got extra cash for odd jobs. Today they were shooting the scene where Dorothy and her companions — the Scarecrow, Tin Woodsman, and Cowardly Lion — were taken by horse-drawn carriage to meet the Wizard. Charles hoped they'd need someone to shovel horse shit. Meinhardt wouldn't scoop dreck, but he'd gladly keep the horse calm between takes with apples and sugar cubes, a few of which he planned to pocket. Between their meager wages and Van Singer's skimming, he was often hungry. He missed his Oma's *Apfelstrudel*, but stolen horse treats might allay his craving.

"I went with Hazel to the Brown Derby last night," Charles said. Hazel Derthick was one of the few women in the cast shorter than Charles. "I won't see her again if you're interested."

"I'm not. She's yours." Meinhardt offered a blank face, practicing his acting.

Charles raised his tiny hands. "I just like company for dinner. Besides, Hazel's eyes are only for you. And near as I can tell, you return her gaze."

Meinhardt fidgeted. He hoped his attraction wasn't that obvious. From now on, he'd direct his eyes elsewhere. Ditto his heart. Wanting something was a worthwhile challenge, wanting someone was too big a risk. Rodge, the legless veteran Meinhardt had met during the year he lived in London before sailing to America, used to say, "If affection does not dictate kindness, let decency do it." Meinhardt wanted to be treated decently, but he didn't count on kindness, and certainly not affection. Normal-size women would automatically reject him, but he shuddered to think a short woman might take him because she couldn't do better. Pursuing work was safer than chasing love.

When Charles and Meinhardt reached the set, a white horse was being hitched to the carriage in a third attempt to shoot the scene. Victor Fleming, the film's sixth director, was impatient. The horse was supposed to change color as it pranced through Emerald City, while the carriage driver quipped it was "a horse of a different color." The crew had slathered the beast with purple paint but the ASPCA objected that it was toxic. Next they tried liquid candy with extra food coloring, but it was too pale and tasted too good. The horse licked it off. Today they were using a paste made of Jell-O powder. Buckets of grape, strawberry, and orange stood at the ready.

The job of shit sweeper had already been given to Joey Polinsky, a troupe member known as The Count, only he wasn't getting extra pay. Baron Van Singer had assigned him dreck duty as punishment for showing up late the day before. A makeup artist claimed to have heard a whining sound coming from the men's room and discovered that Joey, who often drank lunch, had fallen into the toilet and couldn't get out. Meinhardt didn't trust the story. Jack Dawn's crew treated them like children. More than once, Meinhardt had swatted away their hands when they'd lifted him into the barber's chair rather than let him climb up himself. Still, he couldn't deny that yesterday The Count had arrived late and wet. He'd offered him a pair of dry trousers, but Joey had scoffed they were too short, even though he was barely half an inch taller than Meinhardt.

Several other Munchkins had also gathered at the yellow brick road to watch the filming, gossiping about the art department bickering for a week over the color. Charles, who was friendly with everyone, joined them. Meinhardt preferred to keep to himself, but he walked over too so he wouldn't look conspicuous. Midgets could be vindictive if they thought you were uppity. He wanted to stay on their good side if a time ever came when he needed their help.

"Did you hear what Bert Lahr told *Variety*?" asked Little Billy Rhodes.

"No, but I hear you tried to strangle your wife last night."

"Lahr said we brandished knives and developed unrequited passions for normal cast members."

"Judy Garland isn't normal. She's half an inch shy of five feet."

"Little Billy did try to strangle his wife," said Mickey Carroll, a soldier in the Munchkinland scene. "I had to threaten him with my toy bayonet before he let her go."

Charles looked disappointed. "Sounds like all the fun was over by the time Hazel and I got back last night. We should have skipped the Brown Derby and gone to the Hollywood Bar."

Being alone and sober in his room at the Culver Hotel suited Meinhardt better. He felt uneasy about the policemen stationed on every floor, like the Gestapo, but their presence had shifted the midgets' drinking and sex orgies from the hotel lounge to Culver City's nearby bars. He understood that after being persecuted as degenerates in Germany, his peers went overboard flaunting their freedom in America. Nonetheless, he distanced himself from both their present actions and shared past.

Attention turned back to the horse. It liked the taste of the Jell-O mix too, but luckily did not find it as tasty as the liquid candy. Enough stayed on to shoot the scene, even though the director complained that the color was too pale. Something in the powder, perhaps mild doses of horse tranquilizer undetected by the ASPCA, also kept the animal calm. There was no need to feed it apples or sugar cubes. Disappointed, most of the Munchkins left to begin their day's drinking early. Meinhardt, Charles, and a few others hung around, still hoping for another crisis. Their patience was rewarded when Judy Garland complained the ruby slippers were too tight.

"That's because her feet are too big." Hazel lifted her skirt, pointed her own petite toes, and did a tight pirouette. Meinhardt looked, then looked away.

Adrian, the costume designer, asked where the shoes pinched and promised to personally stretch them. He gently pinched Garland's cheek and she giggled. The Munchkins smiled at one another, gratified to see the young star live up to her spoiled-brat reputation. Their satisfaction led to the happy recounting of the other problems besetting weeks of intense shooting. The Flying Monkeys contraptions had failed twice, breaking stunt men's limbs. Rumor had it that special effects maestro, Arnold Gillespie, had designed a full body harness, but the technician who tested it was nearly castrated. Being a eunuch was worse than being a midget.

Scariest of all was Margaret Hamilton, the Witch of the West, suffering second and third degree burns on her face and hands when a trap door failed to open during her fiery broomstick exit from Munchkinland. After a month in the hospital, she was recuperating at home while her stand-in shot scenes that didn't involve close-ups. The midgets jeered that it would be hard to find another face as ugly as hers. It wasn't really her looks they objected to. They instinctively disliked all the regular cast members for being taller and better paid.

Meinhardt shared their animosity, except when it came to Margaret. She was the only star who didn't treat them like pesky children. A kindergarten teacher before becoming an actress, she knew the difference between a five-year-old and a short adult. He also admired her. It took guts to play ugly and court hatred. Of course, it was easier for her. She could wash off her flaws at the end of the day, whereas midgets had no choice but to parade their defects forever.

Chapter 02

Meinhardt took a cab to visit Margaret in her bungalow at the bottom of the Hollywood Hills. Too bad Detroit didn't make cars for little people, but too few had the money to buy them. Nor could he depend on public transit. With a quarter of LA's workers unemployed, bus service had been cut back. He missed living in New York where, until a month ago, a nickel let him ride the subway from the Grand Concourse all the way to Coney Island.

"For you, Maggie," he said, presenting her with a jar of honey and a raw potato.

Her face, naturally thin, was more drawn and pinched with pain. Yet she managed a smile and raised her eyebrows, which were just growing back.

He explained his gift. "Honey to prevent infection and speed healing, potato juice to reduce pain and prevent scars. My Oma had remedies for everything: stomachaches, toothaches ... lash marks."

Margaret's hairless eyebrows shot up again. "You were beaten?"

"My parents got impatient if I couldn't keep up with them. Sometimes they whipped me with a switch to go faster." Meinhardt spoke without self-pity. It was a long time ago and his bitterness had faded with the marks, replaced by sweet and indelible impressions of his Oma. He told Margaret how the Jugend, or Hitler Youth, had once beaten their neighbor Mr. Schwartz and carved a Jewish star into his forehead. "Every day for a month, my grandmother bathed the old man's back and brow with egg whites. Wherever she rubbed her ointment, his body didn't scar." The emotional scars remained, however, just as the mental beating he'd taken before leaving Berlin would linger all his life. Even his Oma couldn't smooth those away.

"Any news of Milton?" Thoughts of his own childhood prompted Meinhardt to ask after Margaret's two-year-old son. She was raising him alone after her recent divorce, and her parents had brought the little boy back with them to Massachusetts while Margaret healed in California.

"Missing him hurts more than my burns." She winced as two salty tears ran down the raw skin on her cheeks. "Your visits are a good distraction for me."

Meinhardt wagged his finger. "As long as you don't mistake me for a substitute child."

"Not as long as you don't misbehave." Margaret gingerly patted her face dry with a tissue. She asked if Meinhardt was hungry or thirsty.

"I'll make tea," he said, "but not to drink." He told her a strong lukewarm brew, soaked in a bath towel, would further ease her pain and promote healing.

"Another of your Oma's tricks?"

"No, I learned that one in London. The British use tea for everything."

"I hear it makes a great witch's brew." Her attempt to cackle turned into a gasp of pain.

9

Meinhardt found the tea bags on the counter. Since her fingers were too sore to pull the cabinet handles, the aide who bathed Margaret had moved things down from the shelves. "Now you live like me," he laughed, "everything low so you can reach." He gently wrapped the burned areas with gauze, covered them with towels, and warned, "Don't let the cotton touch your skin or it will stick. My Oma taught me that. She knew all about fabrics too."

While the tea did its work, Meinhardt told Margaret about his intention to audition for the coroner. She offered to put in a good word for him since MGM "owed" her after the accident.

"Nein!" Meinhardt insisted on earning the part himself. However, since his brief acting experience was limited to the touring midget troupe, he said he'd welcome some advice.

"Don't play cute and cuddly. Use the authority you projected as a barker for Baron Van Singer. And show up for the audition sober. That'll set you apart from the rest." Margaret knew Meinhardt tried to distance himself from the Munchkins' reputation. Years before he and Charles had joined the troupe, the Baron had bought many of them from their parents and brought them from Europe to New York, where he trained them to perform. They were successful until the Depression slashed their bookings. Already angry at being outcasts, they now suffered poverty too. They escaped by sticking their thumbs in the eyes of those who looked down on them.

"I have too much self-respect to act like I'm three instead of twenty-three." Meinhardt paused. "Do you ever worry that playing the witch will make people no longer respect you?"

"Are you kidding?" Margaret snorted. "I was delighted to get the role. I was broke and being typecast as a spinster made it harder to find work.

When my agent said they wanted me to play the witch in *Oz* I was thrilled, because it was one of my favorite books. My students' too."

"I like that you're mean to Dorothy," Meinhardt confessed. "The best line is when you cackle, 'I'll get you my pretty, and your little dog too!'"

Margaret couldn't understand why he and the other midgets hated Judy Garland so much. "She's a poor sweet girl. Did you know she came to visit me in the hospital?"

"Did you know 'poor sweet' Dorothy threw a spoiled brat hissy fit last week because she decided that blue anklets make her legs look fat?"

"Judy is a confused 17-year-old who doesn't know how to handle sudden stardom. She deserves sympathy, especially from the likes of you."

"Why? Most of us were her age or younger when we had to 'handle' the Nazis and their deadly social hygiene policies."

"And did the midgets turn out any better for it?"

Meinhardt admitted most hadn't.

"So, isn't there enough sympathy to go around?" Margaret removed the towel and glared.

"I don't extend sympathy or make excuses for anyone." Meinhardt folded his arms.

"You are so stubborn!"

"Stubbornness comes from a weak will and a strong won't." Margaret loved it when Meinhardt quoted Rodge. His sayings helped buoy her spirits during the worst of the pain.

"Well, if it's any consolation," she said, "Judy lost the battle to get rid of the song 'Over the Rainbow.' She thought it was demeaning to sing it while she stood in a barnyard. Even MGM wanted to shorten the black-and white Kansas scenes and get to the color film quicker."

"Why did she lose that fight? I thought the

11

studio always took her side."

"The director thought the earlier scenes where she pestered Auntie Em and the farmhands really did make her look like a spoiled brat. He figured that singing the song would sweeten her."

"Then they should have cut it," Meinhardt pouted. "I'd be happier if she'd won the battle but lost the affections of her fans."

Margaret declared him hopeless, but smiled before disappearing under a clean towel. They sat in comfortable silence until it was time for Meinhardt to go. He rinsed the used towels and told Margaret to take daily oatmeal baths to relieve the itching once her skin began to heal.

"Goodness, so many remedies for burns! Did you often get burned as a child too?"

"Not really. I learned the itching cure when my Oma treated me for poison ivy. I used to hide from my parents in the woods beside the park. Later I hid there from the Hitler Jugend."

Chapter 03

Dearest Oma,

Wie geht es Ihnen? I'm well, but bored with so much waiting on the set. I thought about visiting the Marx Brothers. They're filming *At The Circus* and their lot must be more fun than ours. I should forgive Harpo. Rodge used to say, "The heaviest thing you can carry is a grudge." Still, Harpo betrayed me with Van Singer. He meant well, but friends should know better.

At least the wardrobe department isn't boring. I look in every day. You'd love sewing the costumes. The wicked witches of the East and West wear striped tights under black silk robes that stream behind them when they fly. Glinda, the good witch of the North, glides in a lace dress of bubble gum pink dotted with rhinestones. She wears a silver crown and waves a glittery wand. There is no good witch of the South. I think it has something to do with American history.

When we're not working or waiting, the other midgets carry on and draw criticism. Even Charles sometimes joins them. It's a relief to retire to my room, alone. The Culver Hotel is elegant — chandeliers, brocade bedspreads, and gold faucets. The chair I climb to look in the mirror when I comb my hair has an embroidered cushion and marble-inlaid armrests. My sole complaint is that there is just one bathroom per floor and my fellow cast members are not very clean. After a night of drinking, the hallways and bathrooms reek of vomit in the morning. The movie's star says at one point, "My! People come and go so quickly here." I wish it were true off screen.

Sometimes I envy the Doll siblings or married couples, who look after one another. It's not that I want to be like them. Taking care of myself is enough. Yet those with families have a sense of purpose. Some don't even bother to learn English. If my year in London was good for nothing else, it taught me to speak the language better. The few who want to improve their lot hatch cockamamie schemes. One thought he could be in baby food commercials and eat for free, as if close-ups wouldn't show the shadow of his whiskers! I don't know which is worse, the absence of ambition in some little people or their bad business sense.

I sometimes question my own dreams. I still want to open a clothing business, but I think about being an actor too. Is that crazy? I have a good voice and an agile body, if only there were parts for me. I'm auditioning to play the coroner, a starring role for a Munchkin. Wish me *Viel Glück.*

Christmas will soon be here and we have the day off. Last night I dreamed I was a young boy

13

helping you roll balls of chocolate and almond *Basler Brunsli*. Do you remember the time I cried with delight when I cut your *Baumkuchen* and saw the circles inside looking like tree rings?

Will you bake for the holiday this year or has your arthritis gotten too bad? Some of the midgets are nearing forty, only fifteen years older than me, and already they have problems with their hearts, lungs, and joints. I don't know if it is from bad living or if illness comes with our infirmity. I feel I must hurry to achieve my ambitions before I too am plagued with ill health.

I bid you *auf Wiedersehen* and *Weihnachtsgrüße*. I will write again before the new year.

Your loving Enkel,
Meinhardt

Meinhardt practiced for the audition every day. He may have lacked other desirable Aryan traits, but German discipline was bred into his genes. He arrived on the set wearing his floor-length navy blue silk dressing gown.

"*Was gibt* with the robe?" Charles asked.

Little Billy Rhodes smirked. "Don't tell me. Mr. Raabe had a beer last night and it made him so drunk he overslept this morning and came to work in his pajamas!"

"You'll see," Meinhardt told Charles. "You know I have a reason for everything I do."

Margaret was standing outside the makeup trailer talking to Mervyn Leroy, the movie's producer. She was in full witch's regalia — pointed hat, pointed nose, pointed fingernails, and pointed chin. Her hands and face were bright green and the thick paint hid her burn marks.

Meinhardt was glad she'd returned to work, until he saw the dark circles under her eyes and noticed she was sucking on a hard red candy. "A cough drop? You are sick, Maggie?"

"No." She slurped. "To make my mouth bright red so my skin looks greener."

Seeing his long robe, she raised her pointed eyebrows, half grown-back and half made-up with black hair to matched the crimped whiskers growing out of her huge chin wart.

"Balance. It's part of my strategy to win the role of coroner."

"You're sure you don't want me to put in a good word with Mr. Leroy? He'll give you the part if I vouch for you. Mervyn is someone you can trust."

"Hah! Like your pal Dorothy, I've been to Oz and seen behind the curtain."

Margaret stroked her chin hairs. "I don't understand. What did you see?"

"Smoke and mirrors. You can't trust anyone to help you. Especially big shot producers."

"Producers are the real wizards. They make the magic of movies happen."

"Believing in wizards, real or fake, opens you to getting hurt."

"Believing in wizards opens you to discovering the best in yourself."

Meinhardt folded his arms across his chest. "Be careful the grease paint doesn't infect the sores left by the burns. Wash it off gently with oatmeal soap and keep applying the raw honey."

Margaret told him to break a leg. She lifted the hem of her robe and then, secure in her ugliness, strode to the witch's castle where the flying monkeys awaited her. Meinhardt raised his own hem and walked confidently to where he could watch the tryouts for mayor. Charles was up against George Ministeri and one of the Boers brothers. He played cute and cuddly, but here the stereotype was fitting. Munchkins would in fact elect a leader who epitomized smallness.

Those auditioning for coroner assembled at the bottom of the three-step semi-circular platform where Dorothy, Glinda, and Munchkinland officials awaited the announcement of the witch's demise. Joining Meinhardt were Little Billy, Jerry Maren, and the other Boers brother.

"Didn't you just audition for the role of mayor?" asked a confused production assistant.

"I'm Henry Boers. That was my brother Theodore."

"Can't you tell?" came a voice from the back. "Henry is a quarter-inch taller."

"Where's Prince Joey?" The assistant checked the sign-up list.

"You mean The Count?"

The producer glowered. "I don't care what his royal ass calls itself. Is he here or not?"

"I believe Mr. Polinsky had a busy night at court." The same voice from the rear piped up, followed by raucous laughter.

When it was his turn, Meinhardt was glad he'd been drinking slippery elm bark tea so he could sing as low as possible without injuring his throat. The resonant depth of his voice never failed to evoke surprise. People expected midgets to talk and sing in high pitched childish voices. Some, like Charles, really did squeak. Meinhardt was sure his smooth baritone would add gravitas to the announcement that someone had been obliterated from the face of the earth.

Since the score was still in flux, Mr. Leroy asked each of them to also sing a popular song so he'd know their vocal range. Billy struck a happy note with "Pennies From Heaven," Jerry went for sad with "The Little Boy That Santa Claus Forgot," and Henry chose the angry and ironic "Small Fry." Meinhardt's mind raced through the tunes he'd sung three months ago on the streets of New York. He opted for the emotionally neutral "Heart and Soul."

It was big back East but just catching on out West, so it would sound fresh.

"Now walk up the steps," the production assistant told them. The other hopefuls looked uncertain. Meinhardt had bet, correctly, that they'd only come prepared to sing and dance. He alone had anticipated they might also be asked to mount the platform and show how they'd unfurl the witch's death certificate. The walk had to be dignified and sure-footed. With their short legs, midgets tended to hoist their bodies up the stairs, a hitched gait that appeared comical, even pathetic. Meinhardt knew the platform steps were shallow but spaced far apart, demanding a long stride. In preparation, he'd stuffed cereal boxes with newspaper and practiced mounting them without swiveling his hips. After a few days, he could climb with his eyes closed.

Billy went up the steps like someone in need of a cane, Jerry took two steps for every riser, and Henry tripped near the top. Meinhardt's feet landed on each step with precision.

Still they weren't dismissed. Mr. Leroy wanted to see them unfurl the scroll declaring the witch dead. The ends were nailed to wooden dowels and the parchment was heavier than it looked. Holding it out to the side with one hand without losing one's balance would be tricky.

Billy couldn't unroll the scroll smoothly. Jerry held it so low, it dragged on the ground. "Careful," snapped the producer as he handed it off to Henry, whose body tilted under its weight.

Meinhardt took it last and smiled to himself. Again, he'd thought ahead. The secret was to set his feet far enough apart to maintain his balance with his arm raised and outstretched. The long blue coroner's robe would make that possible during filming, hiding an actor's wide stance. The problem was the audition. Unless — and here is where his planning paid off — he tried out wearing his

17

bathrobe, which was the same length and shade of blue. Meinhardt risked looking absurd, but if he acted with poise, he'd seem like he was a natural for the part.

He was glad the bathrobe wasn't from the boys' department, which was where midgets usually shopped. It was difficult to find clothes that didn't look like they belonged on a child. Shirts and pajamas were printed with pictures of boyhood heroes. If you didn't want images of cowboys or spaceship pilots, you could choose plaid, but that wasn't flattering on people whose bodies were as wide as they were tall. Faced with either Roy Rogers or Flash Gordon insignia on flannel, Meinhardt had splurged on a custom-made navy silk dressing gown. He'd ordered it cut on the bias so the material would drape, not hang like a wide box, a trick he'd learned watching his Oma. The silk fell in long folds, making him appear taller. Not that anyone saw him wear it at home, but it made him think well of himself, alone in the evening, and dream big at night.

The last part of the performance Meinhardt had considered in preparing for the audition was how to hold his head while reading the scroll. There were three choices. He could look up at Dorothy and Glinda, but that would emphasize his shortness. If he cast his eyes down as he read to the bottom, he'd be kowtowing. But if he looked straight ahead and recited the words on the death certificate from memory, rather than reading them, he'd establish himself as their equal.

Meinhardt faced front, with a mildly aggressive stare, to show death didn't scare him.

Chapter 04

The cast list was posted two days later. Meinhardt got the role of coroner and Charles was the mayor. They shook hands and grinned.

"I'm feeling mighty big." Charles stuck his nose in the air. "*Du auch?*"

"Only if it's a stepping stone to something bigger." Meinhardt stood on his toes.

Hazel walked up to him and curtseyed. "Herr Coroner! My deepest congratulations!"

"Don't forget our Honorable Mayor." Meinhardt waved his hand toward Charles.

"You too, Charlie." She bent her knees slightly, then turned back toward Meinhardt. "I knew they'd pick you. You have the right voice and posture for the part. And the best face."

He thanked her and was about to say something about Charles again when she slipped her arm through his and sang, "I mustn't merely congratulate you. I'd like to help you celebrate too."

Meinhardt blushed and gently moved his arm away from his side until Hazel's slipped out. "That's very kind, but I need to practice my lines before filming starts." He stammered that perhaps Charles would take up her offer.

"We already went out to eat. I was hoping to go with you."

When Meinhardt again declined, she shook her dark curls and pretended to pout, but her eyes betrayed hurt. Meinhardt knew what "putting on a brave face" looked like. He and Charles watched her skip over to where the others waited for the Munchkinland scenes to resume shooting. She whispered in Joey Polinsky's ear. Then she and The Count left arm-in-arm.

Charles winked. "You'll have to give a more convincing performance if you want to play the hard-to-get romantic lead. It'll take more than balancing on your feet in a bathrobe."

Nothing he'd learned from his Oma had prepared Meinhardt for this. The knot in his stomach felt nearly as tight as when he'd faced the treachery of classmates and the Hitler Jugend. From now on he'd stick to the safety of what he knew. And what he knew best was clothing. He went to find the costume designer, who now had the added task of cataloguing the Munchkins' outfits. They'd taken to interchanging parts of their costumes between crowd scenes, forcing the furious wardrobe staff to take hundreds of photos so they could match them on subsequent takes.

"Adrian." Meinhardt climbed on a stool but the six-foot plus designer still towered over him. "I think that padding the shoulders of the coroner's robe would add stature to the role."

The designer looked down his nose. "On the contrary. It will make you look shorter. You're already taller than the other midgets. That's the reason Mervyn gave you the part."

Meinhardt caught his breath. In Berlin and London, even those who saw him as a freak, had recognized the correctness of his fashion advice. As for the winning the role, hadn't Hazel just confirmed it was due to his baritone and bearing? "Then vertical stripes? Or a taller hat?"

"Costumes spring from my imagination, not yours. If you want to sell your ideas, start your own business." Adrian picked up a bolt of red felt and turned his back on Meinhardt.

Mid-morning in Hollywood was early evening in Berlin. His Oma would be cooking a simple dinner of cabbage, potatoes, and onions. The Third Reich was rationing food so Germany could rearm. "Guns instead of butter," was General Göring's slogan for the nation's four-year plan.

"Oma, I am calling with news."

"*Wo liegt das Problem?*" she said in alarm. He rarely phoned. The cost was prohibitive.

Meinhardt quickly reassured her. "*Gute Nachrichten!* I'm the coroner of Munchkinland!"

"*Ich bin stolz auf dich!* I'm so proud. I knew

you would stand out above the others."

"Suppose that's the real reason I got picked — because I stood a little taller instead of because I was the better actor?"

"You remember the *sprichwort* I taught you?"

"We build ourselves up or tear ourselves down by the size of our efforts, not our bodies."

"*Gut!* If you work hard and act smart, decent people will notice." She said it wasn't like him to doubt himself and wondered if he was feeling lonely as the holiday season neared.

It was better to let her think he was upset about spending Christmas alone than because he'd been humiliated by Greenberg, or Hazel. He promised to spend the holiday with Charles, although he was looking forward to a quiet day by himself. He asked after her health.

"Well enough that you don't need to waste money on a phone call to find out. Now, celebrate your accomplishment and then return to the work you are good at. *Ich liebe dich.*"

He said he loved her too and would send her a drawing of his costume. After hanging up, he felt better but still shaken. He needed to tell someone else who would appreciate that his talent had earned him the role. He walked to the witch's castle, where Margaret was melting to death.

"Oh, what a world, what a world. Who would have thought a good little girl like you could destroy my beautiful wickedness? I'm going, oh ... oh!" Meinhardt and the stage hands joined Dorothy, her three friends, and the flying monkeys in celebrating her sizzling demise.

Margaret rose through the trap door and clapped too, but gently, since her hands were still sore. "I hear you also deserve a round of applause," she said to Meinhardt.

"Yes. I got the part. On my own." He hadn't

meant to sound defiant, not with Maggie.

"So you did." She extended a green hand in congratulations, then thanked him again for the home remedies. They'd allowed her to return to work sooner than predicted. If she continued to heal this rapidly, her son Milton would join her in a couple of weeks. "I owe you. Hollywood is a small-minded business, even for big people. If I can ever help you, promise you'll call."

It was time to rehearse his scene. Meinhardt joined the big people and little dog on the platform. The coroner's lines took only twelve seconds but he stood tall and proud for each one. Victor Fleming praised him for nailing the singing and moves on the first try. Meinhardt wondered how he'd feel when he performed the role in costume. Maggie had told him that dressing for the part completed an actor's transformation into character. She said it changed not only your attitude, but your whole body — nervous system, muscles, even the arrangement of your bones.

Because he'd performed so well, Meinhardt was given one more line after pronouncing the witch dead. Standing on the spiraling yellow brick road as Dorothy and Toto set off to Emerald City, he sang, "You'll go down in history." Then he bowed low as they skipped past him. The director called "Cut!" and the shoot was over. Cast and crew dispersed.

Meinhardt, lingering on the set, promised himself that he would be the one to go down in history. Never again would he bow down to anyone.

PART TWO

 And Your Mangy Little Dog Too

Berlin, 1935

Chapter 05

Meinhardt waited for the bus, rereading the help wanted ad: "Knowledgeable salesman sought for gentlemen's clothing store. Must be well-groomed and well-spoken." Applicants were directed to inquire in person at an address whose street name he recognized. His Oma often did alterations for men's and women's stores in this high-priced district, in addition to sewing for her private clients. Only the store's name, Hoffmann's Fine Suits and Haberdashery, was unfamiliar.

Getting the job would be the ideal way to celebrate his twentieth birthday, but Meinhardt wasn't optimistic. The confidence he hoped to project was threatened by the memory of over two dozen failed attempts. At one store, he'd barely crossed the threshold when the owner came out from behind the counter and blocked him from entering.

"What do you want?" The man's broad chest strained the buttons on his duo-toned jacket.

"I'm here about the job, please."

"This is a clothing store, not Circus Busch."

"I refer to the sale's position. We spoke on the phone yesterday." When Meinhardt's shaking fingers had placed the call, his voice, much steadier, had impressed the proprietor with his knowledge of expensive fabrics and skilled tailoring. He'd held out the news clipping, but the owner had crumbled and tossed it on the floor. Meinhardt hastily backed out the door.

The next establishment had hired him as delivery boy, a job Meinhardt felt compelled to take. His grandmother's business had declined as the Depression worsened and he needed to help out at home. The second week, a customer to whom he was delivering a package of mohair vests called the manager to complain that he didn't want a freak touching so much as the wrapping on his clothes. The owner was waiting outside when Meinhardt returned. He handed Meinhardt his lunch pail and apologized for firing him, but said he couldn't afford to lose a client.

Showing up in person today, without even a call to establish his credentials, was risky. Meinhardt had obsessed over how to stop Herr Hoffmann from dismissing him on sight. The pinstripe suit his Oma had finished sewing last night would help. The subtle vertical pleats in the dark gray woolen three-piece made him appear taller and slimmer, while the soft fabric and impeccable styling implied a level of income that matched the store's patrons. The bespoke suit wasn't enough to guarantee a hearing, however, so Meinhardt had devised a strategy to lure the owner into listening before waving him out the door. He would know soon enough if it worked.

Jumping from the bus's bottom step to the pavement, Meinhardt made a solid landing. The successful maneuver, which always threatened his dignity, bolstered his confidence. Then he saw the poster: "Make Germany strong again! Stop the infusion of *Lebensunwertes Leben* — life unworthy of life — into the Aryan bloodstream. Report criminal, insane, dissident, homosexual, feebleminded, and weak persons to the Genetic Health Court. Help purify *das Vaterland*."

He'd seen these signs throughout Berlin, as well as orders for Jews to register themselves. Meinhardt studied people's reactions to them. Those who stopped and smiled had probably voted for the Nazis. The ones who walked past were indifferent or oblivious to the implications. Jews, of course, were not. Nor were people like Meinhardt, who had reason to fear they were next. Anyone with a handicap could sense the posters fifty meters away. Meinhardt swore he could smell the glue on the back before he even saw the ugly words plastered across the front. His nostrils quivered now as the bus fumes dispersed and the air between him and the sign cleared.

In his last year of Gymnasium, Meinhardt's own doctor had submitted his name for sterilization under the Nazis' racial hygiene program. Only the testimony of his English teacher, who vouched for Meinhardt's intelligence, got his name removed from the T4 list. According to the papers, the appeals of over 125,000 other people in the past two years had been denied.

Meinhardt walked around the block twice, eyes cast down to avoid more posters, before he felt calm enough to approach the store. He told himself that compared to threats of sterilization and euthanasia, getting a sales job should be a piece of cake. Tonight, when he ate the *Zwetschgen Streuselkuchen* his Oma was baking, he wanted to do more than celebrate his birthday.

The look on Herr Hoffmann's face when Meinhardt entered was not promising. Aversion was followed by incredulity at the sight of a well dressed midget. Satisfied to have caught the man off guard, Meinhardt prolonged the confused silence by walking up to the bolts of fabric as if he were a customer ordering a suit. "Do you carry the new rayon fabrics?" he asked.

Herr Hoffmann stiffened. "*Nein.* Only natural fibers. If you want cheaper, go to ..."

"*Gut!*" Meinhardt interrupted. "Synthetics do not interest me. Show me your Parisian wool." He fingered each bolt, commenting on the length, crimp, and relative softness of the fibers. "Spanish merino, excellent. The Scottish tweed is durable, but too coarsely textured for my taste. This vicuna jacket is well made. Have you other samples at this level of craftsmanship?"

The owner brought out several suits in

progress, removing the names pinned to the lapels to protect his customers' privacy. "We would of course show the s-s-same discretion should you choose to order a suit, Herr ...?"

"Dark green plaid is not suitable for someone of my proportions." Meinhardt waved away the popular fabric. "And I require a single-breasted coat, not a double."

Herr Hoffman apologized. "I only m-m-meant to show you the triple stitching reinforcing the seams and call attention to details like the mother-of-pearl buttons and silk-lined pockets."

Meinhardt peered closely at the seams and cuffs. "I see you also use silk thread instead of rayon. The fabric lies flatter." He admired the cut. "The London drape favored by the Prince of Wales. Much sought after. The slight intake at the waist and fitted trousers are quite flattering."

"I was several years working for Dege and Skinner on Savile Row." Mr. Hoffman pulled up his tall, slim body with pride. He'd recently returned to Berlin and set up his own shop, but many British customers still ordered bespoke items. Between new clients and his loyal old patrons, the business was growing nicely, even in this severe economic depression.

"I can see why. You carry the best fabrics and know your tailoring." Meinhardt dispensed the barest smile of approval to make the owner feel he was the one with something to prove.

"As do you ...?" Herr Hoffman inclined his head, again inviting Meinhardt's name.

Meinhardt stroked the silk and linen shirts and ties, lamenting to himself that even if he were able to afford such fabrics, a third of the cloth would have to be cut away to fit. He went over to the hat racks and tried one on to demonstrate that in many ways he was no different than a man of normal size. The owner followed him, solicitous, nervous, and curious all at the same time. "What do you think, the fedora or the homburg?" Meinhardt brushed away imaginary lint, feigning offense at the desecration of the felt to keep Herr Hoffman on the defensive.

The proprietor wiped the hat brim. "The homburg. Fedoras are a bit g-g-gangsterish in my opinion, although I do sell a great many of them."

"It must be difficult serving customers in the shop while attending to your tailoring."

"I was training a sales assistant, but he left to join the Gestapo. Now I must begin again. It is a challenge. Few youths have your knowledge. Where did you say your family is from?"

"So you need a new salesperson, preferably someone you don't have to train?"

The owner nodded.

"I might be interested in such a position."

Herr Hoffmann snickered. "At least you would not run off to help Mr. Hitler."

"I am quite serious." Meinhardt replaced the hat and walked behind the sales counter.

The owner, who had resumed following him around the store, stopped and stared. "But how could a person of your stature hold up a full-size suit without dragging it on the floor? Or stretch a shirt across a gentleman's shoulders? Or tie a cravat around a man's neck?"

Mindful of Herr Hoffman's British clients, Meinhardt answered in English, using his best vocabulary. "By standing on step stools upholstered in your costliest fabrics, placed strategically throughout the premises." He explained that he'd studied modern languages in Gymnasium, and stayed up to date going to American movies twice a week. He proclaimed his facility would attract new cosmopolitan German clients as well. "I will prove myself an asset," he declared.

Herr Hoffman's cleared his throat, twice. "Very well. I will give you a try, but the help wanted ad stays in the newspaper. Understand that if someone as knowledgeable as you, but t-t-taller, applies for the position, I will dismiss you. Begin tomorrow."

Chapter 06

His grandmother fussed when Meinhardt got home. "*Mein gut aussehend Kind*, I was getting worried. You stayed out late because you did not get the job?"

He plucked a sprig of parsley from the cabbage rolls and kissed her forehead. "You can't call me your handsome child anymore, Oma. I'm twenty now!" After hanging up his new suit, he told her he'd gone to the American cinema to see a matinee of *A Night at the Opera*. Meinhardt loved the Marx Brothers. Like him, they were outcasts but they managed to slyly triumph over their tormenters. He envied their ability to laugh at themselves as much as they did at others.

As he often did after seeing a movie, Meinhardt acted out his favorite parts for his Oma. He chose the stateroom scene, moving in and out of the kitchen doorway to imitate how fifteen characters forced themselves inside the narrow space.

"Meinhardt, I don't have time for games tonight. I thought you'd be home earlier, maybe with a smile on your face. I'm afraid dinner will burn. I am sorry you did not get the job."

"I am smiling, Oma. I got the job. I start tomorrow."

She caught her breath and crossed her hands over her chest. "*Gott sei Dank!* Thank God!"

"No more weekday matinees, not even to study American English." Meinhardt hung his head and sobbed clown tears.

"Away with you, silly boy. Instead you can wear the gifts I made *eine gute Gesundheit*, in good health." From a hiding place inside her sewing cabinet, his grandmother took out two shirts, a pale gray silk with embroidered cuffs and a creamy linen with small ceramic buttons.

Meinhardt carried them to the window where the sun's last rays glimmered off the silken thread and the overshot pattern in the linen weave. "They are more beautiful than the finest ones I will sell for Herr Hoffman." Real tears webbed his eyelashes. "Now, since you are an equally fine cook, did you also make your delicious *Kartoffel Klose* for my birthday dinner?"

Savoring the cabbage rolls and potato dumplings, Meinhardt recounted how he'd landed the job. "I figured the owner would not dismiss a potential client, especially one who looked like he had a great deal of money to spend. Herr Hoffmann was probably calculating how much he could charge to tailor-make a suit for someone with my proportions."

His grandmother tapped her forehead. "You think smart, like a good businessman."

"I was taught by a good businesswoman." Meinhardt looked at his Oma with gratitude. She'd been raised in a small fishing village, but had moved to Berlin when her husband found a better paying job in a factory. He died when their daughter, Meinhardt's mother, was five. Gretel had supported them by using her sewing skills to earn a steady, if modest, income. As his mother grew up, however, she had rebelled against his Oma's good sense and simplicity, and developed a taste for extravagance. Luckily, she married up and she and her husband were delighted when their red-haired, green-eyed son was born. But when Meinhardt failed to grow, they left him with Gretel lest they'd be branded genetically inferior themselves. They moved to Bonn, where they had two normal children, whose birth announcements Gretel refused to acknowledge. Christmas cards also went unanswered and eventually stopped arriving. With no family history of midgets, Meinhardt's condition was never explained. His Oma blamed his mother for drinking and eating too much *Schaumwein* and *Gänsestopfleber* during pregnancy, but she cared more about raising him to accept what was right about himself than trying to unearth what went wrong.

"You taught me how important it is to respect the customer," Meinhardt now said.

"But first you must respect yourself." His Oma reminded him of Frau Grüber. Meinhardt would never forget the woman who kept changing her mind about the length of an evening dress and became indignant when his grandmother would not alter it a third time without an added fee. "Stupid peasant! Like your retarded boy. His kind don't deserve to live!"

His Oma had planted herself in front of the woman and calmly ripped the silk gown from neck to hem. She dropped it at her feet, pointed to the door, and said "*Vershwinde!*"

Over cake, Meinhardt asked about his grandmother's day. He hoped that with his income, she'd be able to cut back her long hours and worry less about money. At sixty-six, her arthritis was getting worse. Still, she took pride in her fine hand stitching. If only he had his own store, she could work for him and do only as much sewing as she liked. He would take care of her and repay her for the lifetime of faith and devotion she had showered on him.

She took out the lilac marocain crepe dress she was making to show how the tight-twisted wool and silk fibers created a deep cross-ribbed effect. The popular but hard-to-handle material meant

31

using very sharp pins and replacing the needle in her treadle sewing machine frequently so the fabric wouldn't snag. She'd stitched the hem by hand so the heavy skirt swirled and billowed. His Oma could work magic with any material to flatter a woman's body, regardless of her shape.

"Herr Hoffman was impressed with my knowledge of fabrics and tailoring. That too I owe to you." He held his grandmother's fingers. They were still strong but no longer as straight as when they stroked his feverish forehead or wiped away the tears brought on by his classmates' taunting. With no hope that any college would accept someone with his condition, even if he'd been able to afford to go, his Oma's training had given him a future as well as salving his past.

She refolded the lilac dress and Meinhardt perched on a small stepladder to wash the dishes. "You owe me nothing," she said. "It was your own good mind and sharp eyes that let you learn. The store owner saw in you today what I see every day." She pronounced the day perfect.

"Near perfect." Meinhardt dried his hands. "The nice woman ticket seller was not at the cinema this afternoon." He was always relieved when she was in the booth because the man who also worked there made an exaggerated show of leaning down to hand him his ticket.

"Perhaps she had the day off," his grandmother suggested, "or the theater owner changed the ticket sellers' schedules. At worst, she was home with a sniffle."

Meinhardt shook his head. "She was fired. The man told me."

His Oma frowned. "Business is slow all over. I suppose the owner had to let her go."

"*Nein*," Meinhardt said. "She was fired because she is Jewish."

Chapter 07

After a month on the job, Meinhardt was entrusted with opening the shop each morning so Herr Hoffmann could enjoy a second cup of coffee and *Brötchen* at home. Meinhardt loved that time alone to finger the fabrics and study the colors and cuts of the latest menswear designs from Europe and America. There were rarely any customers at that hour, except for an occasional businessman in need of a clean tie after spilling his coffee at a nearby café. Their eyes widened at the sight of Meinhardt. One had muttered *Fick Dich* and left immediately, but most were in too big a hurry to worry about who served them. Only once had a patron, an elderly man with an erect carriage and trim beard, sought his advice on a tie to complement his ecru-flecked suit.

By contrast, Herr Hoffman increasingly asked his opinion on how to display the store's merchandise. Meinhardt knew it mattered which color shirts hung next to one another, and how handkerchiefs were fanned out, belts coiled, and suspenders draped over padded silk hangers.

The owner admitted his surprise. "I didn't think you'd be capable of imaging how things would look up on a shelf or from the viewpoint of someone gazing down into a glass case. Yet you have an eye for how the clothes and accessories will strike those who are your superiors."

"My perspective makes me more conscious of how things appear to . . . taller people." Meinhardt bit his tongue, but decided it was worth it when Herr Hoffman gave him an increasingly free hand arranging the store. Today, however, he wondered if he'd gone too far.

Herr Hoffman skipped the usual morning greeting and spluttered. "Everything's m-m-mixed together." Instead of keeping separate areas for each item, Meinhardt had coordinated two displays. On one side of the store was a navy suit with a sky blue shirt, ties in pale green and yellow, and a straw panama hat. Opposite it was a brown twill matched with shirts, ties, and an umber felt fedora. On the back wall, he'd created a grouping of silk pajamas, dressing gowns, and handkerchiefs, and was half-finished putting together a set of sporting outfits.

"The French call it an *ensemble*, sir," Meinhardt explained. "It's the vogue in marketing women's clothes." He'd observed that whenever his grandmother showed her clients a set of accessories — scarves, hats, gloves — they bought an entire outfit instead of just the dress. He thought the idea would work equally well with men, if not better. Left to their own devices, men saw only what was in front of them. They needed prompting to consider their overall appearance.

Herr Hoffmann raised his eyebrows, but said nothing more. Meinhardt pursued this small opening. "We could do the same in the front windows." He said he'd read about a department store in New York City, Lord and Taylor, that tried this idea with last year's Christmas display and increased sales fivefold. When the owner still looked skeptical, Meinhardt climbed on a stool and pretended to dust a now-empty shelf. From this vantage point he looked his boss almost in the eye. "Let me try it in the north window. Fewer customers approach from that direction, so there is less risk. If it attracts business, then permit me to do the same in the south window."

"Very well, but use this simple suit. And solid colors only." Herr Hoffman handed him a conservative gray flannel jacket and pointed at the row of plain-weave shirts. Meinhardt started immediately, before he changed his mind. When the owner turned his back, he slipped a white-on-white shirt and a tie shot with pale salmon threads into the accessories he carried up front.

He was halfway done when a bell jangled, announcing the arrival of a customer. "Why is there a midget in the shop window? Are you selling clothes or advertising a freak show at the circus?" Meinhardt recognized the man who marched into the store, flashing his plump, ring-laden fingers. Everyone in Germany knew him. His round face and corpulent body, barely encased in a white dress Luftwaffe uniform, had filled the papers when he married actress Emmy Sonnemann.

The pretty dyed-blonde with him today was not his new wife, but whoever she was, she cut a stylish figure. A suit with a belted jacket and fox tails flattered her svelte body. The pencil-thin eyebrows, marcelled upswept hairdo, and pancake hat worn tilted over her right eye, gave her a look halfway between roguish and whorish. She had a camera strapped around her neck and loosely held the leashes of two Scottish Terriers.

"Commandant Göring." Herr Hoffmann, having recognized the fat man too, stood at attention. He spoke slowly to control his stutter. "How may I be of service?"

"First get that poor excuse for a human being out of your shop window!"

Meinhardt began to lower his body to the step stool, but Göring kicked it out from under him. He was forced to slide down from the window ledge on his stomach. As soon as his feet touched the floor, the dogs barked and nipped at his heels.

The woman laughed. "Negus! Stasi! Stop tormenting the funny little man with such a handsome face." She made no move to pull the dogs back.

"Eva, either let them loose to mangle this pathetic monster or restrain them."

She shortened their leashes just enough to remain within an inch of Meinhardt's toes.

35

"Perhaps Frau ...?" interrupted the store owner.

"Fraulein Braun."

"... would care for a c-c-cup of coffee while I wait on the Commandant?" Herr Hoffman indicated an upholstered chair on the other side of the shop.

"*Nein, danke.* I'm enjoying the entertainment." Eva Braun snapped pictures and her grip on the dogs' leashes once again loosened. "Adolf will be amused to see this too."

Herr Hoffman turned back to Göring, who said, "My wife and I are throwing a costume party next month after *Der Freischütz*. You are familiar with the Hunter's Chorus from Weber's opera?" When the store owner nodded, Göring described the outfit he wanted — a medieval tunic with a corded belt to hold his knife, a cape appliquéd with German crosses, and a woven quiver decorated with his personal coat of arms.

The woman smirked and cocked her hip. "And will the hardy menfolk have a late-night hunting party while the fair ladies weave tapestries and prepare to roast the wild boar you bag?"

"*Ja!* We shall hunt down the degenerates and the deformed." Göring glared at Meinhardt, who forced himself not to cower in front of the nipping dogs. "These vermin are an affront to our beloved *Vaterland*. Then, *Liebe* Eva, the womenfolk may fete us with mead."

Herr Hoffmann promised to buy heavy cotton for the tunic and felt for the cape that very afternoon, so the Commandant could return the following day for a fitting.

"Come Hermann." The woman tugged on his sleeve. "I must develop these photographs before lunch and you know how Adolf insists that meals be eaten on time."

"Make sure this scum is gone by tomorrow, or I'll see to it that this store is closed down." Göring kicked the dogs ahead of him and spat on Meinhardt as he marched out the door.

Chapter 08

His grandmother was eating a midday meal of cabbage and potatoes when Meinhardt entered the apartment and slumped in his chair. *"Bist du krank?"* Her hand reached toward his forehead.

"I'm not sick. Herr Hoffmann fired me."

"Gott in Himmel! Was ist das Problem? I know that *you* did nothing wrong."

"It's not what I did, Oma. It's what I am."

She tore through the newspaper until she reached the help wanted section. "So, you will get another job. A better one, where they don't spit on you."

"No one will give a job to someone like me. The government would close them too."

Tears ran down his Oma's wrinkled cheeks. "It is time for you to leave Germany."

"You would come with me?"

"Nein. I'm too old. Besides, the laws can't hurt me, but for you, it will get worse." Last week, a sympathetic client whose husband was in the Waffen-SS had whispered to her that the Nazis would soon pass even more radical policies to protect Aryan purity.

Meinhardt sank further in his seat. "It's only a matter of time before they figure out that extermination is cheaper than locking people up."

His grandmother put a plate in front of him. *"Essen.* With caraway seeds, the way you like it." She dished out the sour cream. They picked up their spoons, but neither of them ate.

Meinhardt wondered where he could go and what he could do. He pictured the store he dreamed of opening. Edwin Hardy Amies, a young designer at Lachasse in London, made clothes for both men and women, but marketed them separately. Meinhardt's idea was to sell them in the same store. Wives, who came to help their husbands shop, would buy something for themselves. The windows would display men's and women's outfits that complemented each other. He was sure the idea would work, but to open such a shop he'd have to save or find a patron. That was hard enough for an ordinary person. New businesses were financed by the government, which invested in military production, not private initiatives. He could try to purvey officers' uniforms, but he had no desire to clothe men who would just as soon kill him.

"It's too bad the Marx Brothers don't live in Germany," he said. "I could work in their movies. With someone my size, they could have squeezed twenty people into that stateroom."

His Oma smiled, as he'd hoped, then got a distant look in her eyes. "Did you know their mother, Minnie Schönberg, was from Dornum, the village where I grew up? Her younger sister and I went to school together. Their father did magic tricks. I'd see the family walk to synagogue Saturday mornings. Christian mothers warned children not to go near them during Lent because the Jews would kill us and use our blood to bake Passover matzo. The family moved to America after Minnie started Gymnasium, and that's where she married Sam, a tailor from Alsace."

"Oma, you never told me you knew so much about the Marx Brothers."

"Not the boys, only their mother. My friend Sadie was half Jewish and knew the family. She used to write me about them, but she lost touch when the elder Schönbergs died. I haven't heard from Sadie in over a year now. I'm worried. Every day there are new laws against Jews."

If persecuted people like Minnie and Sam had the courage to leave, Meinhardt could too. He needn't cross an ocean, just the Strait of Dover. He could look for work in London, on Savile Row. Once he built up a private clientele, he'd open his own place, then persuade his Oma to join him. The English were not like the Germans. They might look at him oddly but the British would be too civilized and polite to openly discriminate against him. "I don't care what they whisper behind my back," he told his grandmother, "as long as they are honest up front."

She reminded him that Herr Hoffmann had worked for a firm on Savile Row and urged him to ask for a letter of reference. "You worked hard for him. He owes you."

"Nobody owes anyone anything in this world, Oma, except for my owing everything to you. I will do it on my own and make you proud of me." He clasped her hands.

"*Ich habe Vertrauen in Sie*, I have faith in you." She drew both their hands to her wet cheek. "*Ich werde dich vermissen.*"

Meinhardt said he'd miss her too, but that England wasn't far away. He'd write every week, and until he earned enough to bring her there to live, he'd visit twice a year. "How could I not come back for your *Pfeffernüsse* at Christmas and your *Bienenstich* at Midsummer's Eve?"

"Oh Meinhardt, remember when you were afraid to eat the *Bienenstich*?" They recalled how, at age five, learning the name meant "bee sting cake" because of its honey glaze, he'd pinched his lips closed and shoved away his fork. He was worried it would sting his tongue and make it swell. "If I can't swallow, I can't eat. And if I can't eat, I won't grow up big and strong."

His Oma had wiped away tears when she reassured him there were no stingers hidden in the batter. Not only would eating the cake not hurt him, but the honey topping would make his voice sweet.

That turned out to be true. Meinhardt had grown up with a beautiful bass baritone.

One memory led to another and soon they began to eat. The upcoming football match between Germany and England, widely covered in the news, prompted them to remember Meinhardt's passion for the sport as a boy. Football was the one game where height didn't matter. The main action was in the legs and Meinhardt's were sturdy. He was coordinated, balanced, and fast. Still, the neighborhood children never chose him for their teams, so his Oma had taken him by bus to the Tiergarten on Sundays, after church, where they kicked the ball back and forth. She'd been spry for a middle-aged woman, retaining the muscles of her rural girlhood. Her wavy reddish-brown hair, which Meinhardt had inherited, escaped its bun as she flew across the field.

"Remember what you said, Oma, when people laughed?" He thought they were mocking him, but she said they were laughing at her, an old lady stumbling across the grass. Now her hair was gray. She still wore it in a bun, but she didn't move fast enough for it to escape its pins.

His grandmother had become as interested in how his leather ball was stitched together as Meinhardt was in dribbling and shooting it. When he came home from school one day, he found her sewing the sections back together, using a tapestry needle threaded with heavy cotton. "You were afraid I'd be angry with you for ruining my ball," he recalled. "Instead I told you to take it apart again so I too could see how it was made." Her influence on his future had started early.

Not every memory was happy. When his grandmother couldn't be there to protect him, he turned to her for answers. "Oma, what should I say when children ask why I'm so short?"

"Tell them most people grow from the

bottom up. Their strength is in their feet so they use them to make their way in the world. You grew from the top down. Your strength is in your head. It is your mind — *Gehrin* — that will take you far in this life."

"Oma, what should I say when people ask where my mother and father are?"

"Tell them your parents are dead."

"But that's a lie."

"It's as good as the truth. It will do."

For almost twenty years, that answer had satisfied Meinhardt as well. No longer. "Oma, I want to see them before I leave Germany," he declared now.

She took a sharp breath and frowned. "It will come to nothing except to hurt you."

Meinhardt, ready to take the risk of leaving home, was prepared to face this one too. "Do you still have the letters my mother wrote you?" he asked his Oma.

"The last one is ten years old. I don't know if the address is still correct."

"I have to start somewhere."

She winced as she stooped to retrieve them from a drawer of old table linens under the flour bin. Meinhardt undid the faded blue ribbon around a packet of five yellowed envelopes. The handwriting was small but not cramped, and wavy rather than curled, like the family hair.

The first letter described their new house, the second her husband's accounting job with a company that made prostheses for war veterans. The third and fourth announced, respectively, the birth of a son and a daughter. Each held a nondescript baby picture. The last letter contained photos of two well-dressed children, a stocky little girl with sausage curls in a lacy dress, and a tall slim boy wearing sports clothes and cradling a football in his arms. His mother said that if her mother wanted to

41

meet her *schön* grandchildren, she and her husband would pay for her to visit Bonn during the summer holidays. "However, we still desire no contact with the boy."

Ten years after writing those words, and two decades after abandoning her son, perhaps she would have a change of heart.

Mutter und Vater,

I write to tell you that I will soon be leaving Berlin to seek a position with a gentlemen's clothing firm in London. My grandmother has taught me well about fabrics and tailoring. I have a good head for business and showed a facility for languages during my studies at Gymnasium.

I think you would be proud of what I have accomplished and can believe in my prospects for the future. I should like an opportunity to see you before I go.

Ihr Sohn,
Meinhardt

Two days later a picture postcard arrived in the mail. On the front was a line of marching youth, the arms of their starched khaki uniforms holding high the Nazi flag — a black swastika inside a white circle surrounded by a bright red rectangle — against a pure blue sky. Hitler's face was on the postage stamp. The card was addressed to his Oma in a familiar, neatly curved script. But the message, in large block print, said: "TELL THE BOY NEVER TO CONTACT US AGAIN."

PART THREE

A Place Where There Isn't Any Trouble

London, 1936

Meinhardt was exhausted, juggling three jobs to afford a room that had been as hard to find as the work to pay for it. More than once, he'd knocked at a house with a vacancy sign, only to have the landlord peer down through the door pane and say it had just been let. Some said nothing at all when they saw him, simply removing the sign from the window.

The house where he'd finally rented a room didn't have a pane, so he found himself face to face with the landlady when she opened the door. Mrs. Mudge, a tall stout woman wearing a faded flowered dress with a billowing skirt and capped puffy sleeves, eyed him suspiciously.

"I ain't got no money for the circus," she said. "Nor charity for the deformed."

Meinhardt propped the door open with his foot before she could slam it shut. He gestured toward the crudely lettered "Room to Let" sign.

Mrs. Mudge glowered. "I want someone what's quiet."

Meinhardt said he followed the German custom of wearing stockings or slippers indoors.

"I suppose someone your size ain't going to tromp about making a great deal of noise." She nudged Meinhardt's small polished shoes with her scuffed lace-ups.

"I have a radio, but I play it very softly and never past ten o-clock," he said. The Braun receiver, his only valued possession, had been a parting gift from his grandmother.

"You don't play that screechy jazz, do you?"

"No, only BBC news and the latest songs, now and then. I hope that's to your taste."

"Can't say I mind a good dance tune." Mrs. Mudge spread jiggling arms and swirled with unexpected grace. "I haven't danced since our wedding, over twenty years ago. Herbie reported for duty two days later and we were too busy elsewise on our honeymoon." She winked.

Meinhardt reddened. He tried not to think about sex. Who would be interested in half a man? He murmured that it must have been difficult when Mr. Mudge went to war so soon after their marriage.

All business again, the landlady asked if he'd have a lot of friends going in and out. Meinhardt said he hadn't met many people yet and was inclined to keep to himself. Mrs. Mudge tsked. "It can't be easy for your type to make friends. I don't imagine the ladies are eager for your courtship, either. Pity. You have a nice-looking face."

Meinhardt forced a smile. He'd swallow his anger in return for a place to live. There was no privacy at the youth hostel where he'd been staying for two weeks, and he couldn't help but think that the late-night whispering between the men in the other beds was about him.

"A quiet tenant who won't upset Herbie is what I'm after." Mrs. Mudge explained. He'd returned from the Great War shell shocked, after seeing his commander's head lying a yard from his body when a shell exploded behind him. Now he was afraid to asleep for fear of seeing that awful sight in his dreams. "Sometimes he wraps a dog leash under his arms and over his head to keep it attached. I lock up the towels so he won't wipe up the blood he imagines is on the floor."

Meinhardt asked if they had a dog and was relieved when Mrs. Mudge said they couldn't, her husband would startle if it barked. The smallest noise set off his tremors and palpitations. He was prone to see animals and strangers as enemy invaders. "He's like to have a panic attack if he sees you," she warned. It had happened with the previous tenant. Mr. Mudge was sleepwalking and came across the unfortunate gentleman fixing himself a piece of toast in the kitchen in the middle of the

45

night. To prevent further trouble, Mrs. Mudge had established new rules. The room, at the back of the house, had its own door directly off the garden. The tenant was not allowed to use the front door or the rest of the house. There was a privy behind the tool shed, and a gas fire in the room for heating and cooking. She'd recently had electricity installed, but it was expensive, and if Meinhardt wanted to use the radio in his room, he'd have to pay extra.

Meinhardt said the terms were acceptable. Being banished from the kitchen wasn't a drawback. Deprived of his Oma's cooking, he subsisted on Weetabix, splashed with milk when he could afford it or coated with marmalade. If he was especially broke, he choked it down dry.

Mrs. Mudge sighed. "Life would be calmer if I didn't have to let the room, but I need the money. After the war, the government listed my husband as sick, not wounded, so they reduced his pension. Rent covers food and a pint now and then, to settle his nerves."

Meinhardt reassured her he'd be a dependable tenant and turn in the rent on time.

"I don't know." She chewed a nail. "Herbie can't abide normal strangers. No telling what he'd do if he caught sight of you. Suppose he heard you talk! Your English is like to be as good as a gentleman's, but there's still a ring of the German to it. I mightn't be able to restrain him."

Meinhardt felt a trickle of sympathy for the poor woman, who hadn't heard a kind word since she and her husband were newlyweds. He'd read that shell shock victims were urged to replace their nightmarish thoughts with pleasant images, like meadows of wild flowers. Cajolery might work on her. "I'm sure seeing you in that flared rose-petal dress soothes Mr. Mudge and banishes those terrifying pictures from his mind." He smiled encouragingly.

"This old thing? I bought it at Gertie's Dress Emporium ages ago!" Mrs. Mudge blushed and spun around again. "All right then," she said at last and took him to see the room.

The mustard-colored wallpaper was blotched with stains and the narrow bed sagged, but the large windows on either side of the door showed a garden brighter and better maintained than the house. He wouldn't mind passing through it on his way in and out, even to use the privy.

"Flowers are free for the looking," Mrs. Mudge said, "but don't be stealing my vegetables like those thieving gypsies and vagabonds."

Meinhardt vouched for the safety of her onions, potatoes, and turnips. He paid the first week's rent and after retrieving his suitcase and radio from the hostel, went directly to Gertie's.

"You expect me to offer you a job?" sputtered Mr. Popham, the proprietor of the dress store.

"Give me a day's try." Meinhardt pitched his voice low. He didn't want to plead.

The owner frowned. He didn't see how hiring a midget could be good for business.

"You have nothing to lose. If receipts are flat," Meinhardt's hands leveled the air, "I'll move on. If sales go up," he raised his hands, "I'll more than earn my keep."

Mr. Popham smiled. "Very theatrical. This is one performance I'd like to see."

Meinhardt surveyed the shoppers pawing through the crowded dress racks and jumbled accessory bins. Most were round and doughy, like Mrs. Mudge. The few who were thin had the pallor of the undernourished, not the healthful bloom of the athletic. Large and small, the women's hems skimmed the tops of their sturdy black oxfords. They hovered around old-fashioned cotton and chiffon dresses with flouncing skirts, ballooning sleeves, and broad patterns. Cheap copies of more flattering current styles — bolero jackets over straight calf-length dresses in bold, solid colors — lay untouched. They passed over toques and turbans in favor of printed head scarves and sprigged bonnets. Gloves and other flourishes they simply ignored.

He approached a woman of medium height and asked if he could be of service. She cast a doubtful glance at the owner, who was enjoying his front-row seat, then frowned at Meinhardt. "What can you possibly know about ladies dresses?" she huffed.

"I know the daffodils on this frock would look lovely on you." He held it a couple of inches from her wide body. "Their color complements the blue of your eyes."

She fingered the shiny fabric. "My husband says yellow makes me look sickly."

"Tell him the color is mimosa." Meinhardt steered her toward the new dresses whose plain shades had been given fancy names: Pernod green, apple blossom pink, carnation blush. He suggested one named for a flower. In the end, the woman still chose a stodgy dress, but she bought a chic mimosa toque and matching elbow-length gloves to go with it.

"A charming combination." Meinhardt spoke loudly so the others, overhearing, might sidle up for a bit of praise and advice too. Most, like his first customer, wouldn't risk a stylish dress, but craving his attention, purchased accessories. Younger women were easier to persuade. One bought a cerise feathered capelet, another an empire-waisted aubergine evening gown. "Now your husband must take you dancing," he told her as she admired her reflection. "You're my heart's desire. I love you Nellie Dean." Meinhardt sang the opening bars of the popular song. The young woman in the purple dress giggled while older women looked on, wistful.

By mid-afternoon, sales receipts at Gertie's Dress Emporium were a third higher than normal. Mr. Popham drew Meinhardt aside. "You're flattery appeals to the ladies. I suppose because it's not threatening, like a real man's. I'll hire you. I'm tempted to pay half rate for half size, but I'll do three-quarters. Even a little bloke needs a solid roof, hot bangers, and a pint."

Meinhardt clenched his fists behind his back. He accepted the job offer.

The day's last customer was a tall, cream-faced, dark-haired woman leading a small boy. She slid last year's dresses along the rack while glancing toward the latest fashions. Meinhardt approached her, relieved to see he was a few inches taller than her son. "Your slim figure can carry the new styles," he told her. The woman blushed and Meinhardt saw with a shock that she was barely older than him. He handed her a dress with a fitted midriff and a skirt that revealed a bit of leg. Reassuring her it was still modest, he persuaded her to try it on.

When she emerged from the dressing room she looked ten years younger. Slowly she turned in front of the mirror. "Mum, you look so pretty!" the little boy said.

The woman sighed. "Maybe next time, if your dad gets that job at the new aircraft plant." After changing back into her own clothes, she looked older than when she'd come in. She thanked Meinhardt for his time, then straightened her shoulders and ushered her son out the door.

It had been quite a day. Meinhardt had a room and a job, but he wasn't ready to celebrate. He pictured the young mother returning home to don a shabby house dress and worn apron. He had more life ahead of him than she did. Today was a good beginning but it was hardly enough.

Chapter 10

When he'd arrived in London, and applied for positions on Savile Row, the clothiers' scorn had increased Meinhardt's resolve to open his own store. He didn't want to continue depending on an allowance from his grandmother. It was his turn to take care of her. To set up his own shop, however, he'd have to earn more than enough to live on, and he couldn't save money on his salary at Gertie's. Swallowing his pride, Meinhardt applied for a serving job at a gentleman's club. The idea had started as a humiliating joke, but he hoped to turn it to his advantage.

The first establishment Meinhardt had approached on Savile Row was Dege and Skinner, where Herr Hoffmann once worked. Although he'd refused to ask his former boss for a letter of reference, he'd learned what type of merchandise they carried, and came prepared to speak about royal crests and cravats. Instead, the store's tailor had spit out a mouthful of pins when the owner snickered that Meinhardt didn't measure up to their standards. At Huntsman and Son, which specialized in sportswear, he'd been offered a job modeling knit coats for hunting dogs. A clerk had woofed as he left. Other forays from No. 1 to No. 38 Savile Row were equally futile.

Meinhardt could sink no lower, so he aimed higher. He walked into Henry Poole and Company, the street's acknowledged founders, whose advertisements boasted that "Young men who want to put up a Good Front will find in our Clothes the biggest return in Style and Quality. We cut your suit *to the Swing of Your Body*. Custom Tailoring means Smarter Dress." He was listening to his tenth rejection in as many tries, when two men strode in. The manager bowed. "Sir Edward, Mr. Graves. Here to fetch your new dinner suits? I trust you'll be pleased as usual with the craftsmanship." He shooed Meinhardt toward the door, but Meinhardt stood his ground.

"What have we here? Is Poole's opening a sideline in sideshows?" The one addressed as Sir Edward rocked back on his heels and looked down his long aristocratic nose at Meinhardt.

"No, sir. I am seeking a position as a salesman. I have experience at the finest clothing store in Berlin. If Poole and Company cannot use my services, perhaps you two gentlemen can direct me toward another establishment along this street that has met with your satisfaction."

Mr. Graves flashed a dimpled smile at the manager. "In fact, we bought herringbones at Gieves and Hawkes and found they rival the quality of jackets here. The vertical pleats in the pockets are quite innovative and in demand nowadays. I expect they're in need of more staff."

Meinhardt nodded as though making a mental note to try there next. He didn't say he'd already been turned away. The manager coughed and flicked his wrist toward the exit again.

Sir Edwards picked up on his friend's mischief. "If that doesn't work out, I believe we're looking for a server at our club." He handed Meinhardt a linen-colored card embossed in dark red script: ***The Arts Club: Where gentlemen of culture, literature, and science converge***.

Meinhardt took the card and left. He intended to throw it out, but it stayed in his pocket where he fingered it on the bus each day between Gertie's and the Mudges's. Serving sherry to snobs was at odds with his image of himself, but he might discover a patron there. People in the arts could be more open to backing a midget and intrigued by his plan to carry clothes for both men and women. From what he'd heard of that crowd, his store would make it easier for them to shop discreetly in public for the cross-dressing fashions they dared to wear only in private.

He entered 40 Dover Street with shame and ambition, dwarfed by the lobby of the 18th century townhouse. Black-and-white checked floor tiles led to a curving staircase with a heavy wrought-iron railing, while a sinking sun, burning through a window on the second floor landing, set fire to the tall oak counter where Meinhardt craned his neck to introduce himself to the concierge.

"Out, mate! The Arts Club doesn't entertain its membership with cheap parlor tricks."

Meinhardt said he'd come about a serving job, and persuaded the concierge to summon the two gentlemen from the billiards room. They looked as surprised to see him as he was to find himself there, but Sir Edward quickly resumed where he'd left off, and what started as a daytime jest turned into an evening job on the weekends. Not only would Meinhardt serve food and drink to club members, he could earn extra as a valet to those occupying the upstairs rooms.

Sir Edward was the first to hire him as a personal assistant. He led him past the founders' portraits and second-floor drawing room into the corridor where a dozen men each rented private quarters. Meinhardt stared in awe at the oxblood red walls, deep green leather armchairs, and Chinese urns whose girth strained the edges of the mahogany end tables on which they rested. A crystal chandelier bathed all the furnishings in muted golden light. The bedrooms, also papered in dark red, were carpeted in blue-and-white Oriental rugs whose checkerboard pattern echoed the glazes on the porcelain urns.

"If you're as fine an expert on attire as you claim, little man, then you may advise me." Sir Edward opened his wardrobe, which was filled with custom-made, but traditional, clothes. Meinhardt asked if he was adventurous enough to try the wider lapels and straight-legged trousers designed by Frederick Scholte, tailor to the royals, as well as the evening mess jackets with cummerbunds that were replacing waistcoats. He further suggested updating solid-color neckties with geometric patterns, stripes, and polka dots. Sir Edward proved enthusiastic about modernizing his wardrobe. Meinhardt wondered if he'd already found his future patron.

Meinhardt quickly mastered the club's routines and tastes. He served meals in the dining room and refreshments in the gaming rooms, where the men listened to the BBC. They turned up the volume to hear about the King's dalliance with the twice-divorced American, Wallis Simpson. "I hope to God the newsmen disgrace her before she disgraces the monarchy," claimed one.

Another retorted. "King Edward will disgrace the monarchy on his own. Hitler will play him for a patsy. Let him marry his strumpet and abdicate to his younger brother George."

The men dialed the radio even louder to hear the news from Germany. Talk of impending war halted their billiard and card playing. Excerpts from the Führer's latest speech boomed out, denigrating the English and Bolsheviks, touting his National Socialists. That Hitler was mad was agreed upon by all the members. There was less unanimity about the glories of marching to war. Those who fought in Flanders and Gallipoli weren't eager to see the nation fight again, while officers who'd escaped action encouraged younger men to prove themselves on the battlefield.

"Enough talk of war," said Sir Edward. "We need lighter diversion!" Meinhardt tuned the dial to a music station and the parlor games resumed. Bing Crosby, the hometown American boy whose smooth voice the club's suave Englishmen adored, crooned

"Pennies from Heaven." Relieved that the men's attention was no longer on his homeland, Meinhardt sang along quietly to himself as he gathered up empty glasses. "You'll find your fortune fallin' all over town. Be sure that your umbrella is upside down. So when you hear it thunder, don't run under a tree ..."

"The little Kraut can sing!" The speaker stuffed a pound note in a dirty glass and passed it around the room. By the time it came full circle back to Meinhardt, the soggy note at the bottom was topped by a stack of crisp, dry ones. The men demanded that he sing more.

"Star Dust." "The Music Goes Round and Round!" To Meinhardt's surprise, one of them asked for "My Daddy Wouldn't Buy Me a Bow Wow" and requests for other bawdy music halls tunes began to flow as freely as spirits. Meinhardt was tempted to refuse, even to throw down his wipe rag and walk out, but each song brought him another glassful of money.

"If the club closes because we're all called to war," said Sir Edward, "you can earn your keep singing for the troops."

"Better yet, go to America. New York has so many freaks, you won't stand out there." Mr. Graves dropped a five-pound note in the brandy that coated the bottom of his glass.

"Guy Lombardo's Royal Canadians!" came one last call. "The Way You Look Tonight."

"He looks short to me!" Sir Edward poked a manicured fingernail into his friend's ribs.

"How De-Lovely!" Mr. Graves nudged back with a suede-patched elbow.

Meinhardt carried the money-filled glasses down to the kitchen. He put the notes in a tea tin to take home, including, after some hesitation, the fiver from Mr. Graves which he dried on a towel. His weary legs carried him back upstairs where he laid out Sir Edward's gray tweed suit and chose a clashing animal-patterned tie to go with it. He unfolded a pair of blue linen pajamas and turned back the pale silk sheets. It was time for Meinhardt to head home and go to bed too.

Chapter 11

Even with singing tips, Meinhardt didn't earn enough to save money. He got a third job on week nights bartending at his neighborhood pub. The Wheel and Wing was named for the bus drivers and aircraft industry workers who came there. Its early closing hour, mandated during the war so factory workers wouldn't show up drunk the next day, meant he could get a decent night's sleep before reporting to Gertie's in the morning.

Working there also gave him a place to go on the evenings he wasn't at the Arts Club. At home, he had to tiptoe in near darkness because of Mr. Mudge. Sometimes he pressed his ear to the radio, but the depressing news made him shudder. Dispensing pints at the pub was no more humiliating than singing for his supper at the club. He even got free meals both places, although the fish and chips dished up at the Wheel and Wing hardly matched the Filet of Sole Meuniere plated on bone china at the Arts Club. It didn't matter. Nothing he ate rivaled his Oma's cooking.

The publican viewed Meinhardt as a person with a problem to solve, not a curiosity. He turned over a milk crate for him to stand on to reach the keg taps, and cobbled together a trolley with a high shelf for Meinhardt to wheel pints to the men's tables. Meinhardt kept a mug in the corner to collect tips. They were less than at the club, paid in shillings rather than pound notes, but they were dry. On slow nights, the men invited him to join their games of dominoes or darts.

55

All the pubs fielded football teams. One day someone said, "We're up against the blokes from Rat Hole on Sunday afternoon. Why don't you come round and watch the game?"

Meinhardt asked if he could be in the match instead of just watching.

"Ho! You mean a little fellow like you can play?"

It had been ten years, but Meinhardt showed off the moves he used to practice with his Oma in the park. With the men's eyes focused above him or down field, he darted around and underneath their legs. After he helped defeat Rat Hole, he was in the starting lineup every week. The one time an opponent called him a "runt," his teammates brawled to victory in his defense.

Meinhardt felt less conspicuous at the pub than anywhere else. It's not that he wanted to escape notice, but he wanted to stand out as a man of accomplishment, not a freak. The frosted front window and smoky light, meant to give customers privacy, shielded him from prying eyes too. Even the worn floorboards, covered in sawdust to soak up spills, absorbed sound better than the thick carpet at the Arts Club. The noise of men enjoying themselves was less raucous here.

Nor was he self-conscious about looking different. The men at the pub had their own share of defects. A lifetime of accidents and fights broke bones they couldn't afford to have properly set; industrial equipment had mangled their hands. Worst off was Rodger Smythe, a veteran who'd had both legs shot off in France and scurried around on stumps. He was nearly twice as old as Meinhardt, but had been younger than him when the shell cut him in half. Yet Rodge was the most upbeat person in the room. Each man got a personal "G'day mate" when he came and "Cheerio" when he left. Rodge also took pride in his appearance. Others arrived in dirty work clothes and boots, but he always wore a pressed shirt, matching tie, and jacket. Even the clips holding his rolled-up pants were made of carved wood or enameled metal. Meinhardt occasionally filched a shirt or tie that Sir Edward was unlikely to miss and gave them to him.

Rodge was also known for his aphorisms. Whatever the complaint, his words turned the mood around. When Petey cursed his no-good son, Rodge quipped, "A watermelon won't ripen in an armpit. Smile sunshine on the lad and he'll fill out and sweeten up." If men groused about being poor, he said "Money buys food, not appetite; a soft bed but not a restful sleep." He'd lick his lips over a plate of pickled eggs and pork scratchings until the others got hungry for a taste. After an evening of Rodge's jollying, men went home cheerful enough to be kind to their wives.

Best were the nights they cried "Give us a tune, Rodge" and lifted him onto the stool of the old upright in the corner. He joked that the piano was missing more keys than he was legs, but the men's voices filled in the gaps. It amused Meinhardt that they cared less for bawdy songs than the sophisticates at the club. They preferred sentimental numbers and anthems for the poor. Meinhardt's baritone blended in easily. He didn't get tips for singing, but sad songs made the men drink more and the mug in the corner of his trolley filled up with coins.

Rodge was also a great fan of American musicals and Meinhardt sang along with him to "Anything Goes" and "A Pretty Girl is Like a Melody." He asked if Rodge knew "You're the Top" and was caught off-guard when Rodge laughed and replied, "That's all I am!" By the time Rodge segued into "I Get a Kick Out of You," Meinhardt knew he turned adversity into a joke. "Shadows would not exist without light," Rodge told him. "Look and you'll find the bright side."

Discovering they both loved movies, Rodge invited Meinhardt to a matinee. Meinhardt considered. It was one thing to be friendly at the pub, another to be friends outside. That took time and cost money. Also, friends could hurt you. He'd seen schoolmates play together one day and be mean to each other the next. Better to keep his own company. He wiped the counter to avoid looking Rodge in the eye. "I don't go to movies. I just catch the songs on the BBC."

"If money's the problem, Helen will sneak us in for free." She was his "lady friend" who worked the ticket booth at the Royal Theater. Seeing Meinhardt's puzzled look, Rodge winked and said, "I only lost two legs, not three." Meinhardt rubbed his rag over the same clean spot.

Even if money were the real excuse, Meinhardt wouldn't want to sneak in and out of the theater. It would make him feel smaller and more invisible than he already was.

"Have you ever been in love?" Rodge asked.

Meinhardt shook his head. He didn't know how to end the conversation, so he returned the question to be polite. When Rodge answered yes, he asked about Helen.

"Helen's a good girl, but it was Jayne who robbed my affections. They say love is selling your heart for free. We got engaged before I shipped out." Rodge touched his empty ring finger.

Meinhardt's eyes inadvertently went to Rodge's stumps.

Rodge looked down too. "Jayne was young and full of energy. I don't hold it against her."

"That makes you an uncommonly good loser."

"A good loser is a bad loser with practice. I'm still looking for the right one. That's why I go to musicals. The guy always gets the girl in the end. Let me know if you change your mind."

Meinhardt knew he wouldn't. He collected the empty glasses as the publican turned on the late-night newscast. "An American court has granted Wallis Simpson a decree of divorce," the announcer said. "The King's Lord in Waiting, Baron Peregrine Crust, is reportedly pressuring her to renounce their relationship and forswear any intention to marry the monarch."

"How much do you suppose Sir Crust is offering the lady to skedaddle?"

"Enough so's if it was me, I'd quit buggering the royal bloke, put it in a poke, and retire!"

The news that followed was about the arrest of protesters in the Battle of Cable Street. Working class residents of London's East End had stopped the British Union of Fascists from marching through the largely Jewish area, intent on smashing shops and busting heads. Several regulars from the pub had joined the protesters when the government refused to protect them.

"It's the rich, not the Jews, responsible for the Depression."

"That's not what Hitler says."

"It doesn't matter who's at fault. Men are out of work and that madman is going to start another war. He's got his eyes on Poland and France, then he's coming straight for England."

The men who worked at the new aircraft plant said the country was more than ready to fight the Gerries this time. They swore there would be fewer casualties than in the last war.

"The officers will be fine. But us working stiffs will be sent to the trenches to have our brains blown to bits. Or worse!" There was silence. No one looked at Rodge.

The piano started up. "The key to happiness is a bad memory and a good drink," Rodge said, and the publican nodded for Meinhardt to wheel around free pints. He and the others sang, quietly at first, then with lusty voices: "My old man said 'Follow the van, and don't dilly dally on the way.' But I dillied and dallied, dallied and I dillied. Lost me way and don't know where to roam. I had to stop and have a drop of tiddly in the pub. Now I can't find me way home."

Dearest Oma,

It is late and I'm tired, but writing to you puts my mind at ease before sleep. I'm happy to say you no longer need to wire money. With three jobs, I can manage, but now I worry about you. Things are bad in Germany. Even your richest clients can't afford custom-made clothes, and all you do are *reparierend* and alterations. The high-toned ladies who come to Gertie's would never have set foot there before the Depression. Thankfully they are more eager for the new styles than those who have always been poor. I persuaded my boss to stock more *modisch Kleider* and he is pleased with sales. I only wish he would give me a raise for what I earn him.

Everyone buzzes with talk of another war. This time they'll kill the Gerries for good. I keep my head down, which (*lächeln*) is easy for me. I want to shout, "Not all Germans are bad!" and tell them how kind <u>you</u> are, but speaking up leads to trouble. You are modest about your goodness, but that is not my nature. I want praise. I need you here to make me as virtuous as you.

I learn more about human nature every day. English persecution is more subtle but just as insidious as German. The rich do not say so openly, but they despise anyone less privileged. With the keen ears of a dog, they listen to how you speak. With the sharp eyes of a hawk, they watch how you dress. Sir Edward claims clothes make the man, *Kleider machen Leute*. Without the suit you made me, I wouldn't have been hired as his valet. When men at the club tell me *gut Arbeit*, it is with the surprise of people who do not expect the imperfect to do such good work.

The labor class is friendlier and more straightforward. The Mudges are an exception, but they act out of fear, not bigotry. Trauma and hardship make people suspicious. This I know.

I still dream of opening my *Herrenmode und Damenmode* store, but I get discouraged. *Geben Sie nie auf* you'd encourage me when I wanted to give up. Rodge, the veteran I wrote you about, says, "If you don't like the way something looks, look at it differently." So I keep trying.

On a happier note, Wheel and Wing beat Bacon Arms in our last football match. I scored the winning goal and didn't mind being carried around on my teammates' shoulders. They do the same with Lester, the team's biggest man, whenever he's the one responsible for a victory.

The weather is turning chilly. London is a bleak city in *Herbst*. I miss the bright colors of a fall day in Berlin. However, the change of season means the holidays are not far away and then I shall be home to visit with you. Until then, *Bleib gesund*, be well, and dream with me.

Your loving Enkel,
Meinhardt

Chapter 12

As outside temperatures dropped, the number of customers inside Gertie's rose. Meinhardt showed them how to drape scarves around their shoulders to hide threadbare spots in their old winter coats. He talked the owner into giving the accessories foreign names. Since the English resented the French and suspected the Germans, they called woolen gloves *guanti*, like Italian leather, and sold knit caps as Spanish *Chilote*. The saleswomen liked these inventions too, but at first they saw Meinhardt as a threat. They talked behind his back, loud enough to be overheard.

"Mark my words. Mr. Popham's going to hire the gypsies next and pay them less than he pays us. Then you, me, and Maude is going to find ourselves out of work and on the dole."

To win them over, Meinhardt lavished praise and dispensed fashion advice. "Maude, you have uncommonly long fingers. Why are you hiding them under mittens? The dark plum *guanti* would look elegant on your hands. Try them on for size." "Rachel, are you secretly whittling away the pounds? A little bolero jacket would show off that new nip in your waist."

He also persuaded Mr. Popham to mark down prices for store employees. The delighted saleswomen made Meinhardt their pet. If he fetched a stool, they'd take down what he needed and pat his head. "Here love, I'll get that." They brought him food, like giving treats to a dog. He pretended to save the shepherd's pie and bubble and squeak for later, then fed the lardy stuff to starving mongrels on the way home. Eating it would have saved him money, but he'd rather get by on Weetabix and pretend it was his Oma's *Kleingebäch*. He was a man, not a corgi.

Meinhardt was rearranging a pile of fuzzy jumpers when a familiar looking woman walked into the store. At first he mistook her for a returning customer until he looked more closely at the bone structure beneath the scarf tied clumsily under her chin. Then he recognized the face from her photograph in *The Daily Mirror*. He approached slowly and asked what she was looking for.

Wallis Simpson held an oversized gray coat

close to her chest but removed her gloves and straw-colored scarf. Meinhardt noted her smooth hands and healthy hair, whose marcelled dark-brown waves cascaded down her high cheekbones from a perfect center part.

"You might want to put your scarf back on," he said, "to keep from being spotted."

The woman's eyes widened. Most people eyed him in fear or distaste, but her concern was for her own appearance. Reporters had been following and hounding her relentlessly.

"Trust me," he whispered. "I can help."

Her taut thin body relaxed but her eyes still moved furtively from side to side. Meinhardt recognized the behavior of someone desperate to remain undetected. He'd never had to run from the press, but he'd often been on the lookout for bullies as a boy, and later for Gestapo hooligans.

The first order of business was her clothing. Unlike working class women who Meinhardt encouraged to look more stylish, Wallis needed to be remade in the opposite direction. He chose a full-skirted rayon dress with a floral print that added layers to her hips. He also suggested a pair of bulky shoes which would not only flatten and widen her feet, but provide sturdy support if she needed to run. The final touch was an oversized handbag that could hold sunglasses and a wig.

Wallis sought reassurance. "You're convinced these make me look frumpy enough?" She had a high metallic voice and a sour mouth that was wider and thinner than it appeared in her photos. Meinhardt realized that she reshaped it with makeup, which she wasn't wearing now.

He answered that she wouldn't attract a first look, let alone a second. For insurance, he advised other ways to help her pass as working class. For one thing, her posture was too erect. He demonstrated how to walk with a weary stoop. Also, her hair should be frizzier. A man at the pub had lamented when his wife accidentally singed her ends with a curling iron. Meinhardt told Wallis to burn the tips of her hair deliberately, but warned her to open a window. "The smell of burning hair, like burning flesh, is a dead give-away."

Next he checked her hands. Although Wallis planned to keep them inside coarse woolen gloves, they had to be roughened in case she took them off. Meinhardt remembered his Oma's red, wrinkled hands after she removed bratwurst links from a water bath and scrubbed the pots. "No more Pears soap," he ordered. Wallis promised to soak her hands in something harsher.

"It's good you left Germany," she said. "The Führer is a wise man, right to condemn Jews, but society needs different types of people, like us, to make life gay and interesting. The British fail to understand this. That is why they dislike me. I should not be sorry if Hitler attacks them." Her light brown eyes were bloodshot. In that respect, she already looked working class.

"When and where will you go?" he asked.

Wallis hesitated and Meinhardt repeated that she could trust him.

"Tomorrow night. By ferry. I'll wire thank-you money if I arrive safely. Be careful."

Meinhardt threw caution to the wind. He told Mr. Popham that he felt ill and went to the Royal Theater. He hadn't been to a Saturday matinee in a month for fear of running into Rodge, but this was a weekday afternoon. The woman in the ticket booth was a pretty blond with a big smile. He wondered if it was Helen. Perhaps Rodge's girl truly had no prejudice. Or maybe, like Wallis, she divided odd people into categories. Jews were bad, while amusing freaks were acceptable.

Meinhardt saw Charlie Chaplin's "Modern

Times," but unlike the antic Marx Brothers, the Little Tramp was too pathetic to make him laugh. He hoped his own hard times would soon be over. If Wallis escaped and sent him money, he could start saving toward his store.

There were still three hours of daylight left before his shift began at the Wheel and Wing. All these months in London, he'd never once spent a weekday afternoon at home. He splurged on paper and colored pencils and caught a bus, planning to sustain the day's hope and excitement by sitting at his small table and sketching the sign he would hang over his shop door. Eager to get started, he opened the back gate and entered the decaying garden. An early frost had killed the flowers and except for a few winter squashes, all the vegetables had been harvested. The path to and from his room would be bleak until spring returned. Meinhardt was imagining how the promise of Wallis's money would brighten his days when a quiet snore interrupted his thoughts.

Mr. Mudge was asleep in a lawn chair under a lap robe. Beside him was an upended milk crate with a cup of tea and a plate of biscuits. His head, loosely leashed to his shoulders, lolled to the right. Meinhardt tiptoed past, clutching his drawing materials.

"A Martian!" The cry was accompanied by the crash of a tea cup hitting the hard ground.

Meinhardt dropped the pad and pencils. "*Nein*, no. I am the renter." He turned around to confront a soft hulking man wearing sagging stained trousers and a gray cabled jumper.

"A Boche! A Gerry Martian!" Mr. Mudge ranted that the Germans had invaded Mars and recruited Martians to help them take over the earth. He hurled biscuits at Meinhardt and ran at him with a shard of teacup. Meinhardt raced past him and locked himself in the privy.

65

"What's going on here?" Through a knothole, Meinhardt saw Mrs. Mudge upright the chair and push her husband into it. The man struggled, muttering that he had to hold the line, but she finally subdued him. When he stopped yelling and trembling, she led him into the house.

Ten minutes later she returned. Meinhardt hadn't dared to venture out of the privy.

"What are you doing here at this hour?" she demanded through the door.

Meinhardt said he wasn't feeling well and had come home early.

"This won't be your home much longer." She threatened that the very instant she found a normal tenant, he'd have to leave. If she didn't need the money, she'd kick him out right now.

From his haven, Meinhardt watched her pick up her husband's scattered tea things and his drawing materials and march with them inside. He waited another hour before venturing out to his room. It was almost dark and he had just enough time to change and hurry off to the pub.

By then he felt sick for real and left an hour before closing time. All the next day he cowered in his room, afraid to turn on the gas light or play the radio, even set at the lowest volume. When evening came, he was sorry the weekend had arrived. It would have been comforting to go back to the Wheel and Wing. Instead, he had to report for work at the Arts Club.

Fortunately, the gentlemen were in a somber mood, leaving Meinhardt free to serve them unnoticed. They listened to news about the recent friendship treaty between Germany and Italy. Several worried it would disrupt their shipping interests in the Mediterranean. Sir Edward twisted his napkin into knots. "I don't like the look of things," he said. Mr. Graves grimaced when the announcer said the BBC would begin television broadcasts to supplement radio news the following month. "Sounds like we're going to get an actual look at the build-up to war."

The next story was a welcomed diversion. "The wire service has just released this news. American divorcee Wallis Simpson appears to have eluded the press and departed England by boat. Speculation on her destination is split between northern Germany and southern France. Buckingham Palace has offered no comment."

The gaming room turned boisterous as the men debated where she'd fled to. "Hitler's mustache tickles her fancy. I predict she'll wash ashore in Germany."

"Göring's parties would suit her, but life in Germany is too austere for her royal tastes, let alone those of our esteemed monarch. The decadence of the French is more to their liking."

"What do you think, little man? Would you be ashamed or honored if the tart turned up in your homeland?" Meinhardt answered that the matter didn't concern him, but it did. If Wallis was in Germany, her Nazi connections might talk her out of sending him money. If she was hiding with friends in southern France, she was more likely to make good on her promise.

Sir Edward took a note from his billfold and passed around a dirty glass. "A song in recognition of our King's beloved," he said, and demanded a chorus of "Mary from the Dairy."

Meinhardt sang, eyes closed and fingers clenched. "My maid Mary she minds the dairy, while I go a-hoeing and mowing each morn." He wondered what the morning would bring him.

He was awakened by an impatient knock on the door. Expecting Mrs. Mudge with his eviction notice, he was unprepared for the courier who handed him a money order, collected his signature, and looked back over his shoulder with curiosity as he exited through the garden.

The wire came from France and the amount was ten times what Meinhardt had expected. He'd helped Wallis escape to another country. It was time for him to make a big change too.

He wrote his Oma that he would come home for a brief visit now instead of waiting until Christmas. "Then I am off for a new life in America. I'm booking passage to New York City."

PART FOUR

Feed Those Hogs Before They Worry Themselves into Anemia

New York, 1937

Chapter 13

Meinhardt warned Mrs. Comfry, the towering director of operations for Macy's Thanksgiving Day Parade, that two of the balloons might scare the children. The dragon's teeth and claws were very sharp, while the policeman's cadaverous mouth, bulbous nose, and staring eyes were truly frightening. Like the Gestapo, he thought. Meinhardt didn't really care whether the balloons made children cry. He just wanted to impress her with his concern for Macy's public image, in hopes he'd be promoted from inflating balloons and swaddling floats to designing costumes.

Mrs. Comfry snapped her measuring tape shut and crossed her heavy arms over breasts as inflated as the cartoon balloons. "Since when does being short make you an expert on kids?"

An association with children was the last thing Meinhardt wanted. He was glad he'd been assigned to women's dresses, a higher status job. The position became available when a German woman left to start a family and Macy's wanted to replace her with someone of the same nationality. The store was proud of its immigrant workforce, which in turn promoted the annual parade.

Like other employees, Meinhardt volunteered ten hours a week in the fall to test balloons for leaks, cut and attach guide ropes, fold tissue paper flowers, and wrap bunting around the floats' platforms. It was tedious work, but he looked for opportunities to catch the eye of the parade's creative designer. If the man liked his ideas, he might get a part-time paying job in the costume division, leading to a year-round position in merchandising or window displays.

"I only want the parade to reflect well on us," he told Mrs. Comfry. "I'm sure the Mickey Mouse and Santa balloons will make children smile. As will the stocking that spills out toys."

"Just do what you're told in the parade shop and then get back to the sales floor."

Meinhardt returned to slicing ropes. Those around him smiled in sympathy and affinity. All were all eager to succeed in this country and a job at Macy's was preferable to laboring in the city's sweatshops or on the docks. Mrs. Pacelli was happier selling Italian gloves than making them, while Mr. Murphy said wielding a pencil in inventory beat maneuvering grappling hooks.

If Meinhardt felt less gratitude than the other immigrants, he shared with them the sting of starting at the bottom and struggling to move up. New York's high-end clothing stores had been as dismissive as those in Berlin and London. He'd tried them all: Saks, Bergdorf's, Lord and Taylor, Bloomingdale's. Even when he lied about having worked in Berlin's finest stores and on Savile Row, they turned him away. At Bonwit Teller, the last place he tried, the manager claimed Germans were barbaric, the Brits had no style, and Meinhardt had no sense thinking he could get a job there. He was patted on the head and gently pushed out the door.

At least his coworkers at Macy's respected him. They dubbed him the "Baron of Bunting" after he showed them how to pin yards of material so it wouldn't sag. He thought they were wasting effort on something that would pass by a million spectators in a minute. It certainly wasn't why he'd crossed the Atlantic, to sell rayon dresses or blow up scary rubber animals.

He was particularly puzzled by America's obsession with Disney. This year's parade attractions were Mickey Mouse's big ears and Pinocchio's forty-four-foot nose. There were also rumors of a Snow White and the Seven Dwarfs float. The movie, to be released in December, was being promoted with a soundtrack recording and a doll. Macy's toy

71

department was stocked.

Meinhardt had his own ideas and related them with coworkers as they cut, wrapped, and pinned. Instead of featuring Disney, Macy's should promote itself. He pictured a beach float. Winter was when people dreamed of lounging on the shore and getting a sunburn. Even if they couldn't go to the Bahamas, they could pretend their living room was Jones Beach. Those riding the floats would wear Macy's line of men's white dinner jackets and sand pajamas, and women's halter tops and bare midriff dresses. The television coverage would be a free advertisement.

"Won't the half-naked models get goose bumps?" asked a listener from Southern Europe.

"Braving the cold," answered Meinhardt, "will make them look like heroes to the crowd."

"But don't people want fairy tale fantasy when they watch the parade?" asked another.

"They'll get a fantasy of sunshine and warmth just as winter sets in."

"What a stupendous idea!" A voice from behind drowned out the skeptics. Nikko Foxx, the parade's creative designer, was as tanned as if he'd just returned from a tropical vacation himself. Foxx flashed a toothy smile and swept into his office, an area christened "backstage."

Mr. Murphy congratulated Meinhardt. "A big idea from a little person. No offense mate."

"None taken," said Meinhardt. He hoped he'd risen in Nikko Foxx's estimation too.

When his volunteer shift ended, Meinhardt walked uptown to the Automat. It cost more than a meal at his boarding house, but he could eat alone in the coin-operated cafeteria. He also had more choices, depending on which tier of glass-fronted doors held the food he wanted. The second row was his limit. Today, German chocolate cake was in the third, so he settled for apple pie. Thankfully, Boston baked beans, an American staple he'd grown to like, filled all four rows.

He wandered over to Times Square. Fingering the coins in his pocket, he calculated he'd need another week's wages before he could afford a movie ticket. The latest Marx Brother's hit, *A Day at the Races*, was at his neighborhood theater. Maybe he should have become a jockey.

Walking around was free, though, and the moonless evening was bright with electric ads for Planters Peanuts and Coca Cola. Beggars mechanically accosted the streams of people, some in clothes as tattered as those with their hands out, others dressed in topcoats and furs on their way to the new hit play *Golden Boy*. The only ones with space around them were the buskers beneath Father Duffy's statue. Meinhardt recognized a Brandenberg Concerto and tapped his feet to *The Music Goes Round and Round*. Knowing it would mean no dessert for him tomorrow, he added his nickels to the scattered coins in the fiddler's violin case and the crooner's hat. Despite being as poor as the panhandlers, the musicians looked happier, perhaps because they worked for their change. Their hopes were no different than his, to be recognized and paid for their talents.

Where the bright lights ended, Meinhardt took the downtown subway home. He'd have preferred walking to save the five-cent fare, but darkness was dangerous. He was an easy target for hungry thieves and joy-seeking thugs. Even Mayor LaGuardia, the domineering "little flower," was powerless to protect people like him. Meinhardt understood how women must feel. He was freer in America than Germany, but he would face barriers wherever he lived.

The next day, after eight hours convincing

housewives that zippers, the latest feature in dresses, were fashionable and mechanically safe, Meinhardt reported to Mrs. Comfry for his assignment.

"Balloons or floats?" He tried not to cower before her towering bulk.

"Neither. Backstage." She wrapped her arms around herself as though hugging a secret.

Looking at her smug face, Meinhardt feared for his job. Had she complained to Mr. Foxx that he'd criticized the balloon designs as too scary? Only after he remembered Mr. Foxx's praise for his beach float idea did Meinhardt's confidence recover. This could be his big break.

"There are twenty-one balloons and floats in this year's parade." Mr. Foxx shuffled the sketches, photos, and advertising circulars on his desk. "I'm thinking of adding one more."

Shots of Disney productions topped the pile. Meinhardt waited for the designer to find the ads for Macy's tropical beachwear. Meinhardt didn't need them for inspiration. The float was already taking shape in his head, draped with glitter-flecked beige crepe for sand and riders on lounge chairs tossing beach balls to the crowds lining the parade route. "Spectators will go wild."

"You think so too?" Mr. Foxx gave up his search among the Disney paraphernalia. "I've never seen the public this excited before. They can't wait for December 21st to get here!"

Meinhardt couldn't see why people would be eager for the first day of winter to arrive, but if Mr. Foxx believed it would trigger vacation fantasies, he wouldn't disagree. Recalling Mrs. Comfry's displeasure with what she perceived as his arrogance, it was best if he acted humble.

"I picture you as Doc, the smart one, but you can be Grumpy, Happy, Sleepy, Bashful, Sneezy, or Dopey. It's your coice." Mr. Foxx spread his hands and smiled.

Meinhardt frowned. What did the seven dwarfs have to do with the first day of winter?

"Clever of Disney to release the film four days before Christmas. A Snow White float a month earlier will ratchet the excitement higher. So, which one will it be?"

"Not Doc," Meinhardt answered.

Mr. Foxx looked at him expectantly.

"*Nein* to the other six as well."

It was Mr. Foxx's turn to frown.

"I am not and I will not play a dwarf." Meinhardt repeated "*Nein!*" seven times.

Mr. Foxx jumped up and thrust a finger toward the door. "Out of my office, out of your job, out of Macy's." He spluttered "out" seven times.

Meinhardt stared straight ahead as he walked to the exit, but he caught the looks of shock and concern on his coworkers' faces. They knew it would be hard for him to find another job.

His eyes avoided Mrs. Comfry, yet he heard her final jab. "Little man with a big mouth."

Maybe he did have a big mouth, and a big ego, but from now on he'd use them to build himself up instead of giving others an excuse to tear him down. Rodge claimed "Troublemakers are like farmers. They turn up the earth so something new can be planted." It was time for Meinhardt to sow a new life. He'd use the honey-sweet bass baritone his Oma loved to earn his living on the street with the other proud buskers. Who knew what opportunities would turn up?

Chapter 14

Meinhardt quickly learned which songs made people toss coins. The nonsensical *Inka, Dinka, Doo* was popular, ditto the upbeat *I've Got the World on a String.* He avoided downbeat tunes like *Hallelujah,*

I'm a Bum and *Brother, Can You Spare a Dime?* except on bright days, when people laughed at themselves. On overcast ones, being out of work and hungry wasn't funny. He also developed a repertoire of Fats Waller numbers, *Ain't Misbehavin'* his favorite. Pedestrians thought a tiny white man doing songs made famous by a large black one was hilarious.

Nevertheless, as temperatures dropped, so did the number of coins in his hat. People hurried past without listening. Others stomped off if he declined a request whose lyrics made him sound Germanic. Despite daily practice to obliterate his accent, traces came out when he sang. Speaking gave him more time to pace his words and control their pronunciation. He flat out refused to perform songs from *Snow White and the Seven Dwarfs*, and felt vindicated when there wasn't a Snow White float in the Macy's parade after all. It was likely a business decision, but Meinhardt preferred to imagine that his former co-workers had protested against building it.

"Mommy, a dwarf!" A red-cheeked child had pointed at him one day near Broadway.

"A singing one! Give us a chorus of *Whistle While you Work.*"

"I'm not a dwarf and I don't sing dwarf songs." Meinhardt launched instead into *It's a Sin to Tell a Lie.*

"Hey Grumpy. Sing the song for the kid."

"Yeah Dopey. Then do *Heigh Ho* so we can all go off to work for a change."

"Maybe he's bashful." There was a loud snicker on his right.

"I'll bash him something to be bashful about!" The threat came from his left.

Meinhardt looked for an opening in the crowd. He remembered arriving home breathless after yet another narrow escape from childhood bullies. His grandmother had held him to her chest until his heart stopped racing, but there was no escape, and no Oma, to help him now.

"*Pennies from Heaven*." A deep voice called the request from a place he couldn't see.

Meinhardt began: "A long time ago, a million years BC, the best things in life, were absolutely free." The man who'd spoken worked his way to the front and whistled approval. When the song ended, nickels, dimes, and quarters rained into the hat. The crowd dispersed.

The man wore no fright wig, and he'd broken his silence, but Meinhardt recognized Harpo.

"Thank you, Mr. Marx." Meinhardt poured the coins through his fingers. "This is more than I usually earn in a week."

"*Bitte*," Harpo replied. "You sing and speak English well."

Meinhardt said he'd studied languages as a schoolboy in Berlin.

"My mother is from Germany." Harpo spoke naturally. "I was born here, but I quit school after second grade. The Irish kids picked on me for being Jewish, and small. Two threw me out the window. It was only the first floor, but I knew if I tattled they'd torture me more."

Meinhardt remembered the classmate who broke his pinky; his Oma fed him pineapple to lessen the swelling. The bullying had gotten worse after the Nazis came to power. "I read that your given name is Adolph. No wonder you got rid of it."

"Nah. I changed my name legally in 1911." He'd inherited the harp from his maternal grandmother and got the nickname at a poker game by plucking high strings if he won a hand, bass notes when the other players lost. It unnerved them and he took home the whole pot.

Meinhardt hesitated. "Your voice ...?"

The silent routine was originally ad-libbed,

Harpo explained, but became a permanent gag after a reviewer wrote that his beautiful gift for pantomime was ruined whenever he spoke. "Actually my voice is deeper and smoother than Groucho's, but the brothers don't compete. We each do our own schtick." He invited Meinhardt to meet them and gave him directions to their film studio in Queens. They'd moved most productions to MGM in Hollywood, but still got their best ideas in New York. Meinhardt agreed to come the following Monday. Harpo puckered up and *Whistle While You Work* wafted softly from his lips. He ran in a circle and skipped off.

The cavernous space of the Kaufman Astoria Film Studio was like an armory. Meinhardt walked between Greek columns toward the sound of gobbling punctuated by laughter until he reached the set where *Room Service* was being shot. Harpo stopped chasing a rubber turkey with a baseball bat and flapped over to introduce him to Groucho and Chico. Meinhardt asked what the movie was about. They took turns narrating a story about a ballroom, a playwright, and a dead body that wasn't really dead. "And they all live happily ever after. *Verstehen?*" asked Groucho.

Meinhardt didn't understand, but assumed he wasn't meant to. He asked why the still lifes of overripe fruits and wilted flowers adorning the ballroom walls were signed by Harpo.

"Didn't my brother confess that he painted?" asked Chico.

"He's terrible," said Groucho. "As a wedding gift to his wife, he gave away all his paintings."

"None of his brothers would take them, though." It was Zeppo entering the studio with his wife Marion, who was carrying a large tureen. "Lunch, boys," she announced. "*Essen!*"

Meinhardt took a tentative taste of broth and

smiled in recognition. It had the distinctive flavor of his Oma's chicken soup. "Grated yams!" he said, and took a second, larger, spoonful.

Surprised, Marion asked how he knew her secret ingredient. He said they cooked it that way in Dornum, the town where his grandmother and Minnie, the boys' mother, had grown up. Marion confirmed that she'd learned the recipe from her late mother-in-law.

"Nu," said Groucho, "you couldn't learn how to make lighter matzo balls too? These *kneidlach* are like are cannon balls. I'd rather chew this." He put his cigar back in his mouth.

"Good German food is supposed to be heavy," said Meinhardt. Marion smiled. Zeppo raised his eyebrows and twiddled his thumbs. Meinhardt took a bite. They awaited his verdict.

"A cannon ball," he agreed, "but a tasty one. The dill and onion explode in your mouth."

"The man's a born diplomat," Harpo declared. "We should give him a part in the movie."

"You'll pay?" Meinhardt would treat himself to a nice dinner at the German delicatessen around the corner from the Automat.

"Five bucks, two matzo balls, and a knish for every take." Groucho shook his hand.

"Second helpings to seal the deal!" Zeppo refilled Meinhardt's bowl. "Look at him. So small for his age."

"He's a midget, you idiot." Harpo bonked Zeppo on the head.

"Midget, schmidget. The boy looks like he hasn't had a good meal in months."

It was true. Busking barely brought in enough to rent his room. The brothers decided Meinhardt needed a gimmick to boost revenue. Something nonverbal to accompany his singing. They deferred to Harpo, who fetched an overflowing prop box and took out the bright pink fright wig he'd worn on stage before switching to a red one that showed up better on film. He plopped the pink wig on Meinhardt's head. "Funny! You look taller too."

Meinhardt looked in a mirror. Unlike Harpo, he lacked the self-confidence to be laughed at. He took the wig off.

Harpo spotted a stack of newspapers on the table. He rolled the top one with the headline facing outward and brandished it on the beat while belting out *Lady of Spain*. "People will step closer to read the headline. Once they're next to you, they'll feel obligated to throw money."

Meinhardt disliked people hovering over him, but if they paid, he'd learn to live with it. "*The Post* or *The Daily News*?"

"*The News*. More lurid headlines." Harpo dove back into the prop box and extracted a purple top hat with a white silk band above the brim.

Meinhardt shook his head.

"Not to wear." Harpo set the hat top-side down on the floor. "To collect your money."

It was perfect. Big enough that it asked to be filled, yet not so big that it was depressing when empty. Meinhardt positioned it to the right of his feet. He launched into *Inka Dinka Doo*. The brothers drew near and Groucho pretended to read the headline on the rolled-up paper. "Man-Eating Squid Discovered Off Miami Coast." They each pitched a quarter into the hat.

Chapter 15

Meinhardt learned to avoid corners with newsboys so pedestrians would get the headlines from him: Amelia Earhart's Plane Spotted (at least weekly), Child Star Shirley Temple Over the Hill, Picasso Paints Graphic Guernica. Harpo wasn't much of a painter, but his acting advice was spot-on. Cautiously, Meinhardt let himself trust someone other than his Oma.

He felt protective toward his good locations. Broadway at 45th was the most lucrative, where his growing repertoire of show tunes attracted theatergoers. At Harpo's urging, he began with two handfuls of coins in the hat to impress passersby that his talent was worth their money. When the hat was full, he emptied it into a pouch, which he tied around his waist and tucked underneath his pants. Some days the pouch grew so heavy, it was hard to walk home. He ate at the German delicatessen every Wednesday, between the matinee and evening performances.

Charles Becker was on Meinhardt's corner on a blustery day when he returned from one of those meals. Until now, Meinhardt's scowl had scared off musicians twice his size. This singer, another midget of all things, smiled cordially, as if welcoming Meinhardt to *his* spot.

"This corner is mine." Meinhardt waited for the man, more than half a foot shorter than him, to challenge back. Instead, he apologized in a faint but recognizably German accent, picked up his cup, and turned to leave.

"Look, a little Mutt and Jeff." A man in a tweed coat and a woman in furs demanded a duet. When the man took out his wallet, Meinhardt nodded for the other midget to come stay. He set his top hat on the ground and began singing *Tea For Two*. The smaller man sang along and danced a soft-shoe, which Meinhardt picked up. Soon they drew a large crowd. During an encore of *The Lullaby of Broadway*, the clink of coins nearly drowned out their harmonizing.

Meinhardt knew he should offer to split the take. "Your hat, your money," the other man said affably. Meinhardt guiltily accepted. He suggested another good corner, two blocks north.

The men introduced themselves. Both were

from Berlin, but Charles had left a year later. "After you got out, *es ging vom schlechten zum schlimmeren*, things went from bad to worse." People like them were branded *Untermenschen*, subhumans unworthy of life. The Ministry of Education ordered those who knew a foreign language to register with the government.

"Does that include people who speak English?" For the first time, Meinhardt worried the racial purity laws might affect his Oma. The worse the economy got, the more the Nazis sought scapegoats. Göring had instituted a four-year self-sufficiency plan to ready the nation for war. Meinhardt shuddered to think of the man who humiliated him bringing down a whole continent.

Charles wished Meinhardt good luck and headed uptown. Meinhardt enjoyed a moment of superiority about his height advantage, then felt ashamed. He was being a little Nazi himself.

A few days later, Charles was back. Meinhardt worried he hadn't been forceful enough, but Charles had just stopped by to visit. "I'm not competitive. Besides, you're better than me."

"There's no difference in talent," Meinhardt said graciously. Charles had a passable tenor and was actually a more graceful dancer. "It's a matter of practice and *widmung*, dedication."

Meinhardt saw that as the reason Harpo garnered respect, not mere laughter. No matter how foolish he acted, he played the harp with seriousness. A reverence for music mattered to Meinhardt too. After his voice settled, his Oma tried to hire a music teacher. Even those who acknowledged his talent told her not to waste money on lessons. So she bought recordings by Anton van Rooy and Leo Schützendorf, and saved for months to take him to a Hans Hotter concert. The appreciation she nurtured continued into adulthood. The pleasure of singing with Rodge, even silly musical hall numbers at the pub, was that both cared about the quality of their performance. Rodge claimed his ear was more sensitive to sweet and sour than his tongue.

"I want to succeed at work." Meinhardt spoke with a fervor that made Charles draw back. He said his *traum*, his dream, was to prove men like Göring were the earth's true little creatures.

Charles had a dream too, though his was more modest and personal. He wanted a happy marriage and children. If his hope could be stated in grander terms, it was to be adopted by his new homeland. "I want to become a citizen and prove I'm a good American," he said quietly.

"I am sure you will succeed in your *traum*, Charlie."

"Charles, not Charlie!" He spoke sharply and this time Meinhardt pulled back. Charles apologized. He wasn't competitive about his height, he explained, but he hated the diminutive name. "I'm a full grown man, not *ein kleines Kind*." Meinhardt nodded in full understanding.

Meinhardt never sought out Charles, but enjoyed being visited during the afternoon lulls. They agreed that being different made them watchful. Meinhardt looked out for enemies, Charles for friends. One day Charles surprised him with an invitation. "Do you want to go to an opera?"

Harpo's advice boosted Meinhardt's earnings, but street wages didn't buy opera tickets.

Charles didn't mean the Met, however. *The Cradle Will Rock*, a controversial opera about corporate greed and unions, was reopening on Broadway. A customer had given him passes to a dress rehearsal. Not even his regulars had given Meinhardt anything other than coins. Although wary of establishing a precedent for friendship, curiosity about the music made him agree to go.

He was disappointed by the opera's heavy-handed symbolism, especially the trite names of the characters: Larry Foreman, Reverend Salvation, even Moll for the good-hearted prostitute. The Marx Brothers' sideways antics had spoiled him. Nevertheless, Meinhardt saw parallels between Mr. Mister's total control of Steeltown and the Nazis' domination of Germany.

Charles on the other hand was ecstatic about the performance. Afterwards, in the lobby, he bounced on the balls of his tiny feet. "It's the American way, fighting for the underdog." That hadn't been Meinhardt's experience. Maybe Charles's friendliness engendered more kindness.

"Gentlemen, welcome!" A youthful six-foot man swept down and slapped their backs. "Orson Welles, director." He looked a bit like Göring, though he was large rather than corpulent.

A photographer asked Welles to stand between the two midgets. The director laughed and posed. Charles, uncertain whether to look up at Welles or straight at the camera, did his best to smile. Meinhardt stepped out of the frame. Wasn't the opera about *not* exploiting people?

"I wish Germans could see this piece." Charles told Welles how government-controlled industries forced citizens to work for the war, fixed wages, and threatened to intern those who protested. Welles asked how the two of them were getting by since escaping.

"Street singers," answered Charles. "We earn pennies but we're free from tyranny."

"Even buskers need to organize!" Welles had a booming voice to match his size.

"Against who?" Meinhardt stepped into the conversation. "We're independent workers."

"Hah!" Welles spread his cape and tossed his thick black hair. "You work for the theater owners whose patrons catch your street act before they go

84

inside to see their shows. The owners should cover your asses for entertaining the customers whose asses cover their seats." He said buskers had the same right to organize as stage and screen actors, and promised to bring a union representative to see their street acts. Then he bowed, spun around, and strode off.

Charles was excited. Joining a union was one more step toward becoming an American.

Meinhardt snorted. "I work for myself. The Nazis are masters of organization and look where that got us."

Dearest Oma,

The weather is cold but I'm warmed by success I never expected. I postponed my dream to sell clothes to the rich and instead sell my voice to whoever passes by. In New York City, this means people from all over the world, although the person I see most is another small German man named Charles Becker. We're friends, yet I keep my distance. I'm afraid a pair of midgets will attract hostile attention. Such fears follow me here from Berlin.

Hören! I met the Marx Brothers. *Stellen Sie sich vor*! Imagine! Their mother, who you knew in Dornum, was very ambitious. Minnie wouldn't let being Jewish prevent their becoming famous. She had faith in her boys, like you in me. Only she pushed harder, maybe because there were five of them! They are cutting on screen but kind in person, generous with advice and food.

I struggle to understand Americans, obsessed with little Mickey Mouse, yet big-hearted and optimistic, even in hard times. They are not like the Germans, who are always depressed. Some are accepting of differences, perhaps because they come from so many backgrounds. As I learned in London, those at the very top and very bottom are the most small-minded and cruel.

I worry about you every day, what with the *verrückt* Nazi rules. You were wise to urge me to leave. I miss you but if I'd stayed, I might be locked away and not even able to write you.

I still dream of the day when you will join me. It is not that this country is better off in the Depression, but here I feel there is a chance that my efforts will be rewarded. Then I will be able to take better care of you. Perhaps the *Optimismus* of the Americans is taking root in me.

Your loving Enkel,
Meinhardt

Chapter 16

Orson Welles never came to watch Meinhardt perform, but another man did. Though nearly as tall as the director, this gentleman was older and held his thin body with the stiff bearing of royalty. He too affected a cape and had long wavy hair that blew wildly in the early winter gusts.

The man stood immobile at the side of the crowd as Meinhardt performed show tunes and a medley of Fats Waller songs. After he'd listened for an hour without putting any money in the hat, Meinhardt grew annoyed. He pointedly faced away from him. Only when the street lamps came on did the man approach and hand him his card. Meinhardt's hopes rose. Perhaps this was the Broadway or Hollywood agent he dreamed would discover him. He read the ornate script:

> ***Baron Leopold Van Singer***
> ***Owner and Manager***
> ***Traveling Midget Troupe***

"Perhaps you have heard of me? The Lilipudstadt?" The man had an Austrian accent.

Meinhardt knew about the "midget city" in a Venice amusement park. Before abandoning him to his Oma, his parents threatened to sell him to a man who "put naughty midgets in cages with lions and tigers and bears." His grandmother later told him such talk was *Unsinn*, nonsense.

Van Singer complimented Meinhardt's singing and said he'd make a good barker. "You have the confidence to part people from the little money they have. Also, your face is handsome, something people don't expect in a midget. It will draw customers."

Meinhardt handed back the card. He had no desire to be part of a traveling freak show.

"You confuse midgets with lumpen dwarves. Midgets are better proportioned and move with grace." Instead of pocketing the card, Van Singer buried it among the coins in Meinhardt's hat. "Perhaps you will reconsider." He bowed. "You come highly recommended."

Stooping to pull out the card, Meinhardt looked up, unable to hide his curiosity.

"Mr. Harpo Marx." Van Singer's smile was triumphant. "He said you had a big talent."

"What gives you the *chutzpah*?" Meinhardt used the word he'd learned from Harpo when he confronted him. "You think because people laugh *with* you, they don't laugh *at* people like me?"

"They laugh at me because I can laugh at myself." Harpo put Meinhardt's purple top hat on his own head and grinned. "*Nu*, don't be so angry. Zeppo's wife is making Shabbas dinner. Come. You'll eat her matzo cannon balls and the weight will calm you down."

Meinhardt didn't want to calm down. He snatched back the hat and stomped it flat. He didn't need Harpo's help or his friendship. He'd find his own way to make a buck.

In a tourist shop on Times Square, Meinhardt chose a panama hat with an orange-flowered band. He bought a paper several blocks from his corner. The front page read "Relapse. Economy Heads Back Down." He rolled it face in. The headline would scare off customers. But they didn't need *The Daily News* to tell them things had taken another turn for the worse. Over the next few weeks, the panama hat, although shallower than the top hat, was never more than a quarter full.

Meinhardt retrieved Van Singer's card from his coin jar. He saw no other way to survive.

Charles was surprised when Meinhardt came to find him. His eyes grew big when he read the card. "*Eine große Chance!*" he declared and embraced Meinhardt. "*Vielen Dank, Freund.*"

"Don't thank me." Meinhardt didn't want the burden of Charles's gratitude any more than that of owing his success to Harpo. "I thought two could negotiate a better deal than one."

Van Singer congratulated their timing. After rehearsing a new show, the troupe would tour twenty cities that spring and summer. Then, in the fall, MGM had contracted with him to assemble over a hundred midgets to play Munchkins in a movie titled *The Wizard of Oz.*

"What are Munchkins?" Charles's voice squeaked with excitement.

"The Baum books, on which the movie is based, describe them only as little blue people."

Meinhardt shuddered. "I suppose I'd rather be a little blue person in warm California than a cold white one in New York."

Charles laughed. Even the Baron smiled, although he didn't give them more money. Still, Meinhardt was glad for a year's guaranteed income, after which the economy might turn around again. Meanwhile, he'd have his way paid to Hollywood, where he could look for a real agent.

His only fear was that he'd run into the Marx Brothers. He also regretted adding distance between him and his Oma, but she would understand. The prospects in Hollywood outshone those in Berlin, London, and New York combined. More than being a meal ticket, playing a Munchkin could be Meinhardt's ticket to fame.

PART FIVE

There's A Storm Blowing Up, A Whopper

Hollywood, 1942

Chapter 17

"It's a good job if you're not claustrophobic," Charles had written, "and our team is short two men." It was three years after the filming of *Oz*, and images of that rainbow fantasy land had been dimmed by a war-darkened world. Hollywood was still making movies, but the rest of the country was making itself ready for war. At Willow Run in Ypsilanti, Michigan, Henry Ford had converted an automotive factory into a B-24 bomber plant. He was hiring ten midgets to work on the bombers because they were small enough to crawl into the wings and buck rivets from inside.

Meinhardt wasn't afraid of enclosed spaces. On the other hand, he wasn't eager to crawl into one to earn a living. Only the fact that he was desperate for a job made him willing to take a Pacific Electric red car to the LA Union Passenger Terminal, where he now waited to board an eastbound train. He felt like he was traveling backwards in time as well as miles. It would be good to see his friend once more, but not to again seek employment he considered beneath him.

Charles had written Meinhardt every couple of months since they and the other midgets had said goodbye on the movie set. He'd married Jessie Kelley, also from *Oz*, and they were now expecting a baby. Charles stayed in touch with everyone, so the letters were full of news about the Munchkins. From him Meinhardt learned that Little Billy Rhodes and his wife got divorced after he beat her up once too often, and that the Doll family scraped by on four-for-the-price-of-one wages for their circus act. Their three normal siblings, still in Germany, said it was good that the little Dolls had gotten out. Meanwhile, Henry Boers was recovering from a mild heart attack, although his brother Teddy was fine. Those two barely managed on occasional sideshow jobs.

Most interesting to Meinhardt, although he'd never admit it to himself, let alone Charles, was the news that Hazel Derthick had married Joey Polinsky, The Count, and taken him back to Hawthorne, Oklahoma, her birthplace. There she gave dance and drama lessons to children under a government-sponsored work program. Joey was content to let her support them while he drank. "I don't know what Hazel expected," Charles wrote, "but The Count sure doesn't treat her like a Countess. She still asks after you." The letter concluded: "Except for me and Jessie, no one is faring well. All the same, I think America is a great country compared to Germany. Come to Michigan and the next time I write Hazel, I can tell her where you are and what you're doing."

Charles had offered to wire Meinhardt the twelve-dollar fare for the two-and-a-half-day train trip. He refused, but had to accept a letter from the plant's foreman to buy the ticket. Under a Presidential proclamation citing the 1798 Alien Enemy Act, Germans, Italians, and Japanese weren't allowed to travel without government permission. Meinhardt wondered if foreign-born Americans would become like the Jews of Germany, their humanity stripped away one right at a time. But as numerous as Jews were in Germany, they were nothing compared to the hordes of Europeans and Asians living in this country. America was built by and still beckoned foreigners like him. *Entlassen!* Leave it be! Meinhardt repeated this phrase to himself, trying to dismiss his worries. He was on his way to see about a job and see the country from a railcar along the way.

The terminal was crowded with soldiers heading to training camps in the Midwest and South. Since troops were given priority, Meinhardt was relieved to get a ticket at all. He bought a one-way fare on the

California Limited to Chicago's Dearborn Station, where he would transfer to the Motor City Special to Detroit's Central Michigan Station. He almost got a round-trip ticket to save money, but he told himself not to decide ahead of time that the job wouldn't work out. "Your mind is like a parachute, " Rodge used to say. "It functions only when it's open."

From the platform, Meinhardt admired the train. The engine was streamlined for speed, its steel and iron frame covered with lightweight aluminum. A poster described the Art Deco design on its exterior as "Armour Yellow with a Leaf Brown roof and undersides." Meinhardt pictured a man's suit in those colors, fine umber wool with yellow stitching around the lapels. He imagined a woman's gold linen dress with chocolate brown stripes radiating from the waist like rail spikes. They'd convey the sense of energy women poured into their new roles in industry.

Even using the booster stool on the platform, it was a stretch for Meinhardt to reach the bottom step of the Pullman sleeping car. For once, he was grateful when the conductor lifted his luggage and gave him a strong hand to grab as well. He kept his small suitcase with him, for fear it wouldn't be transferred from the baggage car when he changed trains in Chicago. Rail travel in the U.S. had a good reputation, but it would never be as precise and efficient as Germany's.

Onboard, Meinhardt was dismayed to see people filling the aisles and standing in the vestibule between coach cars. Other than a pregnant woman and some elderly travelers, soldiers occupied all the seats. He might have to stand for the entire 2,500 mile trip. Instead of worrying about getting a lower sleeping berth the next two nights, he'd be lucky to find enough floor space to stretch out. This was a rare occasion when being short would work to his advantage.

He claimed a small square area for himself and stood astride his suitcase. The exercises he'd invented for the coroner's audition, which he still practiced in hopes of landing another movie role, stood him in good stead as the train picked up speed. He kept his balance while the other standing passengers struggled to get their train legs, and peered under their armpits and out the window as the landscape changed from the city to the open country. Watching the poles that posted the number of miles from the point of departure was mesmerizing. There were 30 poles per mile, with every tenth-mile pole colored-coded, to help him track the train's progress east.

It was a cool day in late fall, but the hot breath of so many passengers quickly raised the temperature in the car. Soldiers opened windows and cinders and smoke from the coal-burning engine blew in. The debris drifted over Meinhardt's head but lodged in everyone else's eyes. Many draped wet handkerchiefs over their noses against the irritation. Meinhardt, safe and low, continued to stare as flat farmland turned into hills and then gradually dried out into desert.

The train stopped at larger cities to squeeze on more passengers. It sped past most small towns but now and then slowed down enough for residents to cheer the boys in uniform. Through the open windows, men in suits and overalls shook the soldiers' hands and urged them to bomb the bug-eyed Gerries and wipe out the slant-eyed Japs. Young women pushed slips of paper with their names and addresses over the sill and gathered the scraps on which the soldiers jotted down theirs. There were promises to write. Rodge used to say "One thing you can give and still keep is your word," but wartime pledges defied good intentions. Meinhardt wondered how many of these encounters would produce letters during the war, let alone romance when it ended.

Heading eastward condensed the hours, and Meinhardt's stomach growled before daylight faded into evening. He went to the dining car early, thinking it would be impossible to find a seat later. The food prepared onboard had a good reputation, and meals would break up the long journey. Maneuvering slowly down the train, he studied each compartment. Chair cars, one level up from coach, had reclining seats and more leg room, a waste of money for him. Parlor cars had swivel chairs and wider windows for the view, but he would have had to stand on the seat like a child to see. He was barred from the lounge cars, reserved for first-class patrons, at the end of the train.

When Meinhardt finally reached the dining car, he inhaled the earthy aroma of roasted meat and potatoes, and the soulful smell of fresh-brewed coffee. His stomach registered pangs of hunger recalling his Oma's sauerbraten; his heart ached with equal intensity for the loneliness of eating meals without her. Although he ordinarily preferred solitary meals to eating with strangers, something about being alone and in transit made him want to at least eat alongside others tonight. Unfortunately, all forty seats in the dining car were taken; some people juggled plates and silverware from a standing position. Reluctantly, Meinhardt retraced his steps.

Arriving back at his coach car felt like coming home. Meinhardt re-occupied his patch of floor space and waited for one of the Negro porters to come down the aisle selling ham and cheese sandwiches, small bottles of milk, and candy. Since coming to America, he'd developed a taste for Baby Ruth Bars and was glad to see them on the porter's tray. He also bought a Denver Sandwich Bar, "the candy lunch," which consisted of two chocolate-covered wafers. It seemed he'd have to subsist on bread sandwiches and candy sandwiches until he arrived in Michigan. He hoped Jessie was a good cook and would serve hot meals during his stay.

Chapter 18

His last good meal before leaving Los Angeles was a surprise lunch with Margaret Hamilton, just hours before he opened Charles's letter. They'd run into each other at Grauman's Chinese Theater, where *The Wizard of Oz* had premiered. Meinhardt was standing under a huge dragon flanked by two Ming Heaven dogs guarding the entrance. Sun glinting off the pagoda's copper roof had nearly blinded him, but the voice calling his name was unmistakable. "Careful those dogs don't bite you! Heh, heh, heh!" Margaret and her son threaded their way through the courtyard's hand and footprints.

"Maggie, you look well. No scars from the burns?"

"Bless your Oma's home remedies." She introduced him to Milton, a serious-looking child who extended his hand. Meinhardt told him he was a handsome little boy.

"I look like my daddy, but he lives far away. I'm not little anymore. I'm five years old."

"You do look like your father, not me, thank heavens. And you are a big boy now." Margaret rested her hands on his thin shoulders.

"Do you go to kindergarten, Milt?" Meinhardt asked.

"I'm Milton, not Milt."

Just like Charles, Meinhardt thought, who hated being called Charlie.

Margaret told Milton he could go fit his hands and feet in the impressions in the concrete while she and Meinhardt found a shady bench, as long as he stayed where she could see him. He left to play, but his large brown eyes sought his mother's every few minutes for reassurance.

"He's almost too well behaved," Margaret said. "He was barely a toddler when he went to live with my parents after I got burned. I thought the separation wouldn't affect him, but he grew up afraid that if he's bad, I'll send him away again. He doesn't see his father much."

Meinhardt looked after the child. He knew how it felt to be abandoned by your parents.

Margaret said that instead of playing cowboys and sports, Milton liked anything to do with movies. Maybe he thought it would keep him at her side. She took him to landmarks, including the Hollywood Forever Cemetery to see the graves of famous stars.

"Didn't he get bored?"

"No. He practiced his alphabet letters by reading headstones. He wanted one of his own. I had to explain that people only got those after they died." She shook her head. "Sometimes I feel buried alive in this town. I expected more work after *Oz*, but except for *My Little Chickadee*, it's been minor roles and radio spots."

"Parts for spinsters are as scarce as those for midgets."

Margaret tried not to appear discouraged in front of Milton, or he'd out-worry her. She'd brought him to Grauman's to see the hand and footprints of living people in hopes he'd make his own in their yard. "Frankly, I'd love to see him play in the mud and get dirty like a normal kid."

Meinhardt had come there today to rekindle his own dying dreams. Van Singer's midget troupe was popular after *Oz*, but they disbanded even before the U.S. entered the war. Americans suspected all Eastern Europeans, not just Germans, of being spies and Nazi sympathizers.

"We were doing our act at a tent in Atlanta, colored people in back, whites up front, when a gang stormed the stage shouting 'Go home Krauts!' and pelting us with maggoty cabbages. The heckling went on throughout the South and Midwest. We were all in debt to Van Singer, who tried to force us to go on performing, but we quit en masse and scattered."

"I'd think you would find a place together. Strength in numbers," Margaret said.

"More likely danger in numbers. When midgets band together, folks get suspicious."

"So that's why you prefer to be alone. You feel safer?"

"Sometimes." He looked around at the crowds. "Other times, more vulnerable."

"And these days?" asked Margaret.

"Neither safe nor vulnerable." Meinhardt turned up his hands. "Just broke."

Los Angeles was booming, manufacturing ships, fighter jets, and tanks for the war, but he couldn't handle the heavy equipment. He asked if Margaret remembered Charles Becker.

"The mayor of *Oz*. With the squeaky voice and dimpled smile. He was the shortest man."

Meinhardt said that before leaving Berlin, Charles apprenticed to be a butcher. The others teased him when he had trouble wielding the saws and big meat cleavers. Their joking got nastier as the Nazis rose in power. He'd fled after they threatened to put him through the meat slicer and feed him to the Gestapo's dogs. Southern red necks were no different than beefy apprentices.

"The best I can do," said Meinhardt, "is a part-time job at a used clothing store where women trade in their ugly old clothes for someone else's ugly old clothes. I show them how to brighten up their outfits with accessories, but really, nothing improves the look of synthetics."

"Nothing improves the look of natural either. Look at me."

Meinhardt rewarded her with a smile. He knew Margaret wasn't after a false compliment.

As if on cue, Milton returned and smiled at her too. She asked if he was hungry and when he nodded yes, offered to treat Meinhardt to lunch. He agreed to join them, but only if they went Dutch. "It's an old German, or Deutsch, tradition," he punned. Margaret's groan was his reward.

They went to Du-Pars Restaurant, a famous hangout where Milton liked to spot undercover stars. Margaret loved the pot pies and her son always ordered pancakes. It was Meinhardt's first time there. As they waited for the street car, he asked Milton what he should order.

"Pancakes <u>and</u> donuts." He nodded for emphasis. "Are you a child or a grown-up?"

"A very short grown-up." Meinhardt looked toward Margaret for help.

"Remember how we said people come in different shapes, sizes, and colors?"

"Like Benny." Milton turned to Meinhardt. "He's in my class and he uses crutches. Big Sam's a grown-up, but he's more like a giant." Margaret explained that Sam was a very large Negro who carried children crippled by polio on and off the school bus. "He also tells the bullies to stop teasing them," Milton added.

"Are there a lot of bullies in your school?" Meinhardt asked.

The boy looked around and whispered their names.

"How do you and the other children treat them?"

"We're nice to them, otherwise they hit us."

"If you're a little person and other people are nice to you," said Meinhardt, "you know it's because they like you and not because they're afraid of you."

"Are there grown-up bullies?" Milton asked.

"Are they mean to you?"

"Yes, but there are nice grownups too. Like your mommy."

"Since when did I become a good witch?" Margaret wiggled her claws; they pretended to shriek with fear. When the streetcar came, she boosted Milton onto the bottom step. Meinhardt signaled for her to board next. He didn't want her to watch from behind as he hoisted himself up.

Margaret let Milton choose their seats. Meinhardt assumed he'd want to sit up front and look out the window, but he led them to the back where he could watch the other passengers.

"I think he studies their characters." Margaret shook her head. "That's my son for you."

"Watch," Meinhardt said. "He'll end up being a more successful actor than either of us."

In the restaurant, Margaret also let Milton choose their booth. Bright red, with a quilted leather back, it offered a clear view of the counter where business was brisk. Margaret got a chicken pot pie and Milton's buttermilk hot cakes came with two pitchers, one for syrup and the other for melted butter. Meinhardt ordered fresh-squeezed orange juice, eggs, and "hand-peeled and cut" hash browns. You'd never know there was a war going on and that food was rationed.

Meinhardt and Margaret caught up on the last three years. He told her he'd convinced his grandmother to leave Berlin and return to her home village of Dornum in case the Allies bombed the cities. Although she was safer there, he still worried about food shortages and forced labor.

"I'm sure she worries about you too. There's nothing stronger than the bond between children and the grownups who raise them, especially when they do it alone." They looked at Milton, cautiously pouring butter and syrup on his pancakes, and taking small neat bites.

"Any love interests?" Margaret asked. "No sense in your good looks going to waste."

Meinhardt squirmed. "I won't be thirty for three years, plenty of time before I think about romance." Shame filled him, remembering visits to the prostitutes on Santa Monica Boulevard. He shouldn't have cared what they thought of his body, yet he did. He couldn't imagine enduring the judgment of a woman who he loved. Margaret made a living playing unattractive people. He wondered if she risked having a social life, but hesitated to ask in front of Milton.

Without embarrassment, Margaret answered his unasked question. She was nearly forty and had no desire to remarry. Her son's love was enough. Meinhardt wondered if his Oma would have remarried if she hadn't had his mother to bring up on her own, and what the rest of her life would have been like without him to raise after that. Taking care of others was an essential part of her nature. He realized with a pang what a sacrifice she'd made by urging him to leave.

"Mommy," Milton put down his fork and wiped his mouth and fingers with a napkin. "Why did those movie stars put their hands and feet in the sidewalk?"

Margaret didn't know. Meinhardt said he'd read that Sidney Grauman got the idea when he accidentally stepped in wet cement during the theater's construction.

"Did the cement man get mad at him?" Milton gripped his napkin.

"I don't think so. Mr. Grauman was the boss."

"It was wrong to step in the cement," Margaret added, "but sometimes when people act badly, it can lead to a good idea."

"Speaking of good ideas," Meinhardt said to Margaret, "Eleanor Roosevelt's giving a talk tonight on Freedom House and human rights. Do you want to go?" He avoided politics, but liked her views on equality. He wondered if she thought of people like him when she spoke about it.

Margaret doubted she could find a last-minute babysitter. Also, Milton grew uneasy when she left him at night. She was gone enough during the day, always looking for work.

"We could join a USO show as a novelty act," said Meinhardt, "a German midget and a New England spinster."

"We'd depress the troops instead of cheering them up." Margaret frowned. "Did you ever think of changing your name? You barely have any accent. You could pass for an American."

"I'll never change my name. It's the only thing that connects me to my parents, especially my father. My Oma understood. She never pressured me to take her last name."

Margaret nodded. "That's why I wanted Milton to keep his dad's name, Meserve, even though it bothers him that his last name is different than mine. Besides, can't you hear children sing-songing 'Mil-ton Ha-mil-ton' just to tease him?" Milton looked up. She winked at him.

"Even if I became John Smith," Meinhardt said, "it's not as if there are more film roles for American midgets than for German ones."

Margaret sighed. "Hollywood is churning out movies and neither of us can find work. It doesn't seem fair. I still think that with your face, you're leading man material."

Meinhardt slicked back his hair and presented his profile to Margaret. "Since Clark Gable and Henry Fonda enlisted, I could be drafted to play their parts. What do you say?"

"Very handsome." She tilted her head coquettishly. "And I could play the nurse who the soldier falls in love with after his plane is shot down and I restore him to health and virility."

"Actually I *was* recruited for a war movie. Did you see the cartoon *Seven Wise Dwarfs*?"

Margaret hadn't. She said it sounded like something she'd take Milton to.

Disney wanted to make a live-action short about the dwarves wisely investing money in Canadian War Savings Certificates and U.S. War Bonds. They asked Meinhardt to take the lead role and chaperone the six children they'd hire to play the other dwarves. When he refused, the studio made a cartoon instead. "Disney pays well, but I won't prostitute myself."

"I would," said Margaret. "The studios and the army are making movies to warn soldiers about venereal disease. By playing an ugly prostitute, I'd do my part to keep our boys clean."

Meinhardt couldn't tell if she was serious. Had her worries about taking care of Milton compromised her morals to the point that she'd play an enemy whore?

"Better yet, I could concoct a witch's potion that turns me into a ravishing beauty who seduces German soldiers and gives *them* a venereal disease." She erupted in a wicked laugh.

Meinhardt relaxed. Her integrity was intact. "You're plucky. Something will turn up."

She nodded. "You know if I'm ever in a position to recommend you for a role, I will."

"Thanks, but *you* know I have to do it on my own."

"What if positions were reversed?" she asked.

"The same. But I don't think you'd accept help either. You're as independent as I am."

"Yes, but not as proud or as stubborn. I have to take care of someone other than myself." She pivoted in the plush seat to wrap an arm around her son. "Milton! What are you doing?"

103

One hand was emptying the maple syrup onto his pancakes and the other was pouring out all the melted butter. The two liquids overflowed the plate, their amber and gold streams merging across the tabletop. This was not the little boy whose mother lamented he was too well behaved.

"So, Milton," Meinhardt said, "you're being bad, like the man who stepped in cement?"

The child nodded and looked at the adults. This time, Margaret beseeched Meinhardt.

"And what good idea will come from this?" It was his turn to sound matter-of-fact.

Milton hesitated, then sank both his hands into the sticky puddle.

"What do you think, Maggie? Should we take off our shoes as well?"

Margaret cackled, Milton grinned, and Meinhardt laughed more heartily than he had since chasing a football in the park with his Oma as a child.

"Morals are better on a full belly." It was an old expression Rodge used when he bought fish and chips for everyone to keep peace at the pub. "What flavor donuts should I order?"

Margaret liked glazed, Milton preferred chocolate, and Meinhardt confessed a weakness for cream filling. "Let's splurge and get a platter with all three," Meinhardt said. "My treat."

"Dutch treat," contradicted Margaret. "It's an old *Oz* tradition."

Chapter 19

Memories of food would have to satisfy Meinhardt's hunger on this long journey. He was tired too, even though it was early by California time. Weary passengers climbed into Pullman berths, freeing up space on the floor. Meinhardt stretched out on a Culver Hotel bath towel, a souvenir from his film days, and folded a sweater on top of his suitcase for a pillow. After a few minutes of anxiety about being stepped on, he was lulled to sleep by the metronomic clicking of the rails.

He woke when his eyelids were pierced by the still-cool rays of a low-hanging sun. The same rhythmic sounds that had lured him into slumber the night before now eased him gently into morning. Snores and steady breathing told him his fellow travelers were still asleep and he savored the quiet solitude. Ambition made him an early riser. Rodge tried to motivate the pub patrons by saying, "If you want your dreams to come true, you mustn't oversleep." But for men who put in a hard day's work followed by an evening's drinking, it was all they could do to drag themselves out of bed. They knew the next twenty-four hours would be no different. Meinhardt, by contrast, never stopped hoping that the day ahead would turn his life around. He didn't know what made Rodge get up chipper, unless it was the hope of brightening someone else's day.

Having spent the previous day looking out the window, Meinhardt spent this one studying his companions. He looked at their clothes for clues about their lives. Some soldiers embellished their regulation outfits as if anticipating the military would soon make their minds as uniform as their khakis. One blonde youth switched his army cap for a lifeguard's sun visor. A dozen slips of paper, pressed on him by women the day before, spilled from his shirt pocket. Another boy, with the sturdy build of someone who'd spent eighteen years plowing the family farm, tied a bandana around his neck. The scarf made a handy face covering when cinders and soot blew into the car.

Civilian outfits were more varied, but often patriotic. Women dressed in the colors of the flag. Men too old to fight sported hat brims, neckties, and pocket handkerchiefs trimmed in red, white, and blue. Only a few dared to dress in subdued browns and grays without so much as a tie clip or cufflink to show their support for the troops. Those same men frowned instead of smiling at the antics of the youth for whom this trip was a last fling of freedom until the war's end, if not forever. Meinhardt suspected them of being isolationists afraid of speaking up amid the bravado of the recruits, but they may have simply been jealous of the young men's vigor, much as the Arts Club veterans of the last war envied those who would see action in the next one.

Midday, the train stopped in Colorado Springs. Among the large crowd boarding was an elderly gentleman in a worn topcoat, who worked his way to the middle of the car bowing and repeating "*Mi scusi*" until he set his battered suitcase next to Meinhardt. When the train lurched forward, the old man stumbled and almost fell on top of him, but Meinhardt gently braced his hands against the man's chest so he could upright himself. "*Mi dispaice molto*, many sorry" the gentleman apologized. Meinhardt steadied the man's suitcase as he slowly lowered himself onto it. "*Grazie*." The old man, pale and shaken, patted his brow with a frayed silk handkerchief.

Soldiers didn't retract their long limbs from the aisles to make standing room for the new passengers. No one gave up his seat to the old man. Meinhardt heard them muttering Dago, Wop, Guinea. Some were about to be killed by Mussolini and his Blackshirts, but that wasn't the fault of this elderly Italian man. He thought of old Mr. Schwartz, beaten by the Nazis, whose bruises his Oma had treated despite their neighbors' disapproval. The taste of the Denver Bar he'd eaten for lunch rose in Meinhardt's throat as addressed the young men sitting opposite him.

"He's elderly and unwell. Perhaps one of you

might offer the gentleman your seat."

The blonde soldier stretched his legs further and knocked the suitcase out from under the old man. He sprawled on the floor, a billfold, papers, and a photograph spilling from his pocket. A pudgy, acne-scarred soldier standing nearby bent to retrieve them.

The elderly man, struggling to sit up, looked dazed, but when the soldier handed him the picture, he grew animated. "*Nipote.*" He lowered his hand two steps to show it was his grandson. Meinhardt leaned over to see the photo of a dark-haired youth in a U.S. Army uniform.

The pudgy soldier read aloud as he refolded the papers. "Fort Leonard Wood, Missouri."

"*Sì, sto andando a vedere il mio nipote. Il suo nome è Vittoro.*"

The recruits understood. He was going to visit his grandson Victor at the army training camp there. Though none gave up a seat, they leaned back as Meinhardt and the pimply-faced soldier brushed off the old man, righted his suitcase, and gently lowered him back on his perch.

The tension in the compartment didn't dissipate, however.

"How about you, *Herr* Midget?" It was the lifeguard soldier again, only this time several others leaned forward with him. "Where do you think you're going?"

"Only place Gerries can travel to is an internment camp," another recruit said. "It's the law." He rattled off four camps the train would be passing as they headed east: Good Shepherd Convent in Omaha, Camp Selma in Kansas, the St. Louis County Jail, and 4800 Ellis in Chicago.

"Let's quarter him and drop off a piece of the Kraut in all four."

"No, keep him whole to repatriate to Germany in exchange for one of our boys."

"Look at him, dummkopf. We can only trade him for half of one of ours."

Meinhardt's trembling hand pulled from his jacket pocket the official document he too was carrying. It was the letter from the plant foreman with a waiver allowing him to travel "for authorized non-combat defense purposes." He explained he was going to Michigan to support the war effort by making B-24 bombers at Henry Ford's Willow Run assembly plant.

"I guess that makes things all right?" The big farm boy's voice was shaky, but the others shrugged in agreement and leaned back. They were saving their energy for the real fighting.

Only the blonde soldier persisted. "How do we know you won't sabotage the planes?"

"He's got a letter. That means he's okay." For the first time, one of the women spoke up.

"Enough!" A large matriarch surrounded by packages glared. "Our boys are fighting for peace. Let's have it on the train."

Everyone was quiet after that, but the battle lines were drawn. In one camp, sprawled in their seats, were most of the soldiers. They surrounded Meinhardt, the farmer, pudgy boy, and Italian grandfather, all of whom occupied the middle of the car along with the women. Meinhardt was surprised to find himself grateful for their community's company and protection. He wondered whether Mrs. Pacelli and the other immigrants at Macy's would be as proud to call themselves Americans if they'd witnessed the scene on the train. He knew from the moment the U.S. entered this war that he'd be marked in yet another way. A recent newspaper article said people who emigrated after adolescence never fully lost their accents. He'd left Germany two years too late.

Chapter 20

Meinhardt wasn't contemplating sabotage, but he was ambivalent about building bombs to drop on the Germans. He hadn't told Margaret, but even if he'd been offered a decent part in a war film, he wasn't sure he would have accepted it. Of course he wanted to see the Nazis destroyed, but Germany was his homeland. His Oma lived there. Who knew if he'd ever earn enough to bring her to this country, or if she'd agree to come. Certainly he'd never go back. All the same, while he wanted an Allied victory, he'd gloated when he read the Arts Club was badly damaged during the Blitz. If not for Rodge, he wouldn't mind seeing the stuck-up Brits obliterated too.

All through last year's bombing of London, he worried about his friend. Letters sent care of the Wheel and Wing went unanswered. He wondered if Rodge's mates carried him into the shelters or down to the tube stations when the air raid sirens went off. Rodge could drag himself into the concrete- or steel-covered trenches Londoners dug in the parks, but those couldn't keep out the rain. Meinhardt pictured his friend hunkering in the dark, trousers soaked to the groin. Fastidious Rodge would be more upset by the assault on his grooming than the threat to his life. Still, he'd try to cheer up those sheltering with him, maybe with a quote from Dickens: "Minds, like bodies, will fall into a pimpled unconditioned state from too much comfort." It was Rodge's standard comeback whenever life's daily miseries threatened to dampen the mood at the pub.

Sometimes Meinhardt's shifting loyalties made him feel petty. That's why he'd gone to hear Eleanor Roosevelt. He read her syndicated column, "My Day," and when the saleswomen at the store weren't watching, he snuck a look at "If You Ask Me" in their copies of *Ladies Home Journal*. The First Lady left no doubt that the Allies had to win and that the principles of liberty and justice we exported around the world should apply at home too. He'd feel better though if she came out in favor of fair treatment for people like him, not just Negroes and women.

Mrs. Roosevelt was speaking at Gilmore Stadium to an overflow crowd of nearly 20,000. Posters linking the military with the home front festooned the stadium's walls. An image of a soldier with a mug in his hand was captioned "Do With Less So They'll Have More." The words on another sign, "Get Some Cash for Your Trash," was a popular Fats Waller song. One poster was familiar to Meinhardt from the used clothing store where he worked: "Go Through Your Wardrobe: Make Do and Mend." There was even a picture of a dark-haired, buxom woman coming on to GIs that warned "Booby Trap: Syphilis and Gonorrhea." He wished he could roll it up and send it to Margaret with a note saying she was more tempting.

Meinhardt maneuvered around hips and ducked under elbows to get within yards of the stage. From the moment Mrs. Roosevelt appeared, he felt a kinship with her stronger than he'd experienced watching newsreels and reading her words. She was less attractive in person and even the adoring crowd murmured about how frumpy she looked. He'd heard her own mother called her an ugly duckling. Maybe being born so plain was what made her stand up for society's unfortunates. Meinhardt hoped to be inspired by her refusal let others define her as a failure.

"Welcome, good people. And you are <u>all</u> good people and good Americans." A sea of men and women cheered and clapped. Waves of admiration and hope flow toward the First Lady. If Meinhardt were taller, the waves would have passed through him on their way her.

"I'm here to tell you about Freedom House,

which the President founded as a clear voice for worldwide democracy." She said every act supporting the war, however small, made a difference to the soldiers and those they were defending. The applause was loud until Mrs. Roosevelt condemned the internment of Japanese Americans. She cut off the catcalls by saying with quiet force, "Don't judge people based on how they look. Give them a chance to show you the intelligence in their minds, the loyalty in their hearts, and the skill in their hands."

When the speech ended, security guards maintained a safety ring around the First Lady. Nevertheless, several people surged against the retreating crowd to get closer to her. Meinhardt followed, letting those in front act like football blockers to clear his way. Mrs. Roosevelt told a woman about her efforts to set up child care centers at manufacturing plants, and listened to the tale of a Negro soldier on leave, who'd been called a nigger by the Army recruiter.

Meinhardt stood directly in front of the great lady. He'd meant to reflect her kindness and warmth, but his voice came out defiant and angry. "You defend the rights of women and Negroes. What about protecting the dignity of the handicapped?"

"Go back to Germany, where our boys can shoot you," someone shouted at his back.

"Kill the pipsqueak here and now," came another voice at his side.

"Let's get you out of here before you start a riot." A security guard lifted Meinhardt from under his armpits and began to carry him behind the stage.

"Let him be," the First Lady ordered. Meinhardt was set down. "The gentleman deserves an answer." She came down into the crowd. Even at ground level, she towered over everyone.

Meinhardt planted his feet for balance and raised his head to meet the tall woman's eyes.

111

"You must speak up for yourselves, just as the Negroes are doing. Take advantage of every opportunity. Anyone willing to work hard deserves to achieve the American dream." She didn't lean over to shake hands, for which he was grateful. Their palms met above his shoulder.

It was exhilarating to have spoken to and touched the First Lady, but Meinhardt wasn't satisfied with her answer. She didn't understand what it was like to be invisible. People paid attention to Negroes, even it if was out of irrational fear. Midgets engendered a curious glance, but then the world moved on. They weren't worth a moment's thought, let alone any action.

Chapter 21

The ground was littered with dirty patches of snow when the train pulled into Detroit. After four years in California, Meinhardt had forgotten the penetrating sting of cold. His enthusiasm for the journey had waned with each mile. Now the bleakness put a final chill on his expectations. He rubbed his arms and scolded himself for being so negative. "The happiness of your life depends on the quality of your thoughts." This Rodge-like admonition was Meinhardt's own invention.

"Of all the things you wear, your expression is the most important." Those words were from Rodge. They would have been hypocritical from anyone else who paid as much attention to his clothes, but with Rodge the sentiment was genuine. Meinhardt was careful about his clothes, but had less control over what he wore on his face. Thinking of Rodge's perpetual smile, he forced himself to meet Charles with an optimistic greeting and matching expression.

They hadn't seen each other in three years. Charles pumped Meinhardt's hand, oblivious to the stares of those around them, and led him toward the exit. Meinhardt lagged behind a step so he could surreptitiously compare himself to his friend. He was embarrassed to realize that he still felt a small thrill about being several inches taller. In all other respects, however, Charles looked happier and healthier than he did. Meinhardt wondered if it was the effect of married life or whether he himself was just tired at the end of a long and disorienting cross-country journey.

A bus took them to Bomber City where Charles and Jessie lived. Most of the 40,000 plant workers, including the other midgets, were housed in temporary dormitories. Some would spend the winter in unheated tents and garages. Willow Lodge Dorm cost $5 a week. Married couples without children, like the Beckers, lived in Willow Court Trailers for $6.50 a week. Recognizing the war could last a long time, Henry Ford was building better housing, due to be completed next year. Charles and Jessie hoped to move into one of these homes before the baby started crawling, but they were afraid priority would be given to normal couples.

"The trailer's too cramped for us," said Charles. "I can't imagine how big people fit."

Space wasn't the only problem. The units were made with shoddy materials and careless workmanship. Cold air seeped under doors and around windows. Hinges popped on cupboards, which were set so high that Jessie stood on a stepladder to reach dishes on the bottom shelf. Though the baby wasn't due until spring, she stuck out the small mound of her stomach. It was a gesture of pride, but perhaps also a hopeful statement that the baby would grow to normal size.

"Sometimes I want the baby to be a midget," Charles had confided on the bus ride.

"*Für die Güte Willen!* What are you saying? Its life will be so much easier if it isn't!"

113

Charles stared out the window. "Of course, but sometimes I'm afraid a normal child will look down on Jessie and me. Not just because he'll be bigger, but because he'll see his parents as ..." Charles turned to face Meinhardt. Their eyes met and filled in all the bad words.

Jessie had been born in this country, not Germany, so the dinner she cooked was pure American: Campbell's tomato soup, Kraft macaroni and cheese, and a store-bought pie from the Wagner Baking Company. The Kraft box on the counter proudly displayed its slogan: "Make a meal for 4 in 9 minutes!" Meinhardt guessed Jessie's love of ready-made foods wasn't because pregnancy made her tired. It was her way of proclaiming she was no different than other housewives.

Instant or not, the food was hot and the coffee was freshly brewed. After three days of cardboard sandwiches and sugary candy bars, Meinhardt was grateful for the hospitality. He'd offered to reimburse the Beckers for putting him up, but Charles refused. Henry Ford paid good wages, although it would be tight when the baby came. They tried to save a little bit every week.

"Mr. Ford deducts 10% from Charles's paycheck to buy war bonds," Jessie said. "It's good for the country and good for us. Maybe our son or daughter will go to college." She sat back from the table so she could thrust the little ball of her stomach farther forward.

"I'm glad to do my part for the war," said Charles. It was consistent with his desire to become an American, so Meinhardt was surprised when Charles added, "but sometimes I feel guilty that my money and my work at the plant are being used to hurt Germans."

When Jessie's eyes widened, Meinhardt suspected Charles had never dared to say this before. "I understand," he said quietly when his friend looked to him for confirmation.

"But here, let me show you what I made." From a cabinet under the sink, Charles pulled a cradle crafted from sheet metal, steel bars, and cockpit cushions he'd scavenged from the plant. He demonstrated how to bolt it to the fold-down window seat with the hardware he'd also taken.

"We're not going to bolt you down, but I'm afraid the window seat will be your bunk too while you're with us." Charles was apologetic. The bed was smaller than a Pullman berth.

Meinhardt patted the cushions. "The accommodations aren't up to the Culver Hotel, but compared to sleeping on the floor of the California Limited, it will be *luxuriöse*."

"Jessie, show Meinhardt what you've been making." Shyly, she brought out a small valise filled with handmade baby clothes. The hems were invisible, the stitches small and even.

"Even my grandmother, a professional seamstress, would admire the precision of your sewing." Jessie watched him finger the tiny garments and blushed with pride.

Charles cleared the table. On the way to the sink, he rested his hand on his wife's stomach and pressed his lips to her rosy cheek. Meinhardt was used to seeing Charles beam broadly at everyone, but the smile he gave Jessie was different, a shining ray meant for her alone.

Never before had Meinhardt observed a married couple so closely. He'd been too worried about his own treatment to notice how his parents treated each other. Had they argued about him? Would Charles and Jessie fight over what was best for their baby? In some ways, he envied them, having a partner who shared your dreams and looked at your body with love, not curiosity or disgust. But marriage could also be a seesaw. It worked fine as long as both sides agreed to play, but if one got off, the other would come crashing down. It was safer to play solo.

Chapter 22

Jessie's hot coffee was doubly appreciated the next morning when Meinhardt awoke with knotted muscles and chilled bones. He trudged with Charles through blowing sleet to the plant, where they stood outside momentarily to take in the scale of the mile-long structure. Inside, workers used bicycles and scooters to get from one end to the other. He and Charles passed more than two dozen assembly stations to reach the area where the wings were built. Rows of wall-to-wall metal jigs held the wings in place, looking like streets of peaked roofs. The factory was its own village, reminiscent of the community of riders who bonded on the train, but here the noise of millions of rivets being forged and hammered was ten times as loud as wheels on the tracks.

It had been a month since the first bomber rolled off the line and production was already behind. The papers had re-christened the Willow Run plant, "Will It Run?" That infuriated the employees. The hardworking crews, hell-bent on proving themselves, included many women and the eight midgets recruited to put together the wings. The foreman was looking to hire two more.

Charles introduced Meinhardt to the team as they crawled in and out of the wings, wiping calloused hands on greasy overalls whose deep pockets jangled with hardware. Charles was the shortest, Meinhardt the second tallest, by an inch. They were all U.S. citizens but otherwise had little in common. Aged 18 to 50, they'd been sideshow performers, janitors, and stable hands before coming north, west, or east to build B-24s. Charles was friendly with all of them, but closest to the two nearest his age.

Winston, one of his friends, was from Kentucky, as were thousands of regular plant workers. So many from that state had come there to find jobs that Ypsilanti, the city where Willow Run had been built alongside the sleepy creek for which it was named, was derisively dubbed Ypsitucky. "Call me Whinny," he told Meinhardt. Raised around horses, he'd hoped to be a jockey, but his big head and bulky body met too much wind resistance. "Least, that's what them thoroughbred owners said." His smile revealed missing teeth. "It weren't cause I couldn't win no photo finish, neither. It were cause I wouldn't look good in the winner's circle photo."

Whinny still loved horses so much that he'd taken a job mucking for a breeder. "Wanted to learn to shoe horses so's I could earn more money, but the other stable hands put the kibosh on that plan too." When he saw an ad for midgets to work in assembly plants in Oklahoma and Michigan, he figured he'd rather crawl through a bomber wing than through more horse shit.

Meinhardt asked why he'd chosen to come to Michigan instead of Oklahoma.

Detroit was car city and Whinny loved automobiles too. "Guess I like anything that'll get me where I'm going faster than these short things." He wiggled his right leg inside the stained work pants. "Figure that when the war ends, they'll need someone to crawl inside car hoods."

"Mr. Ford builds machine to do that," said Harold, Charles's other friend. "Might as well resign yourself to tending the back end of horses again instead of the front end of automobiles."

Harold hailed from Maine and had dropped out of school in fifth grade after being bullied one time too many. He got by on odd jobs for a decade, until his older sister, born normal, lost her husband in an accident at the textile mill. Then she paid Harold to look after his niece and nephew while she went to work at the mill. Unlike other industries, textile manufacturers had always hired women, mostly unmarried girls who came to the cities in search of husbands.

"No hiring freaks, though," said Harold. "We could crawl inside looms and thread warps as easily as we can get into these wings to buck rivets, but the bosses didn't want us around." His sister didn't want him around either once the mill converted to making uniforms for soldiers and set up a child care center for the influx of married women who replaced the enlisted men.

"She was the one who saw the ad," he said. "Midgets wanted to serve their country!"

"His sister wanted Harold to be a patriotic Yankee." Charles directed a crestfallen look at Meinhardt, who understood. Their status as Americans was considered ambiguous.

"More likely she wanted to get rid of me." Harold thought she saw him as a burden she'd be responsible for after their parents died, and wanted him to move far away and make a life of his own. "The word 'Oklahoma' attracted her. To folks back East, that's as good as another country." Michigan was too close, connected to his home state by Canada. Ontario was just across the Detroit River. But she needn't worry that Harold would return. There was no love lost between him and Maine or him and his sister. It was saying goodbye to his niece and nephew that had almost broken him. He wiped his hands on the thighs of his stained denim overalls before carefully extracting their photos from the bib pocket. "Aren't they the cat's pajamas?"

The men crowded around. Meinhardt sensed they'd seen the pictures many times before. He was surprised because cooing over children's photos was something that women, not men, usually did. Then he realized that examining the photos was part of an ongoing debate.

Harold pointed at a slender little girl in pigtails. "This here's Becky," he told Meinhardt. "Six years old and already reading history books."

"Let's see what Meinhardt thinks about Lucas." One of the men prodded Harold to show him the picture of a chubby toddler.

Meinhardt knew he was being asked to judge whether the boy was normal. He hesitated, not wanting to upset the proud uncle or take sides among men he might end up working with.

Harold reassured him. "It's okay. I'm convinced Lucas is one of us." He nodded at the midgets who alternately looked at the photo and at Meinhardt. "My sister won't admit it though. She's so afraid he'll end up like me, she won't take him to the doctor to find out."

"He has a winning smile," Meinhardt said. "Midget or not, he'll do well in life."

Harold rewrapped the photos. As the men returned to work, Meinhardt roamed the plant alone, zigzagging across its millions of square miles, until a whistle signaled lunch. He waited at a table at the front of the cafeteria for Charles to arrive. Peeking inside the lunch pail, he saw Jessie had packed ham sandwiches, hard boiled eggs, leftover pie, and a thermos with two cups.

"Midgets in the last row, left side. Women, middle to back rows, right side." A burly man with a pot belly and short gray hair pointed to the rear.

"Why's a damned dwarf sitting at our table?" A crowd of men gathered. Some wore thick glasses; the rest were too fat, skinny, or old to enlist.

It was like Meinhardt's first day of school. He'd sat at the lunch table with his classmates. Told the seat was taken, he moved, only to be told the same thing. Children draped sweaters over all the empty chairs. He carried his Oma's sausage, bread, and *Lebkuchen* to a window ledge in the back. She'd packed extra cookies in case he made a friend. Thereafter, even on icy days when a wet wind blew through the window's leaded glass frame, he ate lunch there alone.

"Pick on someone your own size, Frank. Cafeteria's got plenty of other tables where you can fill your big gut."

Behind Meinhardt stood a tall blonde woman in bib overalls that matched her dark blue eyes. Charles and his crew bunched together, open-mouthed and bug-eyed, in the doorway.

Frank sneered. "Well, if it ain't our own Rosie the Riveter. What're gonna do, missy, beat me up with those manly muscles of yours?" He flexed his arms beneath his work shirt.

"I'm in better shape than the likes of you," she said. "We all are." Several other well-built women surrounded her, rolled up their sleeves, and rippled their muscles. Meinhardt thought they probably could trounce Frank and his sorry crew.

"Knock it off." It was the foreman. "This is lunch break, not bone break." He declared the disputed table off limits for the day and directed the men to a front table across the room.

They swaggered toward it, but not before Frank said, "Just wait until this war is over and you ladies is back in the kitchen. You're gonna be feeding our mouths instead of giving us lip."

"Please, Rose." The foreman turned to the defiant woman and smiled. "My heartburn. You want my wife to call and threaten you?"

She lowered her arm and grinned back. "Shirley doesn't scare me as much she scares you." Then she turned to Meinhardt and beckoned Charles's crew at the door. "Come on. You're sitting with us." She led the other women and the midgets to a table in the middle.

To Meinhardt's surprise, the foreman

followed and extended a clean hand to him. "Sorry. Frank and the others are good guys, just frustrated they're not young and healthy enough to fight in the war. Still hope you want to work here. I'll check back at the end of the day." Getting an apology from the management impressed Meinhardt. They must really need midgets. If you want to be treated with dignity, he concluded, it helps to serve a unique and useful function.

"B'gosh, these OshKosh overalls *are* easier to sit in than the old ones." A woman stroked the fabric as she lowered herself on a bench. "They made the denim softer, just like the ad said."

"Not ours." Harold slid in next to her, his short legs sticking straight out. "Stiff as ever."

Ford had contracted with OshKosh to manufacture overalls that were bigger in the bib for women and shorter in the legs for midgets. Though OshKosh claimed to discount the price out of patriotism, the custom-made ones were still more expensive than standard issue work clothes.

"Men pay $3.88 a pair, women $4.12. Frank should be charged more on account he needs extra material to cover his fat ass!" The woman who'd spoken swigged Faygo, the local pop, and burped. Charles turned red.

"Dang if we don't pay $4.58," Whinny said. "I guess there ain't enough midgets for them to recoup a price cut, and we don't even get softer denim like the ladies."

"It beats trying to find work clothes in the husky boys department. Let's be grateful for what we've got." Leave it to Charles to look on the sunny side.

The others weren't persuaded. Neither was Meinhardt. Midgets shouldn't have to settle for children's clothes or pay extra for custom-made ones. The cost of his bathrobe had been exorbitant. There were enough midgets in the U.S. and Canada for a smart businessman to make work and leisure clothes that fit that population and sold for a reasonable price. A new dream took shape in Meinhardt's head. "Big People Clothes for Little People."

Excited, he turned to Charles, but he was wedging himself between two women. Seeing the groups intermingle, united against a common enemy, Meinhardt again thought of the train's impromptu community. These factory women could teach midgets a lesson in self-promotion.

"Rose Will Monroe from Pulaski County, in southern Kentucky." The woman who stood up to Frank introduced herself between scoops of cornmeal mush, redolent of bacon, and pickled green beans. She looked nothing like Rosie the Riveter in the familiar poster. That woman had black hair tucked under a red and white polka dot bandana, and her dark eyebrows were knit in a serious expression to go with the slogan "We Can Do It!" This Rosie was not only blonde and blue-eyed, her whole demeanor was jovial and playful. She did have one thing in common with the poster Rosie, however. They both flexed their considerable arm muscles with pride.

"You gals can whomp Frank," Whinny teased, "but I betcha can't beat us little guys. We learned to defend ourselves long before coming here. Building B-24s has only made us tougher."

Taking up the challenge, the women proposed an arm-wrestling contest. Each side chose three representatives to play a round every day at lunch. They'd keep a running score. Whichever team won by year's end had to treat the other to a case of Stroh's, the local beer. Rose and Whinny wanted to compete for bottles of scuppernong wine but the northerners turned up their noses at the thought of this fruity Kentucky delicacy. The women won the first round, 2 to 1.

"So, Meinhardt Raabe from Berlin, are you brave enough to come here to work with all of us strong women?" Rose snapped the lid shut on her empty bean container.

"What's that button above the OshKosh patch?" he asked. He'd noticed it on several of the plant workers that morning. It had the "Winged V" insignia on it, a symbol of the bombers.

"We get them for buying war bonds. A 17-year girl from Ypsilanti designed it." The woman who answered said her people came from Poland. Others chimed in with the countries from which their families had emigrated --- Czechoslovakia, Austria, Hungary --- all invaded by Germany. Rather than seeing Meinhardt as an enemy alien, the view of the soldiers on the train, these women saw someone who'd also escaped Hitler's clutches.

"Rose, you gonna jeer Frank's team tonight?" A twangy voice dispelled the somber mood invading the table. Men had formed baseball teams that summer and were playing into winter to prove their manhood. To free up the field after work, women's teams were relegated to using it before the morning shift when it was too cold and dark to play. They hated conceding to the men.

"Sure thing," said Rose. "Me and Lulu and Mae got us a bet going the Kentucky Coons is gonna beat the bejesus out of the Michigan Mongrels afore Thanksgiving ends the season."

"How much you betting?"

"Sixty-three cents a week. Two percent of our pay is worth watching those goons lose."

Meinhardt calculated. Men got $54.65 a week, midgets $41.40, and women $31.50. He was right that it wasn't enough to be useful. You had to meet a unique need. Midgets were paid more than women because they were harder to find and filled an unusual role. Still it wasn't fair.

A sign on the wall said "Each B-24 bomber

requires 313,237 rivets. How many did you buck today?" Meinhardt pointed to it and told the women they should ask for more money.

"You don't understand," Rose told him. "We're grateful to have any job at all." The other women nodded. With the men gone, they had no other way to feed themselves and their families.

"But you all do the same work." Meinhardt turned to the midgets. "Mr. Ford should pay you what Frank and the other men get every week."

"I don't know," said Harold. "If the ladies ask for equal pay, the bosses might lower ours instead of raising theirs. Can't neither of us expect to earn the same wages as a full size man."

Pitting women and midgets against one another made no sense to Meinhardt. Nor did thinking either group was inferior to the likes of Frank and his crowd. He opened his mouth to say so when he saw the look on Charles's face, part warning and part pleading.

"Every one of you does important work for your country," he said instead. "That's all that matters. To the bomber builders!" He lifted his coffee cup and the others raised their bottles of Faygo. Meinhardt smiled but didn't drink with them. Despite what he'd said, he believed that how people were treated mattered too. If — no when — he started his own business, he would hire and pay people on an equal basis. Even those who were old and overweight, like Frank.

Chapter 23

A whistle signaled the end of lunch break. The men at the front tables glared at the midgets and women as they filed out. Meinhardt was less afraid and more sympathetic toward them now. He knew how it felt to be judged unfit for something you longed to do.

He returned to the wing assembly station

with Charles, where he practiced drilling a hole, inserting the shaft of a universal solid rivet, and bucking the tail end with a hammer until the factory head expanded one and a half times, enough to hold the rivet forever in place. A midget about his size loaned Meinhardt a pair of overalls so he could see how it felt to do it from inside the wing. He filled the bib with MS20470s and crawled through the narrow metal opening.

Whinny inspected his work. "Gotta be done right. Flyers' lives depend on it." With two hammer blows, Whinny accomplished what it had taken Meinhardt twelve to do. The sound of metal beating against metal was magnified in such close quarters. Meinhardt was embarrassed that his body, unaccustomed to sweating, was turning the overall's armpits an even darker blue. The smell worried him too, until he realized everyone would be wet and rank by quitting time.

He wasn't claustrophobic, but after flattening ten pieces of hardware, he was glad to exit the tight space. He couldn't imagine doing hundreds an hour, thousands a day. No wonder Rosie showed off her muscles. It was only a mechanical achievement, though. Meinhardt feared that punching out at day's end, his mind would be as closed and immovable as the ends of a rivet.

The foreman was waiting by the time clock when the shift-change whistle blew. He smiled when Whinny pointed at Meinhardt and gave him a thumbs up. "Seems you made a good impression with the wing crew, not to mention the women. I can offer a two-week apprenticeship at half pay. Once you pass muster, pay rate's the same as the other midgets. What do you say?"

"I'll give it a try and let you know next week." Meinhardt shook the foreman's hand. He and Charles joined the others streaming out of the plant to play ball, get a drink, or go back to the dormitories. Everyone looked tired but there was an unmistakable sense of camaraderie among them. No one walked alone. Winged victory pins dotted the lapels of their coats, like the insignia of a club. Unlike the youth groups of Germany, it was a club whose ideals he could subscribe to.

Dearest Oma,

I am writing from Michigan where Charles wrote about a job at a bomber factory. The labor is hard and dirty, but I must give it a chance. You know how I've struggled to find work.

The evening I got his letter, I met Eleanor Roosevelt. I hoped she'd talk about hiring people like me, but I was disappointed. Perhaps it's too much to expect when she's busy fighting for women and *die Schwartzen*. She said to speak up for ourselves. She doesn't understand. A big black man like Fats Waller can tell bigots *Geh zur Hölle*. Even an average-sized woman can stare discrimination in the face. But it's a tall order for a small man to stand up to prejudice.

I'm glad you are back in Dornum in case the Allies attack the cities. We just had a scare after Japan bombed an oil station in Santa Barbara, 130 kilometers up the coast. Air-raid sirens shrieked and the radio said to prepare for the Battle of Los Angeles. It was a false alarm, but for two hours anti-aircraft gunners fired at the sky, while people cowered in darkness or drove without headlights to escape. I hope you never have to go through such crazy panic and fear.

Like the Japanese, I'm considered a potential enemy alien and have to register with the government. I should be grateful I'm a midget. If I were full size, I'd be seen as a threat and sent to a German internment camp in Kansas, where I could reunite with Dorothy and her dog Toto.

At times when my thoughts are bleakest, I try to revive my spirits by remembering an old Arab proverb Rodge used to recite: "All sunshine makes a desert." Los Angeles <u>is</u> all sunshine, and also a desert for me. Even if there were clouds, it would be hard to find a silver lining.

Ach, forgive me for burdening you. I have a new business idea and still hope to bring you to America when it succeeds. Meanwhile, I'm learning about my adopted country as I check out this factory job. It may be the opportunity Mrs. Roosevelt said to take advantage of. Even if the work itself is bad, one never knows when a good idea will come out of it.

Your loving Enkel,
Meinhardt

Meinhardt did give the job a chance. After a week he cut his bucking strokes from twelve to four per rivet, although he couldn't match Whinny's two. At lunch on the third day, he won a wrestling match for the midgets. He enjoyed hearing more about the lives of other workers. Like Margaret, many of the women were raising children on their own, at least until — or if — their husbands returned from the front. The other midgets, although they hadn't faced the brutality of the Nazis, had horrible enough tales of being bullied and denied decent jobs in the U.S.

Despite his progress and warm welcome, Meinhardt felt stuck. He couldn't wait to escape the cramped walls of the wings and the trailer's walls were another tight boundary. He was afraid of losing his vision, unable to see past their metal and wooden barriers. Seven days after arriving in Willow Run, Meinhardt thanked the foreman but said he was going back to California.

It was harder saying goodbye to Charles and Jessie. He asked them to send a photo of the baby when it came and promised to buy a war bond for its college savings account. To ease his friend's disappointment, Meinhardt pretended that he wasn't physically up to the work. "Not only are you a better dancer, you're stronger than me." He didn't add that moving east would have reversed his westward progress from Berlin to London to New York to Los Angeles.

He was glad he had no family to support. That gave him the freedom to pursue his dream, the newest version. The war wasn't the right time to start a business, but even a menial job in the clothing industry would keep him heading in the right direction. Working in the bomber plant would sap his energy. There were other kinds of fasteners. Meinhardt could use bolts and nails and screws to build a scaffold that would lift him higher. He refused to rivet himself in place.

PART SIX

I Think I'll Miss You Most of All

New York, 1955

Chapter 24

"Stealing from the competition?" asked the tall blonde floor model bending over Meinhardt's drawing of a peacock blue and tomato red cashmere tunic by Cristóbal Balenciaga. She wore Claire McCardell separates. Her flared pants were topped by a navy and white shirt with wide horizontal stripes, a row of shiny rivets at the shoulders, and a polished brass hook below a square neckline. Everything about the sporty outfit was wrong for Big People Clothes for Little People, but this svelte skyscraper, two feet taller him, was born to wear it.

"The competition should steal from me," Meinhardt said, staring into eyes that were as tawny as the woman's golden hair. "Most women are too short and wide to wear clothes like these. They're not made like you."

For two days at the Female Apparel Manufacturing Exposition, Meinhardt had been surrounded by models whose breasts cleared the top of his head. He went to a dozen shows a year for ideas he could re-proportion for people his size. Recently he'd been to Miami, Chicago, and Toronto. New York was more than a business trip, however. It was a pilgrimage, recalling the thrill of arriving here from Europe two decades ago, but also stirring up bitter memories of money troubles and the falling out with Harpo. His financial woes were over, but not the hurt.

"Most people aren't made like you either." The woman's tone was so matter-of-fact that Meinhardt wasn't offended. "Being tall isn't always an advantage. In some ways, you're luckier." Her lips, expertly coated with Rouge Dior lipstick, opened to reveal teeth as bright and regular as the stripes on her shirt. Models paid a lot for dental work, but her look was natural. "Tall people see the dust balls on top of their refrigerators and feel compelled to clean them."

"You can sit wherever you want at the movies and see over every head. We sit in the front row and get neck spasms looking up at the screen." His green eyes dared her yellow ones.

"Not true. We have to sit in the back row. People get angry if we sit in front of them."

"People get angry and accuse us of cheating to get in for children's prices."

"When I was a child, grown-ups expected me to act older than I was. That wasn't fair."

"I'm a grown up and people still treat me like a child. That's even more unfair."

"Your age surpassed your height."

"Your height surpassed your age."

"Poor us." Her laughter soared to the exhibit hall's vaulted ceiling like a cardinal flushed from a rose bush. "I wouldn't want to be any different. Would you?"

Meinhardt closed his sketchbook.

"Celia Posy." She extended a hand with nails painted the same dark red as her lips. "So are you here to steal designs?"

Meinhardt hesitated. It was common for manufacturers to adapt the ideas of top designers for the ready-to-wear market. They only got in trouble if they copied too exactly, and he never did that. Change was the whole point. Even so, he felt uneasy telling her what he was doing.

"Don't worry. I won't report you to the high mucky-mucks. I'm a model, not a snitch." She put a long index finger over her lips and cocked her ear down towards his mouth.

It was an invitation to play, something Meinhardt had never received as a boy. He told her how he adapted styles for the mail-order business he'd started three years ago, and described how he'd belt the Balenciaga tunic at the waist, not the hips, and tone down the tropical colors. Like a child eager to impress a new friend, he boasted that the company grossed in the triple digits and sent out its catalog four times annually to 300,000 midgets in North America.

"May I?" Celia reached for the sketchbook and studied his adaptations. "Narrower belt. Smaller pattern." No change was too subtle for her lion-colored eyes. "This one's tricky. Oh, I see. Moving the hem up a tad to the bottom of the knee makes the legs look a lot longer."

Shy but emboldened, Meinhardt showed her a catalog, explaining how the ads combined his passion for movies and knowledge of clothes. The backgrounds and props came from popular film posters, with midgets in the scenes wearing clothes similar to its stars. His latest featured *Guys and Dolls*. "Shorter skirts and narrower lapels, but hats identical to Brando and Sinatra. People think midgets have big heads because our bodies are short, but they're the same size."

Celia read the line at the top of the order form. "Unlike a child, you never outgrow your favorite clothes." Meinhardt said the idea came from Rodge, a friend he'd met in London before the war and recently gotten back in touch with. Making people smile had doubled sales. Now he sprinkled Rodge's wit throughout the catalog. His next one would have a poster from *The Seven Year Itch* with the line, "Before you scratch an itch, file your fingernails."

"How will you redesign the white dress Marilyn Monroe wears when she stands over the subway grate?" Celia wondered. "Those long, shapely gams are hard to duplicate on a midget."

The skirt would billow to mid-calf instead of the model's chunky thighs, with a caption that said a smart woman didn't immediately reveal everything to a man but saved some for later.

"My mother used to tell me that if a man

tried to snitch a bite of cheesecake before the meal, I should remind him that only boys who finish their vegetables are allowed to eat dessert." Celia rubbed her flat stomach. "My mom made the best cherry cheesecake. I grew up on a cherry farm outside Benton Harbor, a small town in Michigan." She'd come to New York to be a model five years ago, at the age of twenty. Her parents were nervous but they trusted her in the big city.

Meinhardt said he'd left home at the same age and told her about the grandmother who had faith in him. "She too let me go so I could follow my dream." California became home after he landed a movie role years ago. Adopting a wide stance and flourishing his sketchbook, he sang, "She's not only mere dead, she's really most sincerely dead."

Celia's eyelashes, thickened with mascara, fluttered up. "You were the coroner in *The Wizard of Oz*." When the movie was re-released in theaters the year before she moved to New York, she and her girlfriends had seen it five times in one month. "Were you in anything else?"

"My movie career died with the Wicked Witch. It's a cutthroat business, even for normal-size people."

"Modeling is competitive too. It turns girls as mean as witches." Celia's dream was to be a print model. Most of her earnings came from showroom jobs, but she'd worked up to floor modeling at high-end shows like this one, where she hoped to be discovered.

"Someone like you is bound to stand out above the others," Meinhardt said.

"Believe it or not, I'm *too* tall for French couturiers, but I have the lean, athletic body that American designers like McCardell want. Does the active look interest your clientele?"

"Not suitable for my little line, I'm afraid."

"Then can I interest you in a cup of coffee?"

Celia's next break was in a couple of hours. "I discovered a tiny Viennese pastry shop just north of the convention hall," she whispered. "I don't want the others to know. Sweets are a model's weakness and they'd overrun this place."

"You mean Demel's?" Meinhardt whispered back.

Celia's red lips parted in surprise. "How do you know about it?"

"I have an extra sense — my grandmother called it *zusätzliche Sinn* — for baked goods. Whenever my Oma made *Apfelstrudel*, I swore I could smell it halfway home from school."

"Sugar cookies and layer cake are my downfall. Those were my mother's specialties." Celia patted her hips. "American models are allowed more muscle than the French, but not more fat. That's another way you're luckier. You can eat whatever you want."

"Not so. I'd look like a miniature Fatty Arbuckle. I have to watch my health too. Midgets develop heart and joint problems young." It was time he told Celia his age. "I'm forty years old."

"My dad worries about his health. Farming's hard on the body. Of course, he's older than you and has my three brothers to help out. Someday they'll take over the place." Celia sighed. "I'm not sorry I left, but missing my family makes me feel as bare as a cherry tree in winter."

Meinhardt nodded. "Pastry's a comfort. It takes us back to where we came from."

"But I never overindulge," said Celia. "I'm disciplined and determined to succeed."

"Me too. Sweets take the edge off my longing, but work reminds me why I left home."

Celia's voice was as warm as strudel fresh from the oven. Meinhardt could talk to her in a way he couldn't with other women. She held her body erect but there was a looseness about her posture.

He could still see the little girl hanging upside down by her knees from a tree limb.

"I'll meet you at Demel's in two hours," Meinhardt said. "Be sure you're not followed."

Chapter 25

Meinhardt arrived at the pastry shop ten minutes late, so people wouldn't see him waiting if Celia stood him up. He scanned the room for a white and navy striped shirt, convinced she had backed out, until he saw her long legs sticking out from a table beside the display case. She was wearing dungarees, a plain sweater, and loafers. Of course! She couldn't wear designers' clothes outside the exhibit hall. Even inside, she'd have gone through several outfits since he'd met her.

"I was afraid you wouldn't come," Celia said. "People in this business are forever making promises they have no intention of keeping."

"I don't make many promises, but those I make, I keep." Meinhardt couldn't believe she'd kept hers.

"I'm starving." Celia bent in half to peer into the pastry case, which was at his eye level. Their heights were on display like the cakes and pies, but she was oblivious. Either she didn't care what others thought or she was used to being stared at. Meinhardt wondered what it was like to have strangers look at you with admiration.

"Is the apple strudel good here?"

"It's not as crumbly as my Oma's. Strudel is made with *Mürbteig*, literally a short dough, that has lots of butter and no baking powder. It's supposed to melt in your mouth."

"And Dremel's dough?" she asked.

"Not short enough."

"So shorter is better." Celia touched Meinhardt's shoulder. "What about these?" She pointed to a porcelain plate on the top shelf.

"*Palatschinken.* They're like French crepes."

"The French don't like me and I have no use for them." Celia tossed her head. "Besides crepes sounds like creeps and there are more than enough of those in this world."

"I never knew what kind of treat I'd find rolled up inside my grandmother's pancakes."

"They're sounding better."

"If you don't want crepes, try something with *Biskuitteig* or sponge batter. It's light and airy, perfect for filled pastries." Meinhardt indicated two plates on the middle shelf. "These are *buchtein*, pockets filled with apricot jam, and this is *Biskuittroulade*, jelly roll to Americans."

"I got a sweet jelly, a lovin' sweet jelly roll. If you taste my jelly, it'll satisfy your worried soul." Celia's singing voice was thin without being weak. "Meinhardt. You're redder than the jelly! I'm sorry. I didn't mean to embarrass you."

"This is *Gugelhupf.* Soft yeast dough filled with raisins, almonds, and candied fruits. Demel's version is almost as good as my Oma's."

"It looks like my mother's bundt cake. She baked it in a big round pan with a hole in the middle. Only hers had ridges around the edges." Celia draped her hands like fabric folded over the gentle mounds of her breasts.

"Do you like tortes?" Meinhardt's arm swept along the bottom shelf.

"They're my favorite. Tell me about them." Celia snuggled next to him.

Meinhardt didn't move away. "A torte is a flourless cake made with eggs, butter, sugar, and ground nuts. You can sandwich together two or more layers with a sweet, creamy filling."

They split a slice of *Sachertorte*, another of *Linzertorte*, and bought one *buchtein* apiece. Both drank their coffee strong and black. Not until they'd eaten half the food, pausing after each bite to sigh and smile at each other, did they resume talking.

"I was homecoming queen in high school," Celia said, wiping up powdered sugar around the rim of her plate and dabbing it on the tip of her tongue.

"And the homecoming king?"

"Half a foot shorter, but captain of the football team."

"American football." Meinhardt shook his head. "A sport for brutes. Real football is what this country calls soccer. It takes fast footwork and finesse. That was my game."

"I bet you still have some good moves left." Celia slowly licked each finger and opened her mouth for another forkful of *Sachertorte*.

"And after you graduated from high school?"

"Modeling at Chandler's, the town's department store. I helped out at home too, but I knew I could never be a farmer's wife. My folks almost lost the place during the Depression. I was just a little girl, but even then I saw how tough life was for them. Farming is too precarious."

"And modeling isn't?"

"Luck gets you noticed by the right people, but your fate isn't in the hands of a force as fickle and powerful as the weather. My mother cursed every wet spring and dry summer." Celia studied her lacquered nails. "She never lost her spirit, though. Maybe it was all that baking. It was something she could control and it always came out good."

"Tell me about your father." Meinhardt signaled for more coffee. The waiter ignored him. Celia waved the man over. He came to the table and refilled both their cups.

"My dad didn't complain like my mother. He barely spoke, except to my brothers about work." She wrapped her hands around the steaming cup. "When I said I was going to New York, he gave me

137

the money he'd been saving for a new tractor. That got me through the first year."

Meinhardt thought of his Oma sending him money when he moved to London. He hadn't asked and she'd never said she would help him until he could manage on his own. She just did it.

"My mother's love was loud," said Celia. "My dad's was silent."

"My Oma's was both," said Meinhardt. "She was two parents in one."

Celia wiped her hands on the linen napkin. "Would you like to see my portfolio?"

"Isn't the man supposed to invite the woman up to see *his* etchings?"

She pulled a leather satchel from under the table. "I carry it everywhere. You never know when you're going to meet someone who's interested in you. If you wait until later to show him your stuff, he's forgotten you or moved on to the next girl. Models are all pretty much alike."

"You're different Celia. There's a freshness about you that's missing in the others." He smoothed his hands over the soft leather. "You're like a bouquet that doesn't wilt — a posy."

Meinhardt looked at Celia's photos with the same intensity she'd given to his sketches. She laid out two head shots, a set of fashion photos, and, most important, a full-length picture showing the proportions of her body --- feet to knees, knees to thighs, thighs to waist, waist to shoulder, and shoulder to top of head.

"My proportions are simple and easy to remember. Two feet to the waist, two feet to the shoulders, half a foot to the top of my head." Meinhardt touched his red hair, beginning to gray.

Celia ran her finger along his cheek. "You're easy to remember, yes, but simple, no."

"I like that your photos are simple."

Celia nodded eagerly. "Photographers want

to use mood lighting, arty props, and exotic backgrounds. You have to be firm and tell them no, the portfolio is your show, not theirs."

Meinhardt wondered how Celia had learned about the business. He'd picked up what he knew at his Oma's knee, but a cherry farm was nothing like the fashion world.

"I couldn't afford modeling school. Barbizon charged half a year's rent for one charm class."

"You don't need charm classes. Your sunny smile is enough."

"I helped the other girls with their hair and makeup." She grinned. "A knack I developed grooming animals in 4-H club. In exchange, they shared the advice they got in modeling class."

"Like what to put in your portfolio."

"Even more important, tips on how to behave at a casting call. It's as much about how you act as how you look." Celia counted off on her fingers: "Project confidence. Be positive. Show you are self-reliant, organized, and disciplined. Be proud of your ambition."

"I can tell you want very badly to succeed." Meinhardt had never met a young woman so driven. Except Judy Garland, but at 17, she'd already lost the natural charm Celia still exuded.

"Lord knows why, but I do. It's less glamorous than it looks. You're treated like a piece of meat. Travel, room, and meals are deducted from your pay, which isn't much to begin with. Even if you get to the top, they keep you under lock and key."

"To make sure you don't eat too much pastry and get fat?"

"To make sure another agent doesn't steal you away. The best companies hire spies."

"You're better off working on your own," he said, thinking of the partnership offers he'd rejected when his company first turned a profit. "That way you have your freedom."

139

"It doesn't work like that in modeling. Casting calls are almost always done through an agency. Not once has someone gotten back to me on a dry call. Turning up may get you a day's work in a showroom, but I want to do runway shows and most of all, fashion magazines." She opened her satchel wider to reveal a stash of *Vogue* magazines. "I want to be a cover girl."

Meinhardt looked around the restaurant. Models hovered over pastry and looked at their watches, counting calories and keeping track of the minutes before racing back to the exhibit hall. His eyes were only for Celia, but designers had scores of beautiful girls to choose from. In some ways, her dream was even more impossible than his had been. Yet, his had come true.

"What about you?" Celia asked. "What's your story?"

Meinhardt began by telling her what he'd done the night before he left for New York.

Chapter 26

First he had closed his eyes and stroked the yard of red silk with his fingerpads. He'd dipped them in lanolin for a week so they would be smooth enough to glide over the fabric. Next he held the silk to his ear, listening to it swish as he rubbed the cloth between his thumb and forefinger. He buried his nose in the folds of material and inhaled the smell of earth and mulberry leaves. After opening his eyes, he carried the silk to the window, letting the California sunlight play on its shimmering pleats. Last, he sucked gently on a corner. His memory flooded with the sharp taste of *Zimt würzen Kuchen*, the cinnamon spice cake his Oma used to bake at the end of harvest season. It was at this time three years ago that she died. While Dornum's farmers were turning over the soil for a long winter's rest, the ground had been turned under to lay Gretel in her grave.

On the anniversary of his grandmother's death, Meinhardt performed the same ritual he'd created when her childhood friend, Sadie, called to tell him that Gretel was gone. Grieving over his own loss, he hadn't thought to ask Sadie, half Jewish, how she'd managed to survive the war. Meinhardt knew only that he couldn't afford to go to Germany for the funeral and wondered how to commemorate his Oma's memory in America, the country to which he would never bring her.

When the war ended, he'd begged her to emigrate. He was still selling discount clothes and feeling discouraged, but if she came, his optimism would return.

She said no. "I must stay here to work and do penance. We're all guilty."

His grandmother accepted deprivation in her defeated homeland. Food grew scarcer when the Russians cut off supplies from the East. Dornum, a fishing village in the West, survived on the North Sea catch, but it was five years before flour and sugar rations were sufficient to bake a cake. People got thinner. His Oma, despite failing eyesight and worsening arthritis, trimmed material from the seams of their clothes to patch threadbare cuffs, elbows, and knees.

She never complained, but Meinhardt knew she missed fine fabrics and tailoring. For her, sewing wasn't merely a mechanical skill. It was a sensual experience. He decided to observe her death by marrying the queen of cloth to all five senses. His Oma called silk the most beautiful yet the most unforgiving material. In her hands, the natural flaws that snagged less experienced fingers became part of the design. The red silk "ritual of the cloth" that began as a substitute for attending her funeral had thus become for him an annual practice of solace and remembrance.

Sadie had taken care of the arrangements, then asked what to do with the hundreds of weekly letters from him that his grandmother had saved in the seventeen years since he'd left home. She'd found them in a leather suitcase, wrapped in a hand-embroidered cloth.

"Keep them," he said. "Someday I'll come back to visit and you can give them to me."

"I'm 82 years old, like your grandmother," said Sadie. "People don't live forever."

"America has a new president who promises prosperity," Meinhardt told her. "I will come soon, before you die."

"God willing," said Sadie. "But who counts on God these days? I'll leave the letters with my granddaughter Rachel, they should be here whenever you come."

A month later, Sadie wrote to Meinhardt. Her German script, though spidery with age, had the same schoolgirl precision he now missed in his Oma's handwriting.

Dear Meinhardt,

I know you will want to hear about your grandmother's funeral. Many people came to pay their respects. Only your mother was not there, but I do not think Gretel would have minded.

The mourners gathered at Weihnachtmarkt Schloss, the old market place. I was surprised to see Jewish neighbors I thought dead. Like me, they crept back to Dornum 15 years after escaping. Only our love and gratitude for your Oma could induce us to return. Such tales we whispered to one another about how she helped us. The Christians would not look us in the eye.

We walked in a procession to St. Bartholomaeus Church. Inga Schulze, the granddaughter of our old schoolmate Tilda König, played the organ. It was built in 1710 by Gerhard Van Holy and is a national treasure. To have it played at one's funeral is a great honor.

Despite the elaborate setting, I insisted on a simple Lutheran service. Leave it to a Jew to know what a Christian would want! The funeral lasted half an hour and the sanctuary was full of flowers. Afterward, we had coffee and a great deal of food. West Germany's economy has gotten much better these last two years under the Marshall Plan. We are thankful to the Americans.

I was surprised how few prayed during the service. I don't just mean us Jews. Lutherans also lost their faith during the war. Your grandmother grew disillusioned living in Berlin, but she returned to religion when she returned to Dornum. Coming home brought her back to God too.

We sang *Amazing Grace*. The pastor asked me to choose a hymn but I am unfamiliar with the 600 songs in the Lutheran hymnal. I picked *Soul, Adorn Yourself with Gladness*. The title seemed fitting for a seamstress. The pastor said Gretel's favorite was *Go My Children, With My Blessing*. Here is the first stanza: "Go, My children, with My blessing. Never alone. Waking, sleeping, I am with you. You are My own." Jesus is speaking, but the words could be your Oma talking to you. You were always in her thoughts and prayers. She had faith you would succeed.

Your grandmother isn't buried in the graveyard behind the church, which she claimed was too big and fancy. She was laid to rest in a small cemetery outside town, on a rocky bluff overlooking the North Sea. Her parents and others from your family are buried there too.

The pastor said Lutherans regard death as a new beginning. "Those who have faith are assured eternal life with God." Jews do not believe in an afterlife. All that matters to us is the good deeds one does on earth. Gretel, bless her, lived her life as though both were true.

I know you are sad to have missed the funeral. Jews observe the *yahrzeit* or anniversary of a person's death. Perhaps when you come to Germany, it will be on your Oma's *yahrzeit* and you can pray at her grave then. Meanwhile, carry her love and bring honor to her memory.

Sincerely,
Sadie

Meinhardt did not know when he would go back, but the day of her funeral and every *yahrzeit* thereafter, he performed the ritual. It never varied, but immediately after her death, the intensity of his grief resulted in an epiphany. "Now, now, now," the cloth had murmured as he stroked it.

The time to start his own business was now. The idea of Big People Clothes for Little People had grown in his mind during the decade since he'd heard the midgets at the Willow Run bomber plant complain about getting work clothes in their size. He had only to think of his own humiliation shopping in the children's department to realize the need for a company that would let people like him dress like grownups. Mail-order would let them shop in the privacy of their homes. Entrepreneurs were thriving in the post-war economy. The movie industry had spurned him, but California was also the home of scores of new apparel companies. Why not his?

Meinhardt researched the medical and census data on the number of adults under 4'10" in North America before pitching his idea to the banks. Most were dismissive, but one invested in his first catalog. Mail orders poured in. After initially contracting with another manufacturer to sew the clothes, Meinhardt built and staffed his own plant.

Willow Run's human lessons stayed with him too. He hired people of all backgrounds, including women and the handicapped, and paid everyone a fair and equal wage. His Oma had taught him that each piece of fabric had its own character and should be treated with respect. She'd taught him to treat people the same way.

With his Oma gone, Meinhardt had written Sadie about his decision to start the business. He wanted her reassurance that it would be a fitting tribute to Gretel's memory. "My biggest regret," he wrote, "is that I did not fulfill my dream while she was still alive."

Sadie told him what her rabbi said when she and others were overcome with grief at the deaths of so many family members and friends. "In times of loss, memories haunt and torment us, but they can also comfort and save us." Sad as it was, his grandmother's death had saved his wish from being just a dream. He would find comfort in making it come true.

Chapter 27

The success of Big Clothes for Little People was so phenomenal that Meinhardt was interviewed in *Time* magazine. Because the company was moving into larger quarters, the reporter came to his house in the stately West Adams neighborhood of Los Angeles.

Meinhardt described how he assembled the mailing list for the first catalog. He printed postcards that could be mailed in for a free copy and paid to put them next to cash registers in clothing departments for husky boys and large girls. He persuaded endocrinologists and orthopedists, specialists often seen by midgets, to distribute them to patients and bought ads in catalogs for hard-to-fit children and in circus and vaudeville trade publications. After the first year, he no longer needed to pay to advertise. The company took off via word of mouth.

Eager to talk about his fair employment practices, Meinhardt asked whether the reporter remembered Rosie the Riveter, but the young man was intrigued by the low-hanging cabinets. While Meinhardt described his design process, the interviewer was distracted by elongated pull cords, shortened chair legs, and low door knobs. "It's like a house built for children!" Meinhardt was disgusted. The article portrayed him as a curious freak instead of a smart entrepreneur.

Charles was the first to call. "*Time* magazine! That makes you more American than me."

"You're the one who became a citizen." Meinhardt asked after Jessie and the children. Their son, now eleven, was normal, but their daughter, born five years later, was not. After a miscarriage, Charles had alluded to "complications" that prevented his wife from having more.

"Bella is beginning to get teased by her classmates, but she's tough. Still the apple of my eye. I think Robert will make it to six feet. Jessie's partial to him, though she denies it. Parents aren't supposed to play favorites."

Meinhardt wondered about the brother and sister he'd never met. Had their parents told them of his existence? He suppressed the thought. "It's just as well you and Jessie didn't have more children. With one favorite apiece, your family is balanced."

"I'm worried about Robert. Teenage boys already look down on their fathers, and now that he literally towers over me, I'm afraid of losing all his respect. I need to keep him in line so he'll support us in our old age!" Charles's laugh was strained. "I'm not sure how much longer my body can hold up working at the garage." He'd applied for a mechanic's license after the war, but the union kept

146

him out, so he'd settled for a low-paying job as a grease monkey.

"You do your best to support your family. Robert will appreciate that when he's older."

"I'm not as ambitious as you but I try. To tell you the truth, reading the article made me think about starting my own sausage business. I haven't forgotten what I learned as an apprentice butcher in Berlin. There's a large German population in Detroit, and nearby Hamtramck is full of Poles. The war is far enough in the past that people are ready to buy from someone like me."

"Starting a business takes money."

"That's what the banks are for. Also, I'm hoping some friends will invest in it."

"Are you asking me for a loan?" Meinhardt gripped the phone. "Is that why you called?"

Charles's usually squeaky voice was husky. "I phoned to congratulate you. I'm proud of you and you make me proud to be a midget. I saved the magazine to show Bella when she gets older. I want her to know that she can be someone too."

"If she takes after her father, she will. You're a good man Charles. Much nicer than me."

"You're nicer than you give yourself credit for. Think of all the women, Negroes, and handicapped you hire when no one else will. You help little people like me dress with dignity."

"Sometimes it's easier to be nice to a whole group than to one person. The least I can do is send you a gift certificate with the next catalog." To Meinhardt's relief, Charles laughed.

"Robert's the one who keeps outgrowing his clothes. I can't keep up with the expense. By the way, I got another letter from Hazel last week. She and Joey are back together again after that trial separation. He promised to stop drinking. You know they never had any children."

Meinhardt pictured Hazel curtsying and

serenading him after he won the role of coroner. Suppose he'd accepted her invitation to dinner that night. Not that he'd be married to her now, but she might never have gone off with a loser like Joey. "Does Hazel still ask about me?"

"Not anymore," answered Charles.

Margaret Hamilton called Meinhardt next. "Is this the Midget Master of Money? Heh, heh, heh."

"Maggie. It's good to hear your voice. How many years has it been?"

"A dozen or thereabouts. *Time* magazine does have a way with alliteration."

"Why so long?" Neither of them had an answer.

"How about lunch on Saturday? Du-Pars? You won't recognize Milton, he's grown so tall and gangly. Only his eyes are unchanged, as serious as ever. He's off to college next year."

The restaurant looked the same except for being spiffed up in the post-war boom. Its red leather banquettes were reupholstered so there wasn't a crack in sight, and the oversized menus had been laminated. Margaret ordered the chicken pot pie and Milton got pancakes.

"Do you remember when you deliberately spilled melted butter and maple syrup in a big puddle on the table?" Meinhardt asked.

"I didn't!" A mortified Milton turned to his mother. "Did I really? What a brat!"

"No. An observant child who paid more attention to adult conversation than most kids."

Meinhardt patted his chest and said he couldn't eat a meal as hearty as in the old days, but if he ordered the turkey club sandwich, they could share a platter of donuts. "Glazed, chocolate, and creme filling," he said, pointing to Margaret, Milton, and himself in turn.

"What a memory!" she said.

"In your business, you memorize lines. In mine, I recall what people like. How is business these days? I used to listen to you on the radio playing scatter-brained Aunt Eva on *Ethel and Albert*. My favorite episode was when they fought over how to open a pickle jar."

"I adored doing that show. Underneath the comedy, it showed what it was like to make a marriage work. Something I wasn't good at."

"Something I never tried."

"I was sorry when the show moved to television and I wasn't invited. It's been five years since I did a movie. I just finished a stint on *Paul Winchell* and I'm up for a radio drama, but the future's in television. Any interest in acting again?"

"Now and then I think it would be fun to act on the side."

"I could put in a good word. You have a great radio voice and your height won't matter."

"Don't bother, Maggie. My work's too important to take time for that sort of playing."

The pitcher of syrup in Milton's hand hovered mid-air. "My mother's work is important."

"I didn't mean to imply it wasn't." Meinhardt wished he could eat words.

"She teaches Sunday school too." Milton poured the syrup on his pancakes.

Margaret patted her son's arm. "Meinhardt meant that he performs a valuable service no one else does. He's very successful at it. You remember the article I showed you."

Meinhardt cleared his throat. "Your mother's successful at what she does too, Milton. Her talent brings pleasure to a lot of people. Have you decided what kind of work you want to do? I hear you're starting college next year."

"He's at the top of his class." Margaret beamed. "The guidance counselor says he could get a scholarship to an Ivy League school in the East."

149

"I'd rather stay close to home." Milton looked down. "UCLA is a fine school."

"Yes it is," Meinhardt said, "and you'd be near your mother."

Margaret put a finger to her lips to shush him. "You and I weren't much older when we left home." She turned to Milton. "It's a chance to get to know your father, if you — and he — want to. And you'll make new friends who can last a lifetime, long after I'm gone."

"Friendships can be as important as family," Meinhardt said. He looked at Margaret for forgiveness, but her smile was less warm than the coffee cooling in his cup.

Rodge sent a card after the interview came out. The London postmark and familiar script were the first proof Meinhardt had that he'd survived the war. On the outside, a small man in lederhosen scaled a snow-capped peak. "Congratulations! You made it!" was printed inside, and underneath Rodge had written, "I knew your short legs would take long strides to the top."

Meinhardt phoned the next morning, when it was evening at the pub. He could afford the transatlantic call. Rodge didn't want to talk about the hardships of the last decade. "The learned live in the past. I'm a learner. I live in the future." The Wheel and Wing had been damaged in the Blitz, he said, but had been rebuilt. Both the aerospace and automotive industries were thriving in peacetime and the new sign with the pub's old name was regularly polished with pride.

"And the pride of the football field?"

"We smashed Rat Hole last Sunday!"

Rodge offered belated condolences on the death of Meinhardt's grandmother and he returned sympathy for the demise of King George, who'd died the same year.

"Queen Elizabeth will uphold the dignity of the monarchy," said Rodge, "at the same time her sister flaunts convention." A traditionalist, he nevertheless welcomed Princess Margaret's risqué fashion choices. "The Queen is rather stodgy. It's not as if she can't afford to spruce up. It would do the country good to see a tad of sparkle after years of post-war gloom."

"What about you, Rodge? It can't have been easy. I can certainly spare ..."

"No need." Rodge cut him off. "The government upped our disability to match that of the new vets. You Americans are already doing right by us with the Marshall Plan. Just keep earning your big dollars and paying taxes to your Uncle Sam, then Mother England will take care of me."

"I'm sure you can look after yourself. You're a survivor." There was an awkward silence.

Rodge returned to the safety of the *Time* article. "You were always handsome. You've grown distinguished looking now. I quite loved seeing the photos of your special house, too."

"The reporter got a little carried away with the captions. That drivel about the settee with the sawed-off legs: 'The real meaning of sitting *down*' was over, or should I say, under the top!"

"He missed the best one." Rodge chuckled. "The waist-high switch plates with the on and off push-ins for your electric lights? He should have called them belly buttons!"

"I'm glad you wrote, Rodge. I'm glad I called. Let's not lose touch again."

"Friends are like balloons. Once you let them go, you rarely get them back."

Chapter 28

Meinhardt and Celia licked pastry crumbs off their fingers. "Once I made up my mind to start the business," he said, "ideas exploded in my head like popcorn."   He sighed over their empty plates. "American popcorn is plainer than Viennese pastry, but good in its own simple way."

"We grew popping corn on the farm. My mom sends me a huge bag of kernels every fall. Do you still feel bad about not opening your company until after your grandmother died?"

"I suffer from *Schuld*, feelings of guilt, but I would have missed out on important lessons if I'd done it when I was younger." He described his insights at the bomber plant about making a unique product, and hiring people from all backgrounds and treating them with dignity.

"The opposite of modeling," Celia said, "where they hire only beautiful people, pay them as little as possible, and treat them worse than the merchandise. All the fashion world cares about is pleasing customers and making them feel insecure enough to buy more."

"I pay attention to customers too. My Oma taught me about cloth but acting taught me about wearing clothes." He recalled how he felt the first time he put on his *Oz* costume. "Clothes create character. They affect how you think and feel and move. I knew if I dressed midgets in adult clothes, not fat children's sizes, they'd have more confidence and move with more grace."

Celia nodded. The clothes she modeled changed how she saw herself too. "Frills turn me into a gawky little girl. I want to rebel like a brat against the pose the photographer tells me to strike. When I wear sleek, athletic clothes, like the ones Claire McCardell makes, I feel sure of myself. Then I'm willing to work *with* the photographer and the set designer, not fight them."

Meinhardt admired McCardell, whose designs arose from the fabric. Her method was to hold the material up to the light, pull it on the bias, and pleat and crumple it until a style emerged in her hands. She designed the things she needed and other people decided they needed them too.

"That principle is true for me," Meinhardt told Celia. "I know what styles look good on a midget's body and what exaggerates our flaws." He winced remembering when Adrian said wide shoulders on the coroner's robe would make him look shorter. The man was right. "Sometimes disappointment leads to growth. Not that life's setbacks have made me tall."

"And I haven't had enough disappointments to justify my height."

They touched the tops of their heads and saluted each other.

"I heard that President Eisenhower's biggest disappointment was not making the baseball team at West Point," Celia said. "He made the football team, but then he broke his leg."

"Then I'm luckier than Ike. My short unbroken legs can outrun his long busted ones."

"Those legs got you here, with me." Celia pressed her knees to his beneath the table.

Meinhardt's knees exchanged heat with hers through the fabric of their pants. "I'm thinking of a new theme for my catalog scenes --- midgets pictured filling high-level positions in government and industry, with the White House or the Chrysler Building in the background. I'd call the line 'Big Power Clothes for Little People,' but without the wide shoulders."

Celia looked at her watch. "Wide shoulders for big people beckon. If I don't get back, I'm easily replaced." She surveyed the beautiful faces at the surrounding tables.

Meinhardt leaned forward. "You're as unique as the clothes I make. I'm not an unhappy man, but I'm often somber. Being with you makes me feel sunny. You bring that same light to the outfits you

153

model. It's a tough business, but don't ever let it turn you dark."

"Your life's been harder than mine and it didn't darken you. You're like the sunrise, you always come up again." Celia tossed her golden hair and her yellow cat's eyes glowed.

"Failure was never an option, especially after my grandmother died."

"Failure isn't in my plans, either. I don't know what else I could do. Even if I succeed, I haven't thought about what will happen when I'm too old to model."

"Age is one drawback a businessman doesn't have." Meinhardt looked away from Celia's shining face. It was a drawback for an older man to take up with a beautiful young woman. He might never see her again. "Do you have an extra photo in your portfolio? I can pay for a copy."

She handed him a composite card with thumbnail shots of all her pictures. "When are you going back to California?"

"Tomorrow. I've seen everything I wanted."

Celia pressed her index finger against the last sugary crumb on her plate and touched it to Meinhardt's mouth. "Your hotel room, tonight?"

He licked his lips delicately. He'd fulfilled the pledge to his Oma to become a successful businessman. Falling in love wasn't part of that vow. He'd never conceived a plan to do both.

Meinhardt was staying at The Plaza. He treated himself well on trips to New York, although he always ate one meal at the automat. Not out of nostalgia, but to appreciate how far he'd come in fifteen years. The hotel was far from the exhibit hall, so the brisk walk compensated for Demel's pastry. He also liked being across from Central Park. The big expanses of meadow reminded him of the playing field in the Tiergarten, where he used to chase a football with his grandmother.

It would be after ten by the time the show closed and Celia arrived. While Meinhardt waited, he debated what to order from room service. Champagne seemed presumptuous, like a rich man showing off. She might want dinner, but he didn't know what she liked to eat. He opted for fruit and cheese, and a pastry platter. On a whim, he also ordered a large bowl of popcorn.

"I would have gotten here earlier but I was nervous about what to wear. I changed three times." Celia did a runway walk around the room. Meinhardt sat in a chair watching. He was afraid that if he stood, the length of her strides would make him feel shorter. After two laps, Celia perched on the edge of the bed and patted the heavy brocade spread beside her.

Meinhardt wasn't ready for their skin to touch. He gently pinched the silk sleeve of her cream-colored blouse and traced the sharp crease of her black linen pants. Celia stretched out and drew him down next to her. She guided his hands to her breasts.

"You're almost too lovely," he said. "I have to turn off the light to make love to you."

"Leave it on. I want you to look at me and I want to see all of you."

Celia was more experienced than Meinhardt. Unlike the prostitutes he visited now and then, she encouraged him to take his time exploring her body. The backs of her knees were as smooth as satin, and the inside of her elbows had tiny ridges like corduroy. There was a pale velvety nap where she shaved her pubic hair, but her inner folds were densely pleated, reminding him of the marocain crepe dresses his Oma had sewn for her most elegant clients.

Meinhardt was glad his shortness, like most midgets, was in his legs rather than his upper body.

155

Stretched out, his lips came to Celia's nipples and though his feet barely grazed her shins, their genitals aligned perfectly in the middle. Her thinness was deceptive. Years of farm work had made her limbs and torso as sturdy as a tree trunk. He started at the bottom and climbed to the top. Unlike the trees he scaled to escape bullies as a boy, he hugged her with fervor, not fear.

"Your skin is more olive colored than I expected," he said lying beside her afterwards. "I thought it would be pale, like your hair and eyes."

"Artificial tanning and derma dyes," Celia said. "We have to darken our skin to model bathing suits year round. You're pale, though. It goes with your green eyes and red hair."

"Thank goodness I don't have freckles!"

"Says who?" She rolled him onto his stomach and played her fingers over his back. He didn't know he had freckles there. His Oma had never said so when she'd soaped him as a child.

"Lie still." Celia ordered him to keep his face turned into the rumpled sheet. He heard her cross the room to the sideboard and return to the bed before straddling him. One by one, she balanced pieces of buttery popcorn on his freckles and licked them off. "Stop laughing." She began to laugh herself. "You're making them fall off."

Meinhardt rolled over and Celia let herself be pinned beneath him. "You have no freckles so I'll pretend you're a yard — two yards — of Dotted Swiss." He placed a kernel every couple of inches along her thighs and belly and rolled them onto his tongue. Then they threw handfuls of popcorn into the air and opened their mouths wide to catch them. Sated, they snuggled together in the littered bed linens. Meinhardt wished he'd ordered champagne after all.

"Do you have to leave tomorrow?" Celia enveloped him in a long cape of arms and legs.

Despite being encased, Meinhardt felt freer and taller than ever before. "I'll stay the rest of the week." He would call his secretary and housekeeper tomorrow. There was no one else back in California he needed to tell.

"Why me?" he asked Celia. "I'm rich, but not that rich. And I can't help you break into the modeling business. My product line is two feet shorter than the high end you're aiming for."

"You remind me of my father."

Meinhardt was dismayed. "Well, you don't remind me of my Oma."

Celia hugged him. "Don't worry. I'm not looking for a father figure, although I like the idea of being someone's little girl. I missed out on that."

"I never got to take care of someone." Meinhardt had dreamed of providing for his Oma as she grew old, but he couldn't imagine looking after a child who was small and vulnerable.

"You attract me because of what I admire in my father. He's ingenious about adapting things to make them cheaper or more efficient. Otherwise my folks would have lost the farm. My dad's also honest and decent. He's serious on the outside, but he's got a playful streak underneath that only I can bring out. I feel good about myself when I'm with him. It's why I like being with you."

They were quiet for a while. It was well past midnight and traffic noises from the street were sporadic. Even New York was asleep. Meinhardt summoned his nerve. "Perhaps you just like the oddity of having sex with a midget." A whore once serviced him for free merely to add him to her collection of weird clients.

Celia sat up cross-legged and looked directly into his eyes. "You _are_ different than other men but not in the way you think. I'm used to them trying to get me into bed. Sex is all they have on their minds and work is just another way to get it. You're serious about your work, like me. My head may be in the clouds but my feet are on the ground. I don't topple over in stilettos."

Meinhardt eased her back down beside him. "Trusting is hard for me. I'm afraid people are out to ridicule or use me. I want to be able to trust you."

There was silence between them again until Celia said, "I only used someone once."

Meinhardt held his breath.

"It was six months after I came to New York and I still hadn't gotten any work. I lost my virginity to a buyer who said he could get me a showroom job. He was gentle with me and made good on his promise. Maybe it was wrong but I don't regret it. That first job led to others and now I'm in a show where I have a shot at being seen by a top-level designer or photographer."

"Six months! I waited nearly twenty years for a break!"

"I don't have that much time."

"You've got a decade or more. Plenty of time for a career and then a family."

Celia rested her hands on her stomach and closed her eyes. "I can't have children."

"Not yet, of course. But after you're done being a cover girl."

"I mean, I can't ever have children."

"Celia, look at me."

She opened her eyes, but stared at the ceiling. "My ovaries never developed. My friends started getting their periods, so at the end of junior high I announced I had too. I brought sanitary pads to school every month and pretended to have cramps. Finally, when I turned sixteen, my mother took me to the doctor. He told her I wasn't normal."

"You're better than normal. You're extraordinary."

Celia faced him. "I'm so ashamed. I'm not a real woman."

"Why be ashamed of something you can't help? You don't need children to be a woman."

Her laugh was bitter and sad. "I don't know of any world where that's true."

Meinhardt wondered if Margaret would have been as indifferent to her looks if she hadn't had Milton to prove her womanhood. He'd never wanted children. It gave Charles and Jessie as much heartache as pleasure, and growing up without a father, he doubted he'd know how to be a good one himself. Yet for some men, impregnating a woman was a measure of their manhood. "Does my not being a father make me less of a man in your eyes?"

"It's different for men," Celia said. "They're judged on their work. As a woman with no children, I'll never feel complete. Work is a substitute, but it's all I have."

"I still don't understand the impatience. Your athletic looks are what American designers want. You would have landed a job soon enough without trading sex to get it."

"My condition makes me lean and muscular now, but my bones will turn brittle and start to break in my forties if I'm lucky, in my thirties if I'm not." Celia curled into a ball. "All models face getting old. My career will end sooner than most. I don't know how I'll handle being without work and being weak at the same time." She held his hands. "Teach me to stay strong."

He didn't know how Celia could talk about keeping her strength when she'd already been weak. "You need your beauty rest. I'll call you a cab." Meinhardt walked her to the door and as she bent to brush her lips against his, he dug his hands inside the pockets of his robe, out of her reach. The dim ceiling light, reflected in her eyes, turned them a cloudy amber.

After Celia left, Meinhardt stared at his suitcase, unsure whether to pack and leave as planned tomorrow, or stay the week as he'd promised moments ago. It was mid-morning in London, a good time to call Rodge for advice. He had no one else to turn to in matters of love.

Chapter 29

"Celia's half again my height and just over half my age. I don't know what to do."

"If you want advice on how to make love to a taller woman, you've come to the right place. They all stand taller than me." Rodge teased. "The phone feels warm. Are you blushing?"

Meinhardt stammered that he wasn't calling for love-making advice. He wanted to know if Rodge felt diminished next to a woman who overshadowed him.

"I feel like a king. She boosts my stature. People assume the only reason she's attracted to me is because I'm a rich and powerful."

"Maybe they think she's into strange sexual acts."

"There's nothing abnormal about the ladies I see. In fact, they're saner than average. Less worried about what others think of them. They don't care if people stare and judge."

"What if they're after attention? Celia's a model, she lives to be looked at. Dating me guarantees others will stare at her more than they already do."

"Better than having them stare at you and think you're the oddball."

"Do the women you date ever say what it's like for them."

"Helen joked she got a backache and sore knees bending down for hugs and kisses. I once asked if she felt less safe with me because I couldn't protect her in a dark alley. She said she felt more safe because hooligans would feel too sorry for me to attack us."

"If Celia told me that I'd feel terrible."

"I chose to see it as an acknowledgment of good luck, not pity."

"You and I are different that way. I wish I could be as positive as you."

"I know short men who start fights to show how tough they are. Don't go trying to prove your manhood to Celia."

Meinhardt had endured more than his share of fights as a child. He wasn't about to start something he knew he would lose.

"Women assume a handicapped man is funny and kind. He makes people laugh to divert attention from his defects and behaves more decently than normal blokes, who figure they can always get someone else. Ladies also trust us to work hard because we're so used to struggling." Rodge hooted. "I'm the laziest man I know! Unlike you."

"But you are funny and kind."

"And you're not?"

"Celia makes me playful. I want to take care of her, not because I'm compensating for my height, but because she's so young." She was 25 to his 40, the same as Princess Margaret and her commoner boyfriend. "If you saw Celia, you'd swear she was a princess too. Next to her, I'm a common frog. No wonder the Brits are offended at Margaret marrying Mr. Townsend."

"Not all of them. Some are gaga over the romance." Rodge paused. "Do you worry that she sees you as a father figure?"

"She denied that was the case."

"Could falling in love with a giant be your way of finding the mother you never had?"

"If that were true, I'd throw myself at the feet of Eleanor Roosevelt."

"Leave her to me, old chap. She's used to men without a leg to stand on."

Meinhardt would never get used to his friend's biting wit. He never turned it on others, only himself. Rodge maintained that a sharp tongue could cut your own throat and preferred to be the one wielding the knife. "The margin of trust is no wider than the border of your control."

"There's something that bothers me more than our height and age difference." Meinhardt hesitated. His code of honor made him unwilling to betray a confidence, and yet if he didn't share Celia's admission the affair would end with her confession. He needed reassurance. "Celia traded sex for a modeling job. What if she has no integrity? How can I trust her?"

Rodge sighed. "You lack experience in the ways of love and sex. This is the first time in your life you've combined the two. Some people can separate them. Sex is not like business, where dirty money soils your hands forever. Celia made an honest deal. Both sides got what they bargained for. In your place, I'd advise realistic understanding rather than moralistic judgment."

Meinhardt debated whether to tell Rodge that Celia couldn't have children, but decided that sharing something she was so ashamed of was an even bigger breach of confidence. It was easier to let Rodge persuade him she was a good person and turn his doubts back on himself.

"I still don't get what she sees in me. I'm not exactly a tower of strength."

"She sees what I do. A fascinating and sweet man with the energy and determination to face life's obstacles. Someone who is not out to use her for gain or advantage."

"She's so beautiful."

"Your green eyes are as handsome as any Prince Charming's. There's also your fine red hair." Rodge waited a beat. "Or are you losing it, old man?"

Meinhardt laughed and reassured Rodge

that his hair was as thick as ever, if a bit gray.

"You also have a lovely voice. Have you sung to Celia yet?"

"I'll serenade her tonight and every night this week." His suitcase went back in the closet.

Meinhardt flew to New York twice a month, where he stayed with Celia at her studio apartment in Greenwich Village. She refused to be treated to nights at the Plaza.

"You're too independent."

"No more than you. We both insist on taking care of ourselves."

"I want to shower you with pretty things. It's the first time in my life I have the money to buy them and someone to give them to."

"You can bring a box of pastries from Demel's, but we'll cook and eat here."

"Then let me buy you a step stool. I can't even reach the bottom shelf of your cabinets and I don't want your help getting down the Cheerios." They made love chains with the cereal, seated across from each other at her Formica table, and nibbled their way to the center until their tongues met. Celia nailed a low hook on the bathroom door for Meinhardt's blue silk bathrobe.

When they weren't eating or making love, Meinhardt and Celia went to the movies. He loved sitting in the dark with her, out in public yet safe from prying eyes. Both had omnivorous tastes. They shared his handkerchief crying over *Mister Roberts*, sat on the edge of their seats watching *To Catch a Thief*, and shivered at the menace of *Blackboard Jungle*. Musicals were their favorite. After seeing *Oklahoma!*, Celia let Meinhardt treat them to a ride around Central Park in a hansom cab, while he crooned "The Surrey With the Fringe on Top." Later he neighed gently in her ear as he clipped-clopped his way along the trails of her body.

163

While the weather was still nice, they took the subway uptown to walk around the park. However, as the trees became bare in late fall, Meinhardt felt more self-conscious and exposed too. He swore people were laughing at his short legs scurrying beside Celia's long strides.

"This is New York," she said. "People don't notice. Everyone is invisible."

Meinhardt felt being a midget made him stand out, although he conceded there were times it made him disappear. He both welcomed and resented going unnoticed.

"Sometimes I wish I could disappear," said Celia. "I'd blend in and have the freedom to do whatever I wanted."

"What would you do that you can't do now?"

"Walk around the city wearing dungarees and chewing on a blade of grass."

"On you, that would be fashionable. The cover of *Vogue* would proclaim 'Country chic comes to Manhattan wearing blue denim accented by pale yellow hair and golden eyes.'"

"If only I were on the cover of *Vogue*." Celia had every issue for the last five years neatly stacked on top of her bookcase.

"Someday you will be," said Meinhardt. "I have faith in you."

Celia smiled. "I have faith in me too. Just like you had faith in yourself."

"We got it from our families." Whenever they talked about his Oma and her parents, it wasn't long before they untied the string on the white pastry box.

Chapter 30

They spent Thanksgiving in New York. Meinhardt was relieved when Celia refused her parents' offer to pay her fare home, because she would have asked

164

him to meet her there. The fact that she was in love with a midget didn't mean they'd be ready to accept him.

"Be there in a minute," Celia called as he let himself in. "I'm making my mother's dried cherry-cornbread stuffing to put in the bird tomorrow. I bought the smallest one I could find. Is there something like Thanksgiving in Germany? Did your grandmother cook anything special?"

"Who's Celeste Panterdown?" Meinhardt noticed the letter as he set his hat on the mail table. Celia's address was on the front with a return postmark of Benton Harbor, Michigan.

She emerged from the closet-sized kitchen. "That's me," she said.

"I don't understand."

"I changed my name when I came to New York. I thought it would look better on my portfolio." She took the letter from Meinhardt's hand and put it in her apron pocket.

"Why Celia Posy?"

"Posy because a little bouquet to describe a big girl would attract attention. Celia because it sounded European and elegant. Celeste is Midwestern and dowdy."

"Your parents thought it was pretty."

"I haven't told them yet."

"Who are you?" Meinhardt felt cold. He pulled his overcoat around him.

"I'm me. What's the big deal? Movie stars do it all the time." She reached for his hands.

He reached for his hat. "It's expected in Hollywood. Films are about fantasy."

"New York fashion is about fantasy too."

"Well, if it's not a big deal, why haven't you told your parents? Why didn't you tell me?"

"Didn't you ever want to change your name?" Celia's eyes beseeched his. "Hiding your German identity might have gotten you work during the war or a bank loan afterwards.”

“I can’t hide that I’m German. And even though my parents left me, I’d never give up my father’s last name for my Oma’s. I’m not always happy with myself, but I accept who I am.”

“What about being a midget? You don’t accept that. You want to hide from the crowd.”

“I don’t deny my identity.”

“Neither do I. You think you’re the only one whose size makes him an outcast. It wasn’t easy growing up a foot taller than all the men in my town, but I used it to my advantage. Your business helps short people, but you’ll never see your height as anything but a handicap.”

The chill left Meinhardt. He felt warm with shame. Celia was right. She accepted herself better than he did. For goodness sake, even Rodge beat him at knowing and liking who he was.

“Perhaps I’m still the little child not good enough for his parents. My name is the only proof that I’m theirs.”

Celia pulled him onto the couch where they could sit side by side. “Your parents were fools. Or just young and scared. I’m sure they would feel differently if they saw you now.”

Meinhardt pouted. “They didn’t call me after I was written up in *Time* magazine.”

“Not everyone reads ... Oh, Meinhardt!” Celia caught his smile and enveloped him in her arms. “I didn’t mean to hurt you. You’ve overcome hatred and discrimination I can’t even begin to imagine. It’s worse than anything I’ll face for not being a mother.”

They clung to each other, then leaned back, exhausted. It was too soon after fighting to make love, so they window shopped on Fifth Avenue. Like pastry, they savored the latest styles.

“East meets West” was the theme of Lord and Taylor’s animated Christmas display.

"Can you see me draped in yards of shimmering paisley?" Celia unwound her long purple scarf and wrapped it like a shawl around the shoulders of her black woolen pea coat. She strutted up and down, diverting the eyes of the other shoppers away from the store manikins.

"Oriental fabrics were popular when I was a boy. My Oma matched patterns at the seams to make the garment look like it had been woven in one piece in the loom." Meinhardt described how his grandmother measured and cut the material to allow for each millimeter of stitching.

Celia stood still, listening. The crowd moved past, leaving the two of them alone. Soon a light snow began to fall. Meinhardt wished he were tall enough to lick the flakes from her pale lashes. Instead he took her gloved hand in his and pressed them together for warmth. He would learn to claim Celia in public to prove to them both that he thought he deserved her.

They walked on to Bonwit Teller. "Fur," said Celia with disgust.

Meinhardt was surprised. "You model sheepskin and exotic bird feathers."

"I know it's not consistent, but killing small furry animals for the sake of fashion ..." She shrugged. "They're so defenseless."

"I'm small and furry. Do you think I'm defenseless?"

"You're the most well-defended man I've ever met. It's taking all my charm to break you down." She leaned over and draped his arms on either side of her neck like fox tails.

Their noses touched. Meinhardt closed his eyes so he wouldn't see the curious shoppers dividing to walk around them. He let the wind blow away their snide whispers.

"Let's go to the Macy's Thanksgiving Day Parade tomorrow," said Celia. "I've lived in New

York for five years and I've never been."

"I can't." Meinhardt told her about choosing to be fired when asked to play a dwarf on the Snow White float nearly two decades ago, and giving up busking tips rather than sing songs from the movie. "I refused to humiliate myself, even with a job or money at stake."

"I'm not as high minded as you." Celia eyes followed the streaming crowd.

Meinhardt turned her chin back towards him. "You were young and trusting. It takes time to learn people can be cruel and manipulative, and figure out how to stand up to them. By now, you've been in the business long enough to know better. You won't make that mistake again."

Celia faced away from him once more. "It worked for me the first time. I did it again."

"Why didn't you tell me?" Meinhardt's hot breath shot through the icy air like a cannon blast.

She stepped back. "I knew you'd judge me. You worry I'm too good for you, but I'm the one who can't live up to your standards."

"It's a simple matter of self-respect, Celia. My standards are not impossibly high."

"I learned my lesson the second time. I didn't get the job. I never heard from him again."

"That's the wrong lesson. What matters isn't getting the job, it's keeping your integrity."

Celia nodded. "I'm glad I didn't get the job. It made me ashamed of myself. That dirty feeling will never go away. I swear I learned my lesson, the right one."

That night, the studio apartment felt cramped for the first time. They slept poorly on either edge of the pull-out sofa. Celia went to the parade alone the next morning.

All the pain and rejection in Meinhardt's life hadn't prepared him for the helpless anger he felt now. Love wasn't the issue. There was no point asking Rodge for advice. Celia's behavior made him question the possibility of ever trusting her. He decided to call Jennie Grossinger, who he'd met two years ago when Big People Clothes for Little People took off. He'd held his first sales meeting at her hotel in the Catskills, assembling a force of midgets, both men and women, to recruit new customers. They were excited to have jobs and a line of clothing made for them.

Jennie and her staff treated Meinhardt and his associates with respect. The two business owners had a lot in common besides their shrewdness. His German grandmother Gretel and her Polish mother Malke were Eastern Europeans with similar values. Malke, herself an innkeeper's daughter, had passed on a gift for welcoming the humblest guest. Gretel had bequeathed her ease with cloth. Both had died a year earlier. Meinhardt and Jennie commiserated in mourning.

"Jennie, forgive me for calling on Thanksgiving morning. Holiday business is good?"

"The hotel is full. *Auf Holz klopfen*, knock wood, *toi, toi, toi*." He and Jennie also shared old-world superstitions. "But for you Meinhardt, I can always make time. Nu?"

He poured forth his story and his doubts. She exclaimed "Mazel Tov!" over his falling in love, then grew quiet listening to how Celia had traded sex for work.

Jennie sighed. "Not everyone in this world is upstanding. My mother saw her share of dishonest guests and employees taking advantage."

"What did Malke do? Kick them out? Fire them?"

"Only as a last resort. She lived by the doctrine of *Tikkun Olam*, healing the world, and believed most people had it in them to be better." Jennie sniffled. "My mother separated the incorrigible from the redeemable. Occasionally she misjudged a person, but mostly she was right."

"How could she tell them apart?"

"True remorse."

"What does it look like?"

"The fake ones cry loud crocodile tears, the real ones weep quietly."

Celia had been silent last night, but when Meinhardt folded up the couch that morning, her pillow was soaking wet. By the time she came back from the parade, Meinhardt had set the table with a piece of cloth he'd hidden at the bottom of his suitcase to surprise her. The pale yellow silk was the color of her hair, its grain shot through with orange and brown flecks like her eyes.

"It's beautiful." Celia stroked the material with shaking fingers. "It should be draped over antique oak, not my cheap Formica."

Meinhardt steadied her hands. "We've shared our best meals at this table. That makes it more valuable than the most expensive wood."

Celia lit the oven and slipped the turkey inside. They sat on the couch and Meinhardt serenaded her with *Pennies from Heaven*. "If you want the things you love, you must have showers. Make sure your umbrella is upside down. Trade them for a pack of flowers." By the time they'd made slow love and Meinhardt licked the salty tears running down Celia's cheeks, Thanksgiving dinner was ready. They craved something sweet, so they began with dessert.

Chapter 31

Celia was going home for Christmas. Meinhardt had declined her invitation to come, claiming he'd be too tired after the holiday sales rush to make a good impression on her family. She'd extracted a promise that he'd go at Easter when her mother baked her famous bunny cake.

"It's just a plain white cake, but it's really cute."

"Like me?"

"You're cute, but there's nothing plain about you."

Since they wouldn't be together for the holiday, Meinhardt flew to New York in mid-December. He resisted the temptation to splurge on gifts, knowing Celia would feel bad that she couldn't reciprocate. Instead, at the Melrose Flea Market, he bought two porcelain coffee cups, matching cake plates with hand-painted posies, and silver-plated dessert forks.

Celia gasped with pleasure after undoing the red and green knit cloth and cotton batting in which he'd wrapped them. "Now we can dine on Demel's pastry in style."

Together they filled the plates with the *Springerle* and *Lebkuchen* Meinhardt had bought and the gingerbread men with cherry eyes and buttons sent by Celia's mother. They fed each other small bites and when they were sated on Christmas cookies, they nibbled each other.

"I have a surprise for you too." Celia handed Meinhardt an envelope. Inside was a ticket to Claire McCardell's spring runway show in February.

"Why a single ticket?"

"I don't need one. I'm *in* the show!" Celia strutted from wall to wall in her tiny kitchen. "The John Robert Powers agency called last week. If my press photos come out good, they'll recommend me for McCardell's next design spread in *Vogue*."

"That's wonderful! But why do you want me there?" The thought of crowds gawking and camera bulbs popping at the sight of them together mortified Meinhardt.

"Why wouldn't I want you to share the most

exciting moment of my career so far?”

“Because being seen with a freak might hurt your future chances.”

“I’m proud to be seen with you. Your support is my biggest help.”

“So you want me there because you think I can help you get ahead?”

Celia looked puzzled. “No, I meant ...”

“It would make a great publicity shot, wouldn’t it? ‘Six foot four model has four foot six lover.’ A picture like that in your portfolio could advance your career among the avant garde.”

“This is coming out wrong. You’re twisting my intentions.” Celia crumpled into a chair.

“I don’t know who you are Celia. You dishonored your parents by changing your name. You dishonored yourself by trading sex for work. How do I know you didn’t sleep with someone to get this job? It must have been quite a fling to get chosen for such an important show.”

Celia’s sobs were loud. She made no move to wipe away the dark streaks of mascara that carved rivers down her cheeks. “Don’t do this. If you’re uncomfortable going to the show, just say so. I’ll be disappointed but I’ll understand.”

Meinhardt stopped himself from hurling the plates onto the floor. He would maintain his dignity, even if Celia repeatedly compromised hers. He put on his coat and walked to the door.

“You’re a stunted man.” Celia stood over him.

“How dare you!”

“That’s not a slur against your height. You’re emotionally dwarfed. You’re so fixated on your disability that you can’t trust the love of those who see past it.”

Meinhardt replayed those words in the taxi to the airport. They couldn’t be true. He’d loved and trusted his Oma. Celia had only herself to blame. She'd started out a good person, but New York had corrupted her. It was a city of betrayal, from Harpo Marx to Celia Posy.

California was full of phonies too, but behind the glib talk and fancy clothes, people were honest about their intentions. From now on, Meinhardt would save his faith and trust for work, where he controlled the deals. He'd demand of others and expect of himself nothing less than total integrity. Rodge liked to say that "The happiest people are those with a clear conscience or no conscience." Meinhardt half agreed. He was convinced the latter would come to a bitter end, but he vowed to be one of the former. He'd have to trust that someday it would make him happy.

PART SEVEN

And, Oh, What Happened Then Was Rich

Liberty, New York, 1964

Chapter 32

Meinhardt arrived at the overheated lobby of Grossinger's Hotel midday, on the second Sunday in February. He undid the leather buttons of his single-breasted camel's hair coat, a popular item in his company's menswear line. Traveling east during the winter was a trial. After living in California for a quarter-century, he'd grown intolerant of both the chill and the manmade heat.

He was tired and angry. The trip had been a series of insults. Assuming he couldn't reach the counter, the agent at the LA airport had come out from behind it to stamp his ticket and check his suitcase. Then, in New York, when the step on the bus going upstate to Liberty *was* too high, the driver had lifted him into the aisle, deposited him over the wheel well, and placed his legs on the hump so they wouldn't dangle or kick the seat back in front of him. Despite being swaddled in top quality wool, Meinhardt felt stripped of dignity and as vulnerable as a naked child.

By the time he got to the hotel, he almost looked forward to seeing the Munchkins he'd brought together for a twenty-fifth reunion. Apart from Charles, they weren't his friends, but he felt less self-conscious in their company, the same relaxed feeling he had each summer when he held his annual sales meeting here. However, those gatherings assembled two dozen associates, whereas Meinhardt hoped 80 of the over 120 Munchkins would be at this event.

The idea for the reunion had come to him last fall as a strategy to fend off complacency. Business was almost too good. Fashions had changed little in the last decade. Women still wore shirtwaists; men, Italian suits. He was ahead of the trend to shorten hemlines, and educated his clients to avoid Capri pants and wide neckties. All but the most flamboyant midgets, showmen to the core, appreciated the catalog's subdued solid colors. When he occasionally included patterns, they were small and conservative. The goal was for the clothes to divert, not attract, attention.

Having mastered the art of adaptation, Meinhardt needed a new challenge. He was also mindful of the fact that even though he was successful, most midgets his age were not. Charles, who kept in touch with their old cast mates, told him stories about their struggles finding work or paying medical bills. President Johnson's War on Poverty wasn't being fought for them.

When Charles had called last September, he'd teased Meinhardt for missing Michigan's most beautiful season. "If you'd stayed here twenty-two years ago instead of going back to California, you'd be sniffing the crisp fall air and manufacturing clothes in red, orange, and gold."

"If I lived in Michigan, I'd be dreading the arrival of winter and selling blue denim work clothes." Yet he admitted that despite the company's continued success, he wasn't satisfied.

"You could start a line of custom-made butcher's aprons. Jessie shortens mine, but her eyesight isn't what it used to be and some days her fingers are too stiff to sew."

Meinhardt recalled the baby clothes she made when they were expecting their first child, her stitches nearly as small and even as his grandmother's. "How's the sausage business these days?" he asked Charles. When they'd talked the previous spring, it wasn't doing well.

"I'm grinding out a living." Charles waited for Meinhardt to groan. "Actually, it could be better. These days, people don't make a separate trip to the butcher, or the green grocer or baker for that matter. They shop at a supermarket. I'm trying to sell meat to the A&P but they have their own suppliers.

Besides ..." It wasn't in Charles's nature to speak ill of others.

"They don't like doing business with midgets." Meinhardt finished Charles's sentence. A silent nod passed between them over the telephone line. Meinhardt asked about the children.

"Bella's in the high school glee club. The director attached a small platform to the riser so her head's level with the other sopranos. She's hoping to get a solo in the holiday concert." Charles always talked about his daughter first. She continued to be his favorite and, with his encouragement, she didn't yet feel that being a midget would hold her back.

"You and Jessie must be proud of her."

"Jessie is proud of Robert." Their son, born normal, was a junior at Wayne State University in Detroit. "He's got an apartment now with three other boys."

"Can you afford the extra rent?" He'd lived at home his first two years of school.

"Robert's paying it himself. He saved enough the last two summers working on a road crew. I still can't believe a son of mine is over six-feet tall with the muscles of a Charles Atlas."

Meinhardt glanced at the photo from last year's Christmas card. On one side of the tree, Charles stood shoulder to shoulder with Bella. On the other, Robert towered over a beaming Jessie. Their positions signified more than which child each parent favored. Charles didn't want to look small beside his son. He wasn't competitive about height with other midgets, and didn't mind standing among normal people, but when it came to his own boy, Charles felt diminished.

"What it's like with Robert out of the house?"

"To tell you the truth, which I don't admit to everyone, it's a relief!"

Ever since Robert turned ten, Charles had complained to Meinhardt that he overrode his rules on everything from how loud to play the radio to what time to set curfew. By his mid-teens, he no longer bothered to ask his father's permission. He did what he wanted and let his mother defend him. "How is Jessie doing with a half empty nest?"

"She's paying more attention to Bella, which could be a good thing, but it's mostly to criticize her. I'm afraid Jessie will undermine Bella's confidence. As for Robert, she brings him casseroles every Sunday night so he'll have decent food to eat all week."

Remembering Jessie's American-style meals, Meinhardt pictured foil-covered pans filled with noodles, tinned meat, and canned soup. "I hope he appreciates his mother's home cooking."

"As much as any kid his age who'd be happier eating pizza every night." Charles laughed. "Before Jessie puts the casseroles in the refrigerator, she cleans it out. Not just her leftovers, but the other moldy stuff growing inside. Worst are when there's no food, only beer."

"Are you worried about Robert drinking?"

"It's nothing compared to how much Count Joey and Little Billy drank on the set of *Oz*. Robert insists because he's bigger, he can handle more alcohol without it having any effect."

"He's big enough so that even if he gets drunk, he won't get stuck in the toilet like Joey." Meinhardt hesitated. "Have you heard from Hazel lately? Do you know if Joey sobered up?"

"He's been on and off the wagon so many times, I forget where he is at the moment."

"And Hazel?"

"It's been years since she last talked about leaving him. I suppose she stays because being alone is even scarier. At least he's there to remind her of her glory days as a Munchkin."

"She doesn't need him for that. She can see the movie on television." Meinhardt pictured Hazel watching the annual CBS Christmas broadcast of *Oz* while pirouetting around her tattered Oklahoma living room. He envisioned legs withered by age and a heart weakened by sorrow.

"It's a highlight in our family," Charles said. "Jessie makes a big bowl of popcorn and we sit together on the couch. Except Robert. He won't watch, not even to make his mother happy."

Meinhardt heard the pain in his friend's voice. The mention of popcorn called up his own painful memories. A year after he'd walked out on Celia, he'd seen her in a *Vogue* spread for Claire McCardell's spring collection. She'd since made the magazine's cover twice, her pale hair backlit by sunshine. Her sporty look also appeared in the *New York Times* fashion section where the simple but elegant clothes favored by Jackie Kennedy looked good on Celia too. With the distinction between French and American styles breaking down, Meinhardt sometimes leafed through a copy of *Elle* at the airport to see if Celia had broken into that market as well.

"Last year Bella invited three school friends to watch with us," Charles continued. "Jessie was afraid they'd be condescending, but they treated us like movie stars and wanted autographs. You should have seen the look of pride that passed between my wife and my daughter." He choked up. "How do you feel when you see yourself on television?"

"I don't watch the *Oz* broadcasts," Meinhardt said

"I guess after being interviewed in *Time* and having your picture in *Fortune* magazine, your old movie days aren't that big a deal to you."

"That's not why I don't watch. I'm angry that MGM and the big-name stars earn royalties every time it's shown, while the rest of us don't get a penny. Baron Van Singer did a *lausig* job looking after our interests when he negotiated the contract."

179

Charles agreed. "Some of us could really use the money too." Henry Boer was in the hospital after a second heart attack and his brother Teddy was hobbled by a degenerative bone disease. All four members of the Doll family complained of aches and pains but couldn't afford to retire from performing in traveling circus sideshows.

"Disney's releasing an animated film called *Return to Oz* next year. No one in the original movie will make a buck off that, not even the Great Garland." Meinhardt chuckled. "I know you dislike the gossip columns, Charles, but doesn't it give you a little thrill to know that Garland and her third husband Sidney Luft are getting divorced?"

"It just makes me happy that Jessie and I lasted this long. In two years we'll celebrate our silver anniversary. What was it your friend Rodge used to say?"

"Love is more enduring than fame, and you don't have to dress up for it." Meinhardt had a vision. "Charles, that's it! Do you still have your mayor's frock coat?"

"Sure. Jessie has her costume too. We wear them to watch the movie, although they've grown a little snug on us. I can't close the vest."

"I bet everyone in the cast held onto their outfits. And any props they stole."

Charles chuckled. "You haven't sounded this excited in years." He paused. "I don't get it."

"Next year is the movie's 25th anniversary. Between the annual television special and the new Disney film, there's lots of *Oz* nostalgia. I'm guessing the Munchkins own several hundred objects. If we auctioned them off, we could make a small fortune."

"That's brilliant. No wonder you're a successful businessman."

"Thanks, but there's more. If we just hold a memorabilia sale, we'll seem mercenary. Better to have a reunion and drum up publicity. Then, once people are reminded of how cute the Munchkins are, the auction can be our generous response to their affectionate demands for mementos."

Charles whooped with delight. "When? Where?"

It would take several months to contact everyone and get them onboard. Meinhardt would leave that to Charles; they trusted him to protect their interests. "Let's aim for February, at the Culver Hotel."

"The management blacklisted us after those crazy shenanigans."

"Harry Culver died in 1946. The hotel's gone downhill. The new owners will be glad for the attention and the business. It'll give them a chance to spruce up the place."

"I'm convinced," said Charles. "Except a lot of us can't afford a trip to California."

"Meals and tips are on me." Meinhardt did a quick calculation. "Tell me who the worst off are and I'll pay for their plane tickets too."

"Are you turning kinder as you get older?"

"Strictly business. I'll claim a tax write-off."

"What about publicizing the event?"

"One of my shippers is a stringer for *Variety* and knows John Flinn, the columnist who gave the premier of *Oz* a five-star review. He also knows Rich Gold in the New York office."

"What if they bring up all that old talk about drunkenness and sex orgies at the hotel?"

"Today a bad reputation is good press. As long as they give us coverage, the Munchkin memorabilia auction will be more than a sharp alliterative slogan. It will be a financial success."

They talked over the ad campaign. Charles liked "There's a sale blowing up — a whopper!" and Meinhardt thought he could assure the public of a "most sincerely good deal."

"How will you feel seeing Hazel at the

181

reunion? That is, if she and Joey come."

"If they need help getting there, I'll honor my pledge to pay." Meinhardt's image of her twirling feebly in front of her television was supplanted by his memory of a pretty girl spinning with grace and admiration. "Of course, we'll use a rainbow as the auction logo."

Charles was excited, but said parting with their costumes would be hard, especially for Jessie.

"Tell her you'll use the proceeds to send Robert to medical school so he can find the cure for being born a midget."

"I'll tell her we'll use the money to send Bella to college. If midgets can grow up as smart and happy as my daughter, then I say the more, the merrier."

Meinhardt disagreed but replied, "More of us is better for my business too."

Chapter 33

Talking about *Oz* made Meinhardt think about Margaret. Their last meeting, nearly a decade ago, had been marred by his thoughtless remark about her work not being important. He should call her now. Rodge used to say, "You can only cut an apple in half once," but he believed in second chances. So did Margaret. She alone had been forgiving to a young Judy Garland.

"Maggie, it's been too long. I can't believe Milton's almost 30. I'd love to hear what he's up to. Lunch at Du-Pars?" His appeal to her motherly pride worked, although she suggested meeting at a coffee shop near her house. Meinhardt understood she was reclaiming her self-respect, so he let also her choose their seats and didn't offer to pay. They busied themselves with the menu. He didn't relax until Margaret spread three photos on the table, showing a tall, thin man with a beard next to a small dark-haired woman. Both wore peasant blouses.

"Milton's making documentaries in Chile for the Peace Corps."

"I thought he wanted to stay close to home and to you. What changed?"

Margaret laughed. "My son fell in love. He met Nadia at UCLA's Film School and her family still lives in Santiago. They split their time between there and LA. I get to see my two grandchildren half the year. There's a third on the way." She handed Meinhardt more pictures.

He moved the silverware aside to make room. "You have a beautiful family."

Her eyes lingered on each snapshot as she carefully returned them to her purse.

"What about work? I saw in *Variety* that you're the housekeeper on *The Secret Storm*."

"Radio drama's dead. At 61, I'm lucky to get a television gig." She joked about growing more witchy looking. "You, on the other hand, have grown more handsome. The gray around your temples is quite distinguished."

Neither had serious health problems, unlike many others in the *Oz* cast. "Garland has had her ups and downs," said Meinhardt. "I hear she's suing her third husband, Sid Luft, for divorce on the ground of cruelty. He should be suing her. I never understood why you liked her."

"Judy didn't have a chance to grow up. She's still like a little girl."

"You're in touch with her?"

Margaret said they saw each other every couple of months. Garland liked to reminisce now that the movie had become a cult favorite. Meinhardt told Margaret about his idea to auction Munchkin memorabilia. "I don't need the money, but most of the other midgets are struggling."

She nodded sympathetically. "I'm not the type to feel sorry for myself, but if tempted, I remember how fortunate I am." She looked at her hands. "I don't know if I should tell you this, but Sid Luft is selling a big ruby ring Judy gave him so he can pay his legal bills. She can't get it back because the lawyers agree it belongs to him. The New York State Jeweler's Association is auctioning it for charity and giving him half the take. If you have the wherewithal to bid on it, linking the ruby ring to Dorothy's ruby slippers could draw wealthy fans to your sale."

Meinhardt pressed for details. Margaret knew only that the ring was a rare cut and would be auctioned at the jewelers' next convention. Garland wanted to avoid publicity, and her ex didn't want his financial troubles in the news either. "Promise you'll keep the connection a secret, Meinhardt, until after the ring is sold? I'm only telling you so you can help the midgets."

He promised the secret was safe with him. Not that he gave a damn about protecting Judy Garland, but the fewer people competing for the ring, the more it would work to his advantage.

"I wish I could bid on it myself and resell it for a profit," Margaret said.

"Maggie, what on earth would you do with the money?"

"Give it to the Peace Corps. Heh, heh, heh!"

The New York State Jewelers Association annual convention was the second week in February, the same as the Munchkins' reunion. Meinhardt was excited when he learned they were meeting at Grossinger's Hotel. He decided to move the reunion there, telling Charles it would make travel easier for the many midgets who lived on the East Coast. Then he called Jenny Grossinger.

"Ach, I feel terrible." Jennie's gold earrings, inherited from her mother Malka, chimed against the receiver. "We're booked on account of a jeweler's convention. What do you want with the Catskills in winter anyway? Why not Hollywood where you always got summer?"

He described how the Culver Hotel had declined since the Munchkins had stayed there. "They replaced the silk cushions on the lounge chairs with vinyl, and the rust on the claw-footed tubs is thicker than pool scum. Even the rats moved out when room service ended."

"Nu, you can't find another hotel nearby? You gotta go back to the same place?"

"Racy rumors survive. We're still blackballed from every hotel in LA." Grossinger's staff treated his sales associates differently, giving them special care without being condescending. They put footstools under the high feather beds and stepladders in the closets. When the June mountain air turned chilly at night, they could reach an extra blanket without calling for help.

Jennie hated to disappoint him now. "How many rooms you need?"

Meinhardt heard the pages of a ledger turn. He calculated aloud. "Out of 122, I figure one-third no-shows. The oldest is 65. With our propensity for bad health, say five are dead. I think 19 rooms should do it." They could sleep four to a bed, with married couples side by side, and the others two across and two lengthwise. "Being a midget has advantages. We can't reach the second shelf at the A&P, but we can double up in bed when space is short."

"The A&P? Don't even say that name! You'll cast the evil eye on my dining room."

Meinhardt looked at the Grossinger's luncheon menu taped to his refrigerator door and counted aloud with relish: "Three juices, four soups, five hot entrees, six cold entrees, seven desserts, plus your home-baked rye bread, salt-free upon request. My old neighbors in Germany would have

185

conniptions if they knew a born Lutheran like me devoured your kosher food."

Not ordinary kosher, Jennie informed him. In February, an Orthodox rabbi would certify it was glatt kosher to satisfy the Hasidic diamond merchants coming to bid on a rare ruby ring. Her voice dropped to a whisper. "My friend, Maurice Glaubart, president of the jewelers, said it belongs to Sidney Luft, Judy Garland's husband. She gave it to him to match her ruby slippers. She wants a divorce, on account of he beats her. So Mr. Luft, he doesn't want the ring no more."

"Sounds like some ring." Meinhardt acted as though he were hearing about it for the first time. "It'll be worth a lot when word gets out it was a gift from the Great Miss Garland!"

"What do I know from that kind of jewelry? Maurice says the bidding will be very high. It's a silent auction and half the money is for charity."

"A good cause?"

"Resettling Cuban Orthodox Jewish refugees in Brooklyn. They don't like Miami."

"Too much chlorine in the Fontainebleau's pool? Shrimp in the matzo ball soup?"

"Get away with you! So, I'll see you and your friends here in February?"

"You promise to make my favorite kosher egg rolls?" Meinhardt's mouth watered.

"The very same ones what Governor Rockefeller asks for when he stays with us."

"I hear the Pope loves them too."

Jennie waited a beat, mimicking the timing of the Borscht Belt comedians who performed at Grossinger's. "His Holiness told me he's never going back to Kansas."

Chapter 34

Meinhardt surveyed the Munchkins gathered in the

hotel lobby. He and Charles had decided not to mention the auction before the reunion. People might be ashamed about needing money and decide not to come. By waiting to bring up the sale until they were unguarded being together again, it would be easier to admit their troubles to one another. Meinhardt could convince them that nostalgia for the movie made the sale's timing auspicious. In a happy accident of scheduling, *The Wonderful World of Disney* was broadcasting its animated film, *Return to Oz*, that night.

He recognized his company's clothes on many of the midgets, including all four from the Doll family. Daisy, Gracie, and Tiny hugged him; Harry, who'd been in the Lollipop Guild, handed out autographed suckers. Despite the energetic buzz, signs of aging abounded. Tommy Cottonaro, once the robust bearded man, was spindly and nearly bald. His long beard hung gray and scraggly. Others traded notes on their heart, lung, and joint problems. Walking had always been hard. Meinhardt had taken two steps to Celia's one. If he'd stayed with her, he'd be falling behind by now. Unless her bones had weakened to where she could no longer keep up with him.

Charles clapped him on the back. "Why so sad? Is being among us that painful?"

"It's a good turnout. You worked your mayoral charms."

"They loved the idea of a reunion. Nearly two-thirds agreed to come."

"Let me know how much you need to cover their expenses," Meinhardt said. "Tell them an anonymous benefactor, a movie buff, is subsidizing the event." They wouldn't have accepted money from him. His success, while admired, was overshadowed by envy.

Meinhardt counted the couples. Three pairs, married before the movie, were still together. Little

Billy Rhodes and his wife had split years ago. Others, like Charles and Jessie, had met on the set and married afterwards.

"Looking for the Polinsky's?" Charles asked. "Joey's with Little Billy in the Pink Elephant Lounge, having a shot contest. Joey no longer pretends he'll stop drinking." His eyes followed Meinhardt's. "Hazel's in their room, changing. This time she did ask about you."

"I wasn't interested then, and I'm not interested now." Meinhardt picked up his suitcase.

"You fooled me and everyone else. Guess you're just a good actor." Charles winked. "I'm off to find Jessie. See you later."

Meinhardt wedged his way through the noisy lobby. Even dressed in his company's subdued clothes, the Munchkins exuded wildness. They showed off their waning acrobatic skills and harmonized to bowdlerized bits of *Oz* songs. Mingling in a separate area were men in business suits, their shirt cuffs pushed up to reveal oversized gold watches. Each hand sported two or three rings. The New York State jewelers eyed the exuberant midgets and stood up straighter.

At the registration desk, Meinhardt found step stools under the counter. Jennie thought of everything. There were 76 reunion reservations, confirming his estimate. If he was correct about their stash of memorabilia, the auction would be a success too. All he needed was a winning bid on the ring, and he'd net a tidy personal profit while helping the Munchkins. The only snag was that neither *Variety* reporter had come. He was counting on their photos to publicize the sale.

His spirits deflated a bit more when he discovered he was sharing a room with the Boers brothers and George Ministeri, who'd played the coach driver. George pretended to whip people when he was sober, and Leo Van Singer insisted on holding the prop when he wasn't. Because Meinhardt was the last to arrive, he'd have to sleep with his head at the foot of the bed. He missed his usual private room. After taking a deep breath, he threw his unpacked suitcase on an upholstered chair, combed his still-thick hair, and hurried back downstairs to the lobby.

Hazel was in a corner, applauding as the Lullaby League, en pointe, recapped their scene. Avoiding her, Meinhardt turned toward the now overweight trio. If they still had their petaled tutus, they'd fetch a good price. Hidden behind a pillar, he finally studied Hazel. She didn't join the dancers with her signature arabesque, as she'd done on the set. Her thin arms and shins were shrouded in a garish Salvation Army shift. He was torn between embarrassment and pity for her.

Desperate to escape, Meinhardt spotted Charles and Jessie across the lobby and moved in their direction. He wasn't good at small talk, but Jessie made chatting easy. All he had to do was ask about the children, especially Robert, and she carried the rest of the conversation. Nor was he just being polite when he listened. He genuinely cared about his god children.

"You're looking well, Meinhardt." Hazel shuffled between him and the Beckers.

He'd been foolish to think he could duck this moment. He made his mouth smile, hoping his eyes wouldn't give away his dismay. "Hazel, it's good to see you."

"But I don't *look* good." She sneered. "Although I might look better in one your dresses." She put her mouth to his ear. "I hide your catalog in the only cabinet where Joey doesn't stash his liquor. My husband refuses to buy your clothes. He's jealous."

"I admit I've been fortunate in my work. But

189

your dress is lovely, quite colorful.”

Hazel studied the pattern as though seeing it for the first time. “It’s not your business success that makes Joey jealous as much as that thing we had when we were filming *Oz*.”

Meinhardt winced. “There was nothing between us. You liked my voice, I admired your dancing. A mutual appreciation between friends. Charles told me you give dancing lessons.”

“I like teaching little children.” She looked at the carpet. “We had one, you know.”

Meinhardt didn’t know. He would have remembered if Charles had told him. Perhaps Hazel hadn’t told Charles. He wished she weren’t telling him.

“Its lungs were too small. That’s common when people like us have a baby. There was a one in four chance our next child would be normal. I wanted to try again, but Joey didn’t like the odds. It’s just as well, seeing how Joey turned out.” Hazel sighed. “You’ll see him soon enough.”

“Yes,” said Meinhardt, “I’ll see you both at dinner.” He tried edging around her to join Charles and Jessie, who were standing with a large crowd. Much as he’d hate talking with a big group, it would be less painful than a one-on-one conversation with Hazel.

“You could see me alone. Grossinger’s is a big resort. Two little people like us wouldn’t have trouble finding a place to be by ourselves in the next couple of days.”

“I can’t do that, Hazel.”

“Are you with someone?”

He shook his head.

“Is it because I look like the wicked old witch?” Hazel wrapped her arms around herself.

“It’s because it would be wrong.” Meinhardt’s voice sounded harsher than he’d intended. He said more gently, “I know you’re not happy with Joey, but you're still married to him."

"And you're still so moral, Meinhardt. The most upright little man I've ever met." Hazel laughed bitterly. "You're right, of course. It wouldn't change anything. An affair would be just another memory to look back on and regret that things hadn't turned out differently."

Meinhardt had to lift Hazel's spirits, if only to muster the confidence he'd need to get through the weekend himself. "Things may be looking up." He almost patted her hand, but settled for a conspiratorial smile. "I'm making a surprise announcement at tomorrow's brunch. Charles is the only other person who knows, but I'll tell you if you promise to keep it secret."

Hazel crossed her heart. Gratitude flooded her face. "Trust me to keep your secret."

Meinhardt crossed his heart too. "Trust me to keep yours."

Chapter 35

Meinhardt had lost sight of Charles and Jessie by the time he left Hazel, so he circulated around the room. By not lingering with any group, he didn't have to sustain a conversation. He pretended to study the furnishings, which he'd had ten years to memorize, and told people they were in for a treat at mealtimes. On the bulletin board announcing the hotel's events was a sign inviting guests to watch that night's "Really, *really* big Ed Sullivan Show" in the redecorated television lounge. There was no mention of Disney's *Return to Oz*, but Meinhardt thought no one would mind if he changed the channel. Sullivan was on every week; the *Oz* cartoon was unique.

When he could finally slip away undetected, Meinhardt followed two men to the grand ballroom, where the jewelers' trade show was set up. Hurrying past displays of lesser gems, his instincts drew him to the glass cases of precious stones — diamonds, emeralds, sapphires, and rubies. Under a spotlight on a bed of green velvet was a gigantic square-cut ruby ring.

A tall burly guard came from behind the jewelry case and pointedly lowered his head to glare at Meinhardt's left breast pocket, which lacked a name tag. The guard informed him that only members of the association or those with ID numbers to bid on the ring were permitted. He thrust a thick finger toward the exit and Meinhardt, still curious, but intimidated, turned to leave.

"That's my new assistant. He's not a member yet so I couldn't register him. Let him be."

Barely looking up, Meinhardt stared into the face of a short stocky man in a tall fur hat and flowing black caftan. The name tag beneath by his gray side locks read "Itzak Friedman, Diamonds and Rare Gems." The guard scowled, but retreated.

"High scores on all four C's." The Hasidic merchant's finger beat a rhythm on the glass. "Carats, five. Color, pigeon-blood. Clarity, excellent. Cut, very unusual. You know stones?"

Meinhardt admitted ignorance. He knew only that the ring was beautiful, and valuable.

The jeweler nodded. It was rare to find a gem like that cut for a man. Also, the ruby was surrounded by 18 diamonds. In Hebrew, *chai* or 18, stood for life and good luck.

"So, Mr. Friedman, you hope high bids will bring new life to Cuba's Jewish refugees?"

"Call me Izzy. To hell with the Cuban Jews. I'm a businessman. I plan to bid low, sell high, and make a profit. You?"

Meinhardt wondered how much to divulge. Aware now that the ring was worth even more than he thought, he wasn't sure if people who bought movie mementos could afford something so expensive. With Izzy's access to the wealthy jewelry market, Meinhardt considered a partnership, something he usually avoided. He began to explain his plan, assuming a Hasid would know nothing of the movie and the celebrity value it added to the ring.

Izzy interrupted. "My people know all about *The Wizard of Oz*. The Scarecrow's a Jew."

Meinhardt had heard many theories about the movie, but this was a new one.

"What does the Scarecrow *want*?" Izzy asked rhetorically. "A brain, learning. What does he *do*? Like he tells Dorothy, an awful lot of talking. What could be more Jewish?"

"I concede the point." Meinhardt laughed and asked Izzy for his business card.

The Hasid pulled out the sides of his caftan to show there were no pockets. "So we can't masturbate from inside."

Meinhardt turned nearly as red as the ruby.

Izzy guffawed. "I'm in the Manhattan yellow pages under Jew--elers. All one word."

Before they parted, Meinhardt asked why Izzy had intervened for him with the guard.

"I sensed a kindred spirit, another shrewd businessman." His voice turned quiet. "Also, I resented the guard's Germanic behavior."

"I'm German" said Meinhardt.

"Yes, but one persecuted like our kind, not one of them."

The men shook hands. "May the best bidder win," Izzy said. "And try Mrs. Grossinger's kosher egg rolls. They're like nothing my *bubbe*, may she rest in peace, ever made!"

Chapter 36

Meinhardt signed up for the silent auction, returned to the ballroom, and flashed his registration card under the sullen guard's nose. After writing his ID number on the clipboard, he entered an anonymous bid. Each offer had to be at least $500 higher than the previous one. The last bid, possibly Izzy's, was nearly $8,000. Bidding ended at noon Monday, the next day. Mr. Glaubart, the association president, would announce the winner at two o'clock, after the midday banquet.

It was dinnertime. The big dining hall hummed with the midgets' high pitched voices. Meinhardt would have preferred eating alone in a corner, but it was important to socialize with his fellow Munchkins before proposing the auction to them tomorrow.

Charles squeezed over to make room at a table that included the Polinsky's. Joey's alcohol-swollen face was like a child's grotesque red balloon. Beside him, Hazel looked even more pale and gaunt. She and Meinhardt glanced at each other before unfurling their napkins.

With mayoral solemnity, Charles recited the choices on the two-sided menu. "We never ate like this on the set. It was stale Danish and lukewarm coffee for breakfast, hot dogs and coke for lunch. They didn't even give us dinner when shooting ran late. We fended for ourselves."

"Heavy on the liquids, as I recall," said Jerry Maren.

"Didn't you and Harry dip your suckers in vodka before shooting the Lollipop Guild scene?"

"No." Jerry paused. "In beer." Everyone laughed. "American beer. Ach! Terrible!"

Jessie spoke. "Now caterers satisfy every whim, trimming and quartering sandwiches. In our day, even big stars didn't get such finicky treatment, let alone little ones like us."

"We were little but we were never stars," said Mickey Carroll, who'd played the fiddler, the town crier, and a soldier. He was dressed in a Big People Clothes for Little People suit from an early catalog. It may have fit when he bought it, but had gotten too big for his shrunken frame in the decade since. He buttered a second roll and slipped a third one into his frayed pocket.

"Charles was a star." Jessie chucked her husband under the chin, eliciting a modest smile.

"So was Meinhardt." Hazel spoke quietly, addressing her plate. Joey snorted.

"The director treated us like we were interchangeable."

"We got even." Jerry spoke with pride. "Like when we switched the parts of our costumes. They had to hire an assistant to keep track from one day's shoot to the next."

"And they still missed a few. In one scene I'm wearing plaid pants and a yellow coat, then after the camera pans away and returns, I'm in striped pants and a red brocade vest."

Listening to the animated reminiscing, Meinhardt was optimistic the Munchkins would be enthusiastic about the auction. He hoped they'd be willing to part with their costumes. Mickey Carroll deserved a new suit. Meinhardt didn't care if he bought it from his catalog or elsewhere.

Despite the promising chatter, Meinhardt felt the strain of being with so many people. By the time he'd finished the juice, soup, and appetizers, he didn't know how he'd make it through the next five courses, let alone the rest of the weekend. He almost regretted Jennie's marathon meals. Charles leaned over and whispered, "Cheer up. Think of the money." It was good advice. Meinhardt swore he'd refuse to leave before eating a slice of Grossinger's Rum Raisin Pie.

Thankfully, Jennie arrived as his table mates began debating the long column of entrees and side dishes. Their appetites had always outsized their bodies. Tommy Cottonaro used to joke that calling them Munchkins was a misnomer. He'd dubbed

195

them "Glutkins."

"My friend Meinhardt's friends are enjoying themselves?" Jennie stood behind him and Meinhardt felt her warm smile encompass everyone. He hoped the others wouldn't resent his special connection with her. He wanted them to appreciate how kind and capable she was.

"I never saw the Alps before I fled Germany." Little Billy's speech was slurred and his eyelids drooped. He'd lost his drinking contest with Joey. "Lucky I made it to the Jewish Alps."

"And you are getting enough to eat in our American mountains?" Jennie didn't flinch when Billy belched loudly in response. She graciously told him she was glad he was satisfied.

After an awkward silence, the tension eased when Charles, resuming his role of mayor, thanked Jennie for the amenities in their rooms. "We notice little things others take for granted."

"No one is as kind and generous to her customers as Jennie." Meinhardt took her hand and felt fingers as calloused by work as his Oma's, yet still capable of giving soft and soothing comfort. He led the table in a round of applause to cover up his choking voice.

Jennie waved off the praise. "My mother Malke, may she rest in peace, told me a life without sharing was barren." She promised to personally supervise the food for their reunion brunch tomorrow. Then she squeezed Meinhardt's hand and excused herself to visit with the other guests. Before she was out of earshot, the Munchkins resumed debating the dinner choices.

"Roast Prime Rib of Beef Au Jus or Ragout of Veal with Glazed Pineapple?"

"Boiled Flanken with Parsley Potatoes and a side of stuffed Derma sounds good."

"How about Poached Fish with Roe? Or Baked Chicken with Savory Noodle Kugel?"

"What do you recommend?" they asked Meinhardt. "You've eaten here for a decade."

"Everything's delicious," he answered. Then, claiming fatigue after a long day of travel, he skipped the main course in favor of a hasty dessert and bid everyone good night. "Save room for tomorrow," he said on the way out. "You never know what surprises a new day will bring."

Chapter 37

Meinhardt wasn't tired, just weary of the Munchkins. His body was on California time and wide awake. He headed for the television lounge, where guests leaned forward in plump armchairs to watch Ed Sullivan. He didn't have the courage to suggest switching to the *Return to Oz* cartoon, but he wasn't that disappointed. Sullivan's awkwardness in the clubby celebrity world mirrored Meinhardt's, while the offbeat variety acts reminded him of better days on Van Singer's circuit.

Tonight's big attraction wasn't Chinese plate twirlers or dancing horses, however. To an audience of screaming and fainting teenage girls, Sullivan introduced the "fine youngsters" from Liverpool known as The Beatles. Meinhardt understood why the reporters from *Variety* hadn't shown up at Grossinger's. They were in New York City covering John, Paul, George, and Ringo.

He'd heard them on the radio. The tunes were catchy, even if the sentimental lyrics cloyed. They needed to grow up and experience pain. Still, they'd be a hit. Their manager knew what he was doing. Lads in Britain and America would copy the haircuts, free walking advertisements.

With half the U.S. watching, CBS ramped up suspense before the last song by replaying a clip of the Beatles' arrival. Frenzied fans inundated the floodlit tarmac. Meinhardt was drawn to Ringo

Starr, the drummer. He stood four inches shorter than the others, who were six feet tall in their Cuban heels. Ringo didn't build himself up with shoe lifts. Meinhardt wondered if that signaled self-acceptance, or was another gimmick exploited by the group's savvy manager.

Ringo was also the funniest during the press interview. Perhaps his humor had been a defense against childhood bullies. Wit had occasionally saved Meinhardt too, until it became a liability; the Nazis thought it disrespectful. Only Rodge was impervious to slights. He claimed "a hundred pinpricks heal invisibly, only a stab leaves a scar." Meinhardt disagreed. A lifetime of small wounds could leave a mark deeper and more permanent than a single big assault.

He didn't know Ringo's stance on bullying, but liked his impudence. When a reporter asked what he thought of Beethoven, Ringo quipped he liked him, "especially the poems." The levity was momentarily punctured when the cameras panned to a sign reading "John F. Kennedy Airport," a reminder that Lee Harvey Oswald had assassinated the President a mere two months ago, and in turn been shot two days later by Jack Ruby. For a moment, Meinhardt had an irrational fear that his pursuit of the ruby ring would end in another loss. Then the Beatles came back on the air and closed with "I Want to Hold Your Hand." His confidence rebounded.

Buoyed and still not sleepy, Meinhardt went to watch Rodney Dangerfield's act at Grossinger's Playhouse. He couldn't summon the same appreciation for laughter that he had with the Beatles. When the audience guffawed at the comedian's famous line, "I don't get no respect," Meinhardt swore Dangerfield looked to him for confirmation. He didn't want to be seen as a fellow loser. Self-conscious, he looked to see if he was the only one sitting stone-faced, and was surprised to spot Izzy and his black-hatted colleagues in the audience. Seeing Meinhardt, the Hasid wiggled his ring finger and turned up his palms. Who would win the bidding? He grinned, as if to say they were well-matched adversaries for whom the contest was professional, not personal. The gesture restored Meinhardt's good mood. Once again, he dismissed the idea of partnering with Izzy. Why trust another shrewd businessman? He'd find a buyer on his own.

It was midnight and Meinhardt despaired of growing tired, but rest was essential before tomorrow's reunion. He couldn't fall sleep without one more look at the ring. The ballroom was empty, save for a new guard who yawned before checking his credentials. Three more bids had been entered since dinner. Meinhardt topped the last one by $500, then upped it another $1,000.

Chapter 38

Moonlight, reflecting off the snow and shining through the window, provided enough light for Meinhardt to find his way around the room. The Boers brothers were snoring and George was probably still in the bar. Glad he wouldn't have to make conversation, Meinhardt eased into bed.

Two hours later, he gave up on sleep and went downstairs to the library of books donated by hotel guests who'd finished them. He hoped someone had left behind *The Spy Who Came in From the Cold*. In the silent lobby was a man coming in from the cold. He wore a navy greatcoat with a muffler around his jaw, like a caricature of a toothache. Meinhardt counted three rings on each hand, but they were too flashy for him to be a late-arriving jeweler. It was Ringo Starr.

He followed him to the ballroom. The guard, awake now, showed no sign of recognition when he checked the Beatle's numbered registration card and gave him permission to enter a bid. Ringo stared at the ruby ring, scribbled on a scrap of paper, then scratched his ear. The muffler, knocked askew, released a telltale lock of hair, which he shoved back into place. He looked up at the guard. "Pounds to dollars," he sighed, not hiding his accent. "I'm not much good at math."

Meinhardt stepped forward. "Perhaps I can help. Do you know the exchange rate?" He did the conversion in his head and Ringo wrote his bid on the clipboard. Neither seemed to find it odd that a German midget was conversing with a disguised Englishman at this eerie hour.

Ringo looked glum. "Two more raises and the price will top me limit."

Meinhardt averted his eyes. He was burning to know what Ringo had written, but he was scrupulous about respecting people's privacy and the auction's anonymity.

"Bloody beautiful, ain't it?" Ringo stared at the ring like a schoolboy hopelessly in love.

"Bloody valuable too." He led Ringo from the spot-lit ballroom to the dim lounge, where, in the corner, a few Munchkins barely held up their heads while footstools propped up their feet.

"The ring sings to me." Ringo closed his eyes, as if listening.

"The sound of money?"

Ringo shrugged. "I'm no better at money than math. Too sickly growing up to learn me numbers. Spent more time in hospital than school." While in the sanitarium, he'd gotten good at ring toss and began wearing rings as a reminder he had a talent for something. "My folks could only afford cheap ones, but they were a magic protection against being called short and stupid."

"You aren't stupid. I heard you on Ed Sullivan tonight. You're quite clever." Meinhardt expected a denial of his identity, but Ringo grinned and extended his hand.

"You're not even that short, Mr. Starr, at least from where I stand."

Ringo's smile widened, before he stopped himself.

"It's okay. I joke at my own expense before others can make fun of me. Their reaction is a barometer of how comfortable they are."

Ringo let a laugh escape. "I joke about me height too. I trust folks won't use it against me."

Meinhardt didn't bother to disagree. Ringo would learn soon enough about the world's capacity for cruelty. "What about the drums?" he asked. "Another ring of magic?"

"Nope. Reality." Ringo had always loved music, but with lungs too weak to play a horn and legs too spindly to stand with a guitar, he'd taken up drums. Sitting in the back, his size was hidden. "Drumming puts me in control. It holds the rest of the music together."

"I sang on street corners. There weren't any drums, so dancing provided the beat that held everything together." He remembered the agility with which Charles moved on Broadway, and Hazel's graceful pirouettes on the movie set. "Unfortunately, I was never a good dancer."

"I knew right off I was a good drummer. I could feel the beats without counting them." Ringo was scolded for being ambidextrous as a child, but it gave him a unique drumming style. The song told him which hand to lead with. It didn't matter that he'd never studied music. Drumming freed him from his body. Like the rings, it drew attention to his hands, not his height.

"You're taking a big risk for this ruby ring," Meinhardt said. "What makes it so special?"

"For one, it's me birth stone. I'll be 24 in July. For another, it's the first time in me life I'm close to affording something so grand." Brian Epstein, the Beatles' manager, had warned him against getting ahead of himself. Stardom could be fleeting and it could go to Ringo's head. Still, Brian had okayed his sneaking off and promised to cover for him until the next day, when Ringo was due in Washington to rehearse for the group's big concert at the Coliseum.

"Stardom can be even shorter than you think." Meinhardt pointed to himself.

Ringo looked at him quizzically and hoisted himself onto a bar stool. Meinhardt did the same. Ringo nodded his approval. "I watched American westerns on the telly when I had to stay home. You mounted that stool as if it were a horse."

"A horse of a different color." The reunion had made Meinhardt nostalgic.

"That's it! The joke about stardom? You were a Munchkin!" Ringo put two and two together. He'd seen the reunion sign in the lobby. "I watched reruns of *The Wizard of Oz* too."

Meinhardt was surprised but pleased to discover another unlikely *Oz* fan at Grossinger's.

"That means we have two things in common." Ringo did a drum roll on the bar. "We're both short." He beat a second, more elaborate roll. "And we're both in show business."

"You could add we're both horses of a different color." Meinhardt did a brief rat-a-tat.

"All I ever wanted was to be part of the group, but I'm a natural loner. Have you seen our movie, *A Hard Day's Night*? Sad to say, that's the real me."

"Being a loner suits me," said Meinhardt. "No chance for others to reject you. Or worse."

"No chance for acceptance, either," said Ringo. "I'll continue to take my chances."

"Be careful about trusting others, especially when you're famous."

Ringo studied his hands. "I trust Brian Epstein. I think I can trust you."

"Epstein. He's Jewish?"

"Homosexual too. A double loser some say, but I believe he'll make the four us winners."

Meinhardt shuddered. Mr. Epstein wouldn't have lasted long under Hitler. "Why do you trust him?"

"Brian inherited his talent for judging people from Queenie."

"He's related to the Queen?"

Ringo laughed. "Queenie is Brian's mum. Her name is Malke, Hebrew for queen."

Malke, the same as Jennie's mother, who was also a good judge of people. According to Jennie, Malke had an instinct about who to hire. During the Depression, she knew who could be trusted not to steal food and linens. Those who suffered the most were the most trustworthy.

All the talk of trust exhausted Meinhardt. He was ready for sleep, but dreaded going back to his crowded room. On a whim, he asked if Ringo trusted him enough to let him stay with him.

"You're not a friend of Dorothy, are you?"

Meinhardt said none of the Munchkins liked Judy Garland.

"I mean, you're not like Brian? 'A friend of Dorothy' is code for being homosexual."

Meinhardt was taken aback. As a midget, he'd been suspected of being retarded, a thief, and many other things, but he'd never had his sexuality questioned. "Of course not!"

"Not that I wouldn't trust you if you were," Ringo said. "Nothing wrong being that way."

In all his efforts to hire minorities and the handicapped, Meinhardt had never considered homosexuals. He was ashamed not knowing if any were on his staff. Recovering his composure, he explained to Ringo the problem with booking rooms and said he'd rather sleep on Ringo's floor than share a bed with three old cast mates. "Even small people need their space."

Ringo smiled. "Makes me feel like a star providing sleeping quarters to my entourage."

They stopped in the grand ballroom one last time before going upstairs. Despite the early morning hour, Izzy was coming out. Meinhardt wondered if the blue and white stripes peeking below his caftan's wide hem were a prayer shawl or pajamas. Did the shawls come in different lengths? Could there be an untapped market for his line of clothes among short Orthodox Jews?

Ringo was impressed. "He must really care about helping Jewish Cuban refugees. If I get rich, I'm going to give lots of money to charity."

"You want to meet a real philanthropist, talk to Jennie Grossinger, not some jewelry salesman. I'm a salesman too, and if I were to bid on a ring like that, I'd do it purely for profit." There was no point in Meinhardt tipping his hand that he actually was one of the bidders.

"I think you're softer than you let on." Ringo wrote down his top bid and shook his head. "It'll never hold up until noon tomorrow."

"Even if you lose, who knows what's over the rainbow."

Meinhardt was rewarded by a drowsy smile from Ringo, who removed his muffler and rubbed his eyes like a sleepy child. A bellhop, arriving for the 4:00 AM shift, stopped and stared. Meinhardt urged Ringo toward the elevator. "You'll need a better disguise tomorrow, and I can't help on that score. You may be the shortest Beatle, but you're a giraffe compared to me."

Chapter 39

As daylight crept under the heavy brocade curtains,

Meinhardt stretched and was surprised when his toes touched the end of the bed. Then he remembered he was lying on a Victorian settee. Warning that fame and fortune were fickle, Brian had nevertheless let Ringo indulge in a suite with a sitting room. At his age, Meinhardt was grateful he hadn't had to sleep on the floor.

Leaving Ringo to dream, he went back to his own room to shower and change. The Boers brothers were already at the reunion. George, buttoning his coat, winked and said, "Missed you last night. I heard Joey passed out in the lounge. Were you keeping Hazel company?"

Meinhardt bundled up for the quarter-mile walk to the ski lodge. If not for the jewelers, they'd be meeting in the ballroom. He appraised his coat. The company's winter outerwear line sold well. To make them warm but not too heavy for a small person's frame, he'd lined them with the lightweight cashmeres and silks his Oma used as protection against Berlin's icy winters. His customers gladly paid the modest premium. Hats he discounted, since midgets didn't need special sizes. He'd purchased his own blue wool hat at an airport ski store, along with the nonprescription sunglasses he now used to hide his tired eyes. Thank goodness his eyesight was still keen. His Oma, although she never complained, had been heartsick when her vision no longer allowed her to sew with the precision of her youth.

As promised, Jennie had laid out a lavish brunch in the wood-paneled room. A big stone fireplace roared. The Munchkins were giddy from eating cheese Danish and remembering their past glory. Instead of being competitive about their height, they compared how many inches they lost since turning forty. Old rivalries were forgotten in lieu of gossip, and Judy Garland's alcohol and marriage woes circulated with glee, particularly the low ratings for her last televised special.

205

Charles struck an upbeat note. "*The Wizard of Oz* gets good TV ratings."

"They didn't show it this year. I guess on account of the Kennedy assassination."

"Not that we get broadcast royalties. Damn Van Singer." George Ministeri stood up. The Munchkins applauded. "It's great to see everyone, but face it, we ain't doing so great."

"Meinhardt's doing well." Hazel's voice was soft but clear. Joey, leaning against her in a semi-drunken stupor, drew away. She said more loudly. "Maybe he can give us some advice."

Joey snorted but the others looked at Meinhardt expectantly. He walked in front of the blazing fire. The flames dancing behind him riveted their attention as he began his prepared speech. He thanked them for buying his clothes and helping to make his company a success. "Most of you haven't had the same good fortune. Neither did I at first. When we left *Oz* murmuring 'There's no place like home,' no warm welcome awaited us, only more storms."

"The circus is dead. People don't come to the big top when they can stay home and see acrobats on Ed Sullivan." Harry Doll sounded near tears. His three siblings rose to console him.

Theo Boers struggled to stand on child-size crutches, supported by his brother, still weak from his last heart attack. "I got this bone disease that's getting worse, while Harry here is fresh out of the hospital. I don't know how we're gonna pay our doctor bills."

One at a time, the Munchkins stood to recite their stories. Drawing on his thirty years of sales experience, Meinhardt waited for just the right moment to announce his plan. They had to be feeling needy and ready for help, but not so disheartened that they were incapable of hope.

"After the tragedy our country has just had,

people long for an earlier and simpler time. I predict a growing wave of nostalgia for *Oz*, especially the sweet innocence of the Munchkins."

"Us? I thought we were notorious pimps and whores!" Raucous laughter broke the mood.

Even Meinhardt smiled. "The press pushed that image to sell papers, but to the public, we're the sweet little girls of the Lullaby League and mischievous tykes of the Lollipop Guild."

"What good is either reputation when MGM owns all the rights and gets all the profits?"

Meinhardt raised a finger to quiet them. "We own our costumes and props. Suppose we held a Munchkin memorabilia auction and kept the proceeds?" Seventy-eight faces stared at him.

Joey used Hazel's shoulder to push himself to a standing position. "I ain't gonna sell my only piece of happiness to some sorry-ass crybaby who wishes we were still living in Camelot."

"The Count's right. Being in that movie was the best thing that ever happened to me."

There were murmurs of agreement. Meinhardt was afraid he'd miscalculated.

Hazel stood. "The happiness I got looking at my costume lasted a couple of years. Now, when I see it at the back of the closet, it reminds me of squandered hope. I'm all for Meinhardt's idea." She sat again and pulled Joey down after her.

Meinhardt looked at her with gratitude. He forced himself to stand there calmly. It was better to let support build gradually from the crowd rather than try to push the advantage himself.

Charles stood on his chair. "As the mayor of Munchkinland," he began, and smiled at the appreciative laughter. "I know it's hard, but if we don't free ourselves of the past, we won't have any future. Isn't it better to invest in ourselves and, if we have them, our children?" He rested his hand on Jessie's shoulder. Her eyes stayed on her plate, but she lifted her hand to cover his.

"Would we invite any big stars or crew members who are down on their luck to join us?"

"No!" There was a chorus of boos. "Munchkins only." A chorus of cheers.

"Would we each get the profit from our own things, or pool the money and split it?"

Charles glanced at Meinhardt, who nodded for him to continue speaking. "Twenty-five years ago, we were one community. It was an imaginary one, but I say we form a real one now. I'm for sharing it equally." He looked at the frail Boers brothers. Everyone's eyes followed his.

Joey struggled to his feet again. Sounding less certain, he nevertheless whined, "I'm not sure I trust Mr. Raabe. How do we know you're not plotting to rip us off for your own benefit?"

Knowing Joey's pugnaciousness had sealed the deal in his own favor, Meinhardt pushed his edge. "I'll donate the coroner's cloak and hat." He mimed unfurling a scroll. "Also, the parchment declaring the witch 'most sincerely dead.'" Joey's bravado deflated.

"I've got the mayor's coat, hat, and vest." Charles squeezed Jessie's hand. "I'll add them to the pool, but I can't afford to donate them. We've got a daughter to put through college."

The Lullaby League still had their headdresses and tutus, while their counterparts in the Lollipop Guild were willing to auction their patched shorts, striped tights, and curly-toed shoes. Mickey Carroll offered a treasure trove of costumes and props from the three roles he played. "How about your barrister's wig?" he asked Little Billy, who was now wide awake.

Billy ran his hand over his bald head. "You want me to give it up just when I need it?" He waited until the laughter subsided, then said, "Sure!" Meinhardt saw hope in his eyes.

The members of the Doll family announced that in addition to their costumes, they'd "borrowed" a good witch's wand and a wicked witch's broomstick. The Boers brothers had each walked away from the set with a flying money suit. "Don't ask!" they joked, before anyone had.

All told, there were over 400 mementos. Meinhardt said nothing about the ruby ring, first because he didn't know if he'd win the auction, and second because he planned to keep the profit if he did. Even without the ring, there were enough items for the auction to give a big boost to the midgets. He stood at the door to see them out, uneasily accepting hugs and handshakes.

Hazel held back, the last to leave. "Don't worry about Joey. He'll come around."

"It's his choice," answered Meinhardt. "The sale will be a success with or without him."

"I made a choice twenty-five years ago." Hazel bit her lip. "It wasn't a successful one."

"It was my choice that forced you to make yours. I'm sorry."

"You made the right choice for you. I'm responsible for my own decisions." Hazel's face brightened. "Do you think we'll make enough money for me to open a dance school? Hawthorne, Oklahoma has a lot of little would-be Lullaby League ladies."

"I guarantee it. A studio with an oak barre so you can teach them do an arabesque."

Fifteen minutes before the bidding closed Meinhardt was back in the ballroom. The last offer was $1,000 above his self-imposed limit. Spurred by the Munchkin's enthusiasm, he raised the bid by $2,000. He stared down the whispering jewelers on his way out, where he met Izzy coming in. Meinhardt wondered whether the Hasid would judge his final bid unwise or top it. He pictured the frenzied crowds greeting the Beatles. Sometimes abandoning self-control had its rewards.

Chapter 40

Ringo was wearing a terrycloth guest robe covered with a paisley chair scarf when Meinhardt checked in on him. His hair had been slicked back with the hotel's complimentary conditioner.

"You look like an escapee from a home for the aged and infirm."

"I wanted to sneak downstairs for a last look at the ring. I bet the Jewish guy won." Ringo stared sadly at the one empty finger on each hand. "At least the money will go to a good cause."

"If that's your idea of a disguise, better leave costumes and hairstyles to your manager."

"I'm hungry."

The young waiters would recognize Ringo in the dining room, even if the jewelers didn't. Meinhardt offered to bring him lunch so Ringo could eat in the sitting room. "Jennie has a policy she calls 'Take it back for a snack.' She'll think I'm getting it for myself for later."

Ringo agreed, but warned that due to his many childhood illnesses, he could only eat bland food. Meinhardt told him not to worry. All kosher food was bland.

The jewelers were having a banquet luncheon before the winner of the silent auction was announced. Jennie left the table with Izzy and his friends when Meinhardt came in. She wrung her hands. "There wasn't enough food at the reunion?"

He patted his stomach and Jennie's knuckles. "You left us groaning with pleasure. And mouths too stuffed to open for another bite."

"My mother Malke, may she rest in peace, said 'Flies can't get into a closed mouth.'"

Meinhardt explained he was getting food for

later, and asked a waiter to prepare a tray of cold borscht, blintzes with sour cream, egg rolls, and pound cake. On his way out, Jennie pointed to the egg rolls. "Like I promised you, no?" She put another dollop of sour cream on the blintzes.

Back upstairs, Ringo devoured the egg rolls and wondered if Grossinger's delivered by air to the U.K. "Maybe someday, I'll be rich enough to fly them in. Brian would love them."

"I wouldn't mind a delivery in Los Angeles now and then, and I'm rich enough to pay for them now." Meinhardt said it was also a terrific business idea and he'd suggest it to Jennie. But the time had come to go to the ballroom and find out the ring's fate.

Ringo insisted on going along. He wasn't worried he'd be recognized. All eyes would be on the winner. At Meinhardt's urging, however, he put on the greatcoat. The conditioner was rinsed out, but his hair had reverted to its telltale mop. Meinhardt handed Ringo his own knit cap. "Here's something of mine that will fit you, as long as your head doesn't swell. Better wear my sunglasses too."

The ballroom was festooned with dark red ribbons. All eyes were on the officials conferring at the display case. Meinhardt was relieved. He found a place for himself and Ringo at the back.

The jewelers' association president mounted a small platform and described the ring's rarity and provenance. A representative of the Cuban Jewish refugees thanked everyone for their generosity and said the final bid was twice as high as they'd hoped. Neither mentioned why Mr. Luft wanted to get rid of the ring, or why he was donating only half the profits to the Cubans.

Ringo did a silent drum roll on Meinhardt's shoulders. The president took the clipboard from the security guard who'd thrown him out and announced, "The winner of the man's five-carat, 18-diamond, square-cut, ruby ring, for the grand sum of $20,000, is bidder G-187."

Ringo and the Hasidic jewelers looked toward Izzy. The rest eyed one another.

Meinhardt walked forward and hoisted himself onto the platform. "I deal in clothing, not jewelry, but I recognize beauty when I see it. Also a worthy cause. I too was forced to leave my homeland." There was polite applause; a few flashbulbs popped. Meinhardt handed over a check and the jewelers parted to make way for him as he returned to the back of the room.

Ringo had taken off the sunglasses. He looked pained, then puzzled. Last he smiled. "You're not just a businessman after all. You're a philanthropist too, just like Jennie Grossinger."

"What I said up there? I have nothing in common with those refugees. This is strictly a profit-making venture."

Ringo's hands dangled at his sides as though weighed down by their rings. "Why get rich and famous if you can't use your money to help others? I thought you were different underneath the bluster. You were right. I should learn to be more careful before trusting people."

"I run a business that helps midgets. I don't need another cause. Someday you'll learn that good deeds don't change the world. In the end, only money counts."

Ringo ripped off Meinhardt's hat and thrust it at him.

Meinhardt hesitated. Accepting it would sever their tie and he'd grown fond of the lad. He could offer to sell him the ring. In installments. With interest. They'd stay in touch while Ringo paid it off. When he was ready to collect it, they'd have a reunion at Grossinger's. If the band's fame fizzled before then, Meinhardt would refund the money.

Minus the interest.

Ringo looked at him expectantly, but when Meinhardt didn't say anything or take the hat, he threw it on the floor and stalked out. Meinhardt was about to run after him until he felt the solid weight of the gem in his palm. The ring was too valuable to let it go and the *Oz* auction was the perfect venue to sell it. It would mean a big profit for a little person. Later, he could decide whether to donate some to the Munchkins' pool or give Hazel extra to open her dance school.

Meinhardt faced the cold on the first leg of his journey home to the warmth of LA. There was lots of work ahead — collecting and cataloguing the memorabilia, arranging publicity, and smooth-talking the Culver Hotel into hosting the auction. Returning to the Culver would be a homecoming of sorts. Not that he believed there was no place like home, or intended to click his heels like Dorothy Gale or a Nazi functionary. But if he hoped to move forward with his life, going back to the home of his first success in America was not a bad place to start.

PART EIGHT

Now Which Way Do We Go?

Los Angeles, 1970

Chapter 41

Meinhardt parked his custom-fitted Gremlin between two limousines and walked to the Cinema Center Films studio lot. The audition for *Little Big Man* was in an hour, enough time for him to get inside the mind of his character. In the scene synopsis, tiny Jack Crabb, who the Cheyenne name Little Big Man for bravery, teams up with Merriweather, a snake-oil salesman. Out of the crowd they pick a midget, Meinhardt's hoped-for part, to be their confederate, promising their medicinal elixir will make him grow. When the illusion fails, angry customers try to tar and feather the conniving duo. The fast-thinking midget claims to smell smoke and tells the crowd to run for their lives, allowing the pair to run the other way. Crabb nicknames him Little Little Man for saving their lives and persuades a reluctant Merriweather to make him part of the act. The script was serviceable, but Meinhardt thought it would play better if the snake-oil salesman were not so evil. He should be like Professor Marvel in *Oz*, revealing a kind heart beneath the bluster.

Director Arthur Penn called for the first take. Dustin Hoffman, playing Crabb, and Martin Balsam, cast as Merriweather, took their places. Meinhardt tried not to be awed by them. He acted his part as written, until the snake-oil salesman told him to get lost. Then, instead of letting Crabb speak for him, he himself pleaded for a job, hoping the two stars would go along with the improvisation. Looking skeptical, but intrigued, they did. In the end, Meinhardt's character convinces them that the fat farmer's wives who came to see the show would prefer an elixir that made people smaller. Little Little Man, presumably once full size, would be proof the potion worked.

Penn yelled "Cut" and ordered the crew to

set up for a second take. Martin Balsam silently applauded Meinhardt. Dustin Hoffman walked to a table full of flowers and began to string leis. Meinhardt followed and surreptitiously measured himself against the actor, guessing him to be under five and a half feet. He wondered how he'd achieved stardom in unlikely, even risky roles, including unappealing characters like Ratso Rizzo. Hoffman was the rare man who seemed comfortable being short. Could Meinhardt absorb that same ease playing alongside him?

"Are the leis for the next scene?" Meinhardt smiled. "Do you need any short Hawaiians?"

"No. Making leis was one of my jobs as a struggling actor. I still do it to relax." Hoffman admired his handiwork. "Some people discover what they're good at and convince themselves it's what they want to do. Some know what they want to do and convince others they're good at it. I can't remember whether my skill or desire came first, but I had both." He draped the finished lei around Meinhardt's neck. "May the Great Spirit keep you from being tarred and feathered."

"Do you think Merriweather's character gets what he has coming?" Meinhardt asked. "Or does he deserve more compassion than the part calls for?"

"I tend toward sympathy myself, but mobs and movie studios don't necessarily agree."

"What about Penn?"

Hoffman looked at the director, who was busy making notes. "Arthur's as inscrutable as a cigar-store Indian."

"Take two," shouted Penn. "This time let's do it the way the script is written."

The rest of the audition hadn't gone badly, but Meinhardt couldn't say it had gone well. Acting hadn't been in his dreams for three decades. He no longer needed the money. Business was thriving in an era whose fashions --- miniskirts, platform shoes

216

for both men and women --- were disastrous for midgets. His classic styles made them look good. He should have been satisfied.

Still, thoughts of reviving his acting career arose after the success of the *Oz* auction. The Munchkins made out well, and he'd sold the ring for a fifty percent profit. *Variety* had headlined the sale "Boffo Hit a Boon to Nostalgia Biz" and followed up with an interview and photo spread focused on Meinhardt's achievements, not his scaled-down house. The celebrity had whet his appetite for being in movies again. As before, he wanted an individual role, but his search for a dignified part seemed futile. The only ones available were as demeaning as current fashions.

Meinhardt wanted fame, but not at any price. It had to be earned. Rodge used to say that ideas don't work unless you do, and Meinhardt agreed. He'd had a brush with false fame a few years ago that had almost soured him on getting back into show business. Working with respected artists like Arthur Penn and Dustin Hoffman would be a real achievement, nothing like that earlier experience. Just thinking about it made him ashamed he'd been seduced by glamor.

Chapter 42

Shortly after the memorabilia sale, Meinhardt got a late-night call from New York City, where it was early morning. "Mr. Raabe?" The voice was flat and soft. Loud music in the background blared screaming vocals over thumping drums and screeching metal. "It's Andy Warhol."

According to *Variety*, Warhol bought all the auction items that came multiples, including the trios of Lollipop Guild and Lullaby League outfits. The magazine called him an *Oz* aficionado. He reportedly slept on a futon mounted on a platform of the original yellow bricks.

Meinhardt wanted to believe it was really Warhol calling, but he was skeptical. He asked if there was a problem. A few cast members had second thoughts about giving up their costumes, delaying shipments, but he thought everything had finally been collected and sent to the bidders.

"No problem." Silence. Meinhardt waited. There was murmuring and then another person got on the line. "We are making a movie," said a breathy woman's voice with a heavy German accent. "Andy wants you to come to The Factory to be in it."

Warhol simultaneously fascinated and repulsed Meinhardt. He admired his marketing skill, but was appalled by his weirdness. He didn't want to be another freak in his circle of Superstars. On the other hand, it was as if Warhol had read his mind about wanting to act again.

"Shooting starts next Wednesday night," the woman continued. "We will see you, yah?"

Fear of being in a film full of weirdos wasn't the only reason for Meinhardt's misgivings. It was years since he'd gone back to New York, a place scarred by memories of poverty, Harpo's betrayal, and his breakup with Celia. He was torn between rage at her behavior and guilt that he'd been too harsh. After decades of living in Hollywood, where people changed identities all the time, Celeste Panterdown styling herself as Celia Posy, and using the bedroom as a stepping stone to the runway, no longer seemed so egregious. What if he ran into her? She no longer appeared in fashion magazines. At 40, was she too old to model? Or had the disease disintegrated her bones? Meinhardt was afraid the sight of a disfigured Celia would make him crumble too.

Irritated with his own indecision, Meinhardt called Rodge at the Wheel and Wing for a gentle prod. "What is that awful noise?" he asked when the publican put his friend on the line. It was the same harsh music he'd heard playing in the background at The Factory.

"Heavy metal. The lads like to bang their heads to it."

"Not as melodious and graceful as *Shall We Dance?*"

"Head banging is a type of dancing that doesn't require legs. I've grown rather fond of it." Rodge sounded upbeat, but frail. At 75, he'd defied the doctors who pronounced him nearly dead half a century ago. He was all for Meinhardt reviving his acting career. "Life's too short to wake up with regrets. All you have to lose is feeling bad that you didn't try."

"I was hoping for something more mainstream. A Warhol film could be suicide."

"Death by art. Sounds to me like an admirable way to go."

"Hanging out with freaks could endanger my reputation. It might depress clothing sales."

Rodge chuckled. "Associating with me hasn't stunted your business or growth. You'd already reached full height when we met."

"And my presence couldn't pull you down any further. Quite a pair we make."

"We're both one-offs." Rodge became serious. "What are you really afraid of?"

"Losing self-respect. Business could double tomorrow and a wonder drug could make me twice as tall, but I'll never have your self-confidence. I care too much about how others see me."

"Don't you think there are days when I wake up having already given up? The older I get, the more I'm tempted to race myself to the grave." Rodge's voice was muffled, as though he'd lowered his chin to look at his stumps. "When I feel that way, I give my butt a proverbial kick, put on a natty outfit, and go on about my business. The down-on-their-luck blokes at the pub count on me to remind them that if they lack the courage to start, they've as good as finished."

"Being cut down made you taller in spirit, Rodge. I don't think I can rise to your height."

"Don't be your own coroner. Repeat after me: 'I am not really, most sincerely, dead.'"

Meinhardt dutifully sang his line before admitting, "I'm also afraid of running into Celia, or at least meeting up with my memories of her. I've stayed clear of New York for a long time."

"Lost love! It turns us into avoiders or seekers." Rodge reminded Meinhardt how losing his fiancée Jayne had motivated him to keep looking. "That's why I still go to the movies. A good love story revives my hope that true romance is just around the corner."

"I don't think Andy Warhol makes that kind of movie."

Meinhardt flew to New York two days early to face his demons and calm his nerves before shooting started. The woman on the phone hadn't said how long filming would last, so he booked an open-ended stay at The Plaza, where he and Celia had first made love. The hotel was still grand.

It was also the same time of year, early fall. He wandered Central Park, remembering how he and Celia, a redhead and a blonde, had made each other garlands with leaves of matching colors. Schoolchildren played in the dwindling golden light of late afternoon. He wondered if Celia still felt like a childless freak, if she'd ever married or adopted. Perhaps she'd been so busy modeling that having a husband and children didn't matter. On the other hand, if her career was over, it might bother her now more than ever. He pushed such thoughts aside. He'd made his own peace with being alone. Rodge was right. Life was too short to wake up with regrets.

220

Demel's was still there, its display case, linen napkins, heavy silverware, and china cups unchanged. Meinhardt fortified himself with *Sachertorte* and *buchtein,* the jam-filled pastry pockets he and Celia had gobbled on their first date. He debated bringing an *Apfelstrudel* to The Factory. He didn't want to seem ingratiating. Besides, Warhol and his Superstars appeared to subsist on coffee, booze, cigarettes, and amphetamines. It was possible, however, that drugs and alcohol gave them a sweet tooth. He bought a tray that was half cake, half *Brezeln.* The German pretzels, soft and chewy in the middle but thin and crisp on the ends, would go well with beer.

When Meinhardt walked into The Factory, there was no table, so he set the baked goods down on a stack of carpet sample books. The tray, covered in foil, blended with the walls and ceilings, which were spray painted silver. The lone exception to this decorating scheme was a red couch where three people half-heartedly pawed one another in a simulation of sex. Meinhardt averted his eyes. Others slept on silver lame chairs or stood in small groups, smoking, snorting, or swallowing whatever it was that kept them awake. A few paced around the room's perimeter. No one seemed to notice Meinhardt's entry except for Warhol, who stood in a corner, arms folded, watching everyone's moves. Meinhardt sensed he didn't want to be approached.

"Guten Abend." A German voice, familiar from the call, wished him good evening and introduced herself as Nico. She was tall and blonde, like Celia, with porcelain skin and chiseled features. "Andy, come meet Scroll," Nico yelled above the toneless, thumping music. She led Meinhardt to the middle of the room where the wooden floor was encrusted with paint. "That's your stage name in the credits, but no one actually calls you that in the film. It's a silent movie."

221

Meinhardt stiffened. He would not work with people who referred to him as troll.

"Not troll, scroll. Like the parchment you read announcing the wicked witch is dead. Andy loved the gesture where you unfurled it. Very theatrical, yet economical. Like Andy."

Warhol glided over, his white hair a stark contrast to his black turtleneck. Most people in the studio wore solid black. A few were wrapped in swirled patterns of phosphorescent colors. "The movie's title is *Door*." Warhol pointed to a foil-covered door, nearly invisible against the wall. Wrinkles in the silver paper around the doorknob made it faintly distinguishable. Warhol looked at his watchless wrist, cried "Gee whiz! We start shooting in an hour," and returned to his observation post across the room.

The brief conversation must have signaled to the others that Meinhardt was worthy of their interest too, because Superstars surrounded him, shoving one another aside to introduce themselves. "Holly Woodlawn." A tall woman with bouffant golden curls and wearing a slinky silver lame dress with a black lace shawl, put a masculine hand on his arm. "I'm an heiress."

"Haroldo, all you'll inherit is the dirt in the Puerto Rican slum where you were born." Meinhardt recognized Ultra Violet, flashing a lavender smile and peering out through oversized purple glasses. When another woman with a long nose proclaimed herself "Viva, video artist," Ultra Violet wilted like a week-old lilac. "Billy Name, film director and decorator." The young man pointed to the silver walls and red couch. "All my idea" he said before pushing Viva behind Holly. The four of them looked at Warhol, children competing for daddy's attention.

"Joe Dallesandro." Warhol fluttered his hand toward a bare-chested, well-muscled man with a handsome face and a wide smile. The others ushered

Joe to the front, where he enfolded Meinhardt in a bear hug. With his nose just below Joe's armpit, Meinhardt stopped breathing until he was released. "Everyone's in love with Joe," Warhol said quietly. Heads nodded, but their eyes were downcast. Their beauty contest was as fierce as the midgets' over height.

The crowd dispersed, except Nico. Meinhardt asked her whether he should practice any movements or facial expressions. "No," she said. "Billy just wants you to stand in front of that door for an hour. The clothes you're wearing will be fine." No lines, actions, or costumes. What kind of movie had Meinhardt gotten into? Nico looked disappointed too. "I tried to talk Billy into letting me do costumes. I was a seamstress in Berlin before I became a model and a singer."

Meinhardt stopped breathing a second time. "My Oma was a seamstress in Berlin. She left during the war and went back to the town where she was born. The city wasn't safe."

Nico nodded. "My father was injured in the war. He fought for Germany, but after he got hurt, the Nazis sent him to a concentration camp for medical experiments. He died there."

They stared at each other in silence. "Andy can be quite Germanic," Nico said. "He's very precise and controlling in his paintings and films, yet he wants everything to look natural."

More people arrived, some not much taller than Meinhardt, others of average height or above. A few wore flamboyant clothes and makeup, but most appeared ordinary and seemed as perplexed as Meinhardt as to why they were there.

Billy Name aimed the spotlight, and told Joe Dallesandro, the tallest in the room, to stand to the right of the doorknob. The camera whirred as Joe occasionally shifted his weight, groomed his hair, or

223

massaged his biceps. After an hour, a man named Fred took his place, followed an hour later by Luna, a dark-haired teenager so stoned that she teetered until Billy barked "Stand up." Otherwise the director remained silent, offering neither encouragement nor guidance. Warhol continued to observe from his corner, motionless except for his darting eyes.

After three hours, Meinhardt had gone through the carpet samples, thumbed a stack of art books, and stared at people nodding off or necking on the couch. He was angry and bored. When Billy summoned the fourth person, he summoned the nerve to ask when his turn would come.

Billy looked at the oversized watch upside down on his right wrist. "In seven or eight hours." Each person would be replaced by one imperceptibly shorter. Halfway, the audience would notice that the current person's head was barely above the doorknob. Succeeding heads would reach and then fall below it. Joe, the first person, was six feet tall. The last would be two and a half, for a running time of 22 hours. Meinhardt would be in the middle, just as viewers got curious about how low the film would go. "You're the star, the movie's turning point."

"Since you don't need me until then, I'll leave now and come back tomorrow morning."

Billy smiled mischievously. "Stay. You never know. I might decide to change the plot."

Meinhardt considered his options. Billy wasn't telling cast members to do something, nor was he telling them not to do something. Suppose Meinhardt moved in a distinctive way to add interest to his performance? Dancing was out. He lacked the grace of his friend Charles. He could mouth a running commentary about the orgy on the couch. The audience would only see his wide-eyed stare and fluttering lips, not the action. It would be his inside joke. At this point he was too exhausted to care, but afraid to fall asleep. As much as he told himself that underneath their poses, the people at The Factory were as human as anyone else, he didn't trust them to act decently. He wondered if that was how normal people saw midgets. It was a sickening thought.

At noon, following a short elderly woman and a boy junior high school age, Billy finally called Meinhardt. He stood in position, having lost the desire to perform. All he wanted was for it to be over. Midway through his hour, Meinhardt inadvertently yawned. No one else had done this.

"Good," Billy said. "Just what we need to mark the movie's climax."

When the next person replaced him, Meinhardt asked Billy if he could finally leave.

"No. You must stay until the end. I have to take still photos of everyone for the credits."

"Why not take the photos now? You don't have to adjust the movie camera for an hour."

"I'm using the door as the backdrop for the stills too. Only it's going to be open."

Meinhardt was fed up. "Stop the camera, open the door, and take the damn photos. Then close the door and resume shooting. With editing, who'll know the difference?"

Billy looked at him aghast. "That wouldn't be authentic. Andy wants 22 continuous hours in the life of a door." He turned to the other side of the room for confirmation. Warhol nodded.

It was late at night when the shooting finished, early morning when the stills were done. Warhol played back the film. Those who appeared early watched in narcissistic fascination. The others asked to be awakened when they were on. Billy gave his watch to Joe and crashed on the couch.

"Will you stay for the premiere?" Nico handed Meinhardt a cup of coffee. He had no idea where it came from, but it was hot, strong, and expertly brewed. He wanted a piece of strudel to go with it, but sometime during the night, the pastry and pretzels had disappeared.

"I can't stay in New York that long. I have to get back to California."

"*Nicht so lange.*" Nico smiled. "There's nothing to edit. The movie is premiering this weekend at The Waverley, in Greenwich Village. Vincent Canby from *The Times* will be there, Andrew Sarris, Pauline Kael, and the Boston, Chicago, and LA papers. *Variety*, too, of course."

The Waverley was near Celia's old apartment, a place Meinhardt didn't want to revisit. Nor did he want to sit through a replay of *Door*. Nothing worthwhile had happened, other than him discovering The Factory manufactured celebrity for its own sake. It wasn't like his factory, which made a useful product, or the bomber factory, where something all too real was produced.

Not that Hollywood was ideal. It could also be shallow and self-obsessed. Some called it Tinseltown, as fake and shiny as The Factory's walls. But studios produced films for an audience that was bigger than its stars and a handful of fake intellectuals. If Meinhardt pursued an acting career in LA, he could balance the fantasy of celluloid against the real work of his business.

"I'm more suited to manufacturing clothes than manufacturing celebrity," he told Nico.

She kissed him lightly on either cheek. "It's good to find your groove, but don't stay in it so long that it becomes a rut."

Chapter 43

Images from The Factory flipped through Meinhardt's mind like an album of overexposed photos as he walked to his car after the audition. *Little Big Man* was a far cry from *Door*. Arthur Penn would say more about the passage of life in two hours than Andy Warhol had in twenty-two.

On the way home, Meinhardt turned into Safeway, pulled the handbrake, and pushed the button to lower his seat. Getting around LA was easier since he'd gotten a car. Grocery shopping could wait another day, but now he craved a bag of Baby Ruth Bars. Denver Sandwich Bars had comforted him on the long train ride from California to Michigan nearly thirty years ago. They'd been discontinued, but his taste for sweets during emotional highs and lows hadn't disappeared.

Milky Way and Three Musketeers were on sale, so Baby Ruth Bars had been moved to the fourth shelf. Looking down the aisle, Meinhardt confirmed there was no one was around to see him. He took the candy off the bottom two shelves, grabbed the third, hoisted himself up, and reached to the fourth. If he poked a bag of Baby Ruths at the right angle, it would land in his cart.

His arm was raised when a voice screeched, "What're you doing?" Meinhardt jostled the bag too hard. It bounced off the cart's rim and onto the floor, where it split open and released a cascade of chocolates. A gangly stock boy shoved them back in the bag. "We could get sued if you fell and got hurt." He handed Meinhardt a new package. "All you had to do was ask."

Meinhardt threw the package on the bottom shelf and walked out of the store.

He drove home, ordinarily a place of solace, where he never had to climb or ask for help. Today, however, he was too rattled by the screen test and the humiliation of being scolded by a boy one-third his age. He longed to hear Rodge jollying him, "Fall on your arse? Be glad your nose isn't broken. Fall on your face? Be glad your arse has only one crack." It was one his few ribald expressions and never failed to jolt Meinhardt out of feeling persecuted and discouraged. You couldn't feel sorry for yourself when you thought about the difficulties a legless man faced.

A phone call to London, where it was the wee hours, would have to wait until tomorrow. One of the lads would have taken the aging Rodge home long before. Meinhardt had never seen how his friend managed to reach things in his rented rooms. They'd tacitly respected each other's privacy. He pictured a hot plate, and crates with food and clothes, neatly organized on the floor.

It was just as well he hadn't bought the Baby Ruth Bars. He needed to stay in shape to act again. Instead, he'd relax in the antique claw-footed bathtub, where someone his size could lean back and stretch his legs with room to spare. While the tub filled, he skimmed through the mail and stopped at a letter with a London postmark. It wasn't in Rodge's precise, old-fashioned handwriting. Feeling more uneasy than when he'd come home, he turned off the taps and read.

Dear Mr. Raabe,

I'm sorry to tell you Rodger Smythe died suddenly last week. We was all with him at the Wheel and Wing. He stopped playing "I Want to Hold Your Hand" on the upright — he loved the early Beatles — and keeled over. Massive heart attack, gone "faster than a pint disappearing down a thirsty man's gullet." No warning, no fuss, just the way Rodge would have wanted it.

Rodge was a first-class bloke what played dad, brother, and friend to us. We was riled up when the Conservatives took the election this June. Not even Fleet Street saw it coming. Our real dads is on the dole and we can't even count on being pennyboys, so we pinched a load of pipes from a plumber and was off to break glass and bash heads until Rodge blocked the door. He told us, "The pursuit of happiness is the chase of a lifetime. If I can keep running after it, so can you!" We was ashamed. Rodge always said the earlier you tripped someone heading down the path to destruction, the easier it was to turn them around. He turned me and my mates around. We ain't giving up. Some of us is even talking about college. A life changer, that was Rodge.

He held you up as an example. Told us how despite being a midget and what them pillock Nazis done in Germany, you became a movie star and ran a big business in America. It meant a lot that you didn't forget him when you was famous. I was with him when you phoned after the Beatles broke up. He reassured you about Ringo, said he'd do fine on his own. Rodge believed, "If you're down, help someone else look up. You'll make yourself feel better." He helped us, but he felt best helping someone he admired, like you. Carried himself taller, no disrespect intended.

The union hall was packed for his funeral service. Everyone from the pub was there, the neighborhood folks, old Great War vets, and Rodge's girlfriends. He liked when we teased that he had more luck with the ladies than the handsomest of us! A mystery woman wept in the back. I wonder if you know who she was? Rodge wasn't religious. He joked he was from "The Church of St. Francis of Sass Easy." But everyone who spoke said Rodge was like a gift from God.

You and Rodge was friends a long time. When his landlady cleaned out his room, she found a folder with photos from your movie and a couple of articles about you. Rodge wrote stuff like "My friend!" and "Bravo!" in the margin. Should I mail you the folder? I'm afraid he didn't leave much else behind. Rodge's keepsakes were his words, not his possessions.

229

My condolences and sincere regards,
Pete Campion

The news was too big for Meinhardt to take in. He focused on details, like the call about Ringo. Rodge had told him that "Drummers set the pace. Ringo will figure out a new beat for his life." Meinhardt had remained unconvinced, but grateful Rodge hadn't turned his concern into a joke.

He couldn't identify the mystery weeping woman, but instinct told him it was Jayne, the fiancée who'd abandoned Rodge when he came home legless after the First World War. After listening to the eulogies, he wondered if she regretted the choice she'd made half a century ago.

Meinhardt folded the letter. Did reading about all the people who loved Rodge flood him with regrets of his own? He didn't worry what others would say about him. His accomplishments spoke for themselves. Instead, he worried whether there would be someone like Pete Campion to tell people he'd died. Who would care enough to want to know?

Chapter 44

A week later the casting director called. Her voice was warm. "Mr. Penn was impressed with your reading of Little Little Man. Making the snake oil salesman sympathetic was an interesting plot twist. He was also touched by the compassion you aroused for people with your affliction."

Meinhardt winced, but held his tongue. He wanted the part. "When do rehearsals start?"

"Mr. Penn hasn't made up his mind. We'll let you know."

"But I do have the part?"

"We'll let you know."

It was a good sign that Meinhardt had been

called directly, instead of through his agent, but he still felt powerless. He thought of phoning Margaret for sympathy about the fickleness of show business, but they hadn't spoken in five years. After patching things up before the auction, he was hurt she hadn't called to congratulate him on its success. Maybe she was angry he hadn't thanked her for the tip about the ruby ring. Or was still upset he'd told Milton long ago her work was unimportant. If so, his own struggle to get back into acting meant justice was being served.

Margaret's own career had revived lately. If Meinhardt called her, she might misconstrue it as his attempt to use her. He <u>would</u> be using her, but as a consoling friend, not to pull strings. He missed her. Rodge had cheered him with self-mockery; Margaret's self-deprecating wit made him laugh at his own foibles. She was a forgiving person. Look how caring her son had turned out. If Meinhardt took a risk, would Margaret extend forgiveness and kindness toward him?

"Maggie. You don't mind that I'm calling you?" He covered the receiver and held his breath.

"Meinhardt! It's good to hear your voice. Are you still living in LA? What's happening in your life?" She sounded even warmer than Meinhardt remembered from their days on the set.

"You're not angry at me?"

"For pronouncing me dead? In a movie? You haven't gone daft since we last talked?"

"Angry I implied your work as an actor was less important than mine as a businessman?"

Margaret was puzzled until he reminded her of their lunch when Milton was getting ready for college. "My son is 33. Do you really think I'd hold onto a grudge that long? At my age, it's hard enough to remember my lines, let alone an offhand remark from fifteen years ago."

"We're both stubborn people, Maggie."

"You more than me."

Meinhardt had to agree.

"Besides, it's easier for victims to forgive and forget than perpetrators. Guilt is harder to let go of than anger."

"I doubt the Germans feel guilt."

"Denial is part of their personality. You should know. But Meinhardt, we're not talking about crimes against humanity. You committed an unintended slight. It was no big deal."

"Then you're not still angry?"

Margaret laughed. "Your every utterance does not determine the course of human events. The world doesn't revolve around you. If it makes you feel better, you are hereby absolved."

Meinhardt exhaled and felt the tension leave his shoulders. He made another confession. "I was angry when you didn't call me after the Munchkins' auction was written up in *Variety*."

"I must have been in Chile." With her career over, she'd gone to help Milton and his wife Nadia. They'd adopted two street orphans in addition to raising their three biological children.

"So you're a grandmother five times over. *Herzlichen Glüückwunsch!*"

Margaret filled him in. Milton wanted a big family after growing up an only child. He and Nadia worked on community development projects outside Santiago. Margaret had extended her stay to teach local women about the importance of nutrition and immunizing their babies, and to open a child care center. Her background as a kindergarten teacher came in handy.

"Conditions were bad there?"

"You can't imagine. There's so little food the children look like they're half their age. It's not just their bones that are small, their brains are stunted. They'll never lead normal lives."

Meinhardt's self-pity now seemed petty. "But you are helping to make it better."

"You do what you can. It's never enough. At times I was ready to give up."

"So you came back?"

"Yes, but not because I was discouraged. My agent called Chile out of the blue. After a decade without working as an actor, I suddenly have my choice of television and movie roles."

"Witches are back in fashion?"

Margaret cackled. "Turmoil over the war is pressuring networks to find villains outside of government. Only brave directors like Robert Altman dare speak against the misuse of power."

Meinhardt described his audition for *Little Big Man*. "Arthur Penn is willing to demonize the government too. He gets away with it because he uses humor and big-name stars."

Margaret wished him well getting the part. "It's funny how my career took off at the time I was least interested in reviving it. Sometimes we get what we want when we don't want it."

"Not me. I've only been successful when I wanted something and went after it."

"Milton and Nadia are like you. Relentless!"

"You raised Milton right. You must be proud of him."

"His intensity can be hard to take. The same seriousness that made him such a worrier as a boy makes him fret about the world today. Sometimes I wish he'd stayed in Chile so I could put a few thousand miles between us at the end of a visit instead of just driving crosstown."

"No wonder you urged him to go away to college. Not to help him grow up, but to give yourself a break."

"You exposed my nefarious scheme!" Margaret let out another wicked laugh. "I do like having them here. I get to see the grandchildren more often. And now that I'm nearing 70, its comforting knowing Milton and Nadia are nearby if I need help."

Meinhardt thought of Pete Campion and the other young men who took care of Rodge in his final years. Charles and Jessie had their children. Who would help him? "Shall we have lunch while we're both mobile and not under strict dietary restrictions?" he asked Margaret.

"Du-Pars still makes great pancakes, pot pies, and donuts. We go there all the time."

Margaret's willingness to have lunch with him there was the final sign that she bore no grudges from that long-ago day he'd slighted her. Nonetheless, Meinhardt hesitated. He wasn't eager to sit through a meal with five demanding grandchildren.

He needn't have worried. His old friend knew him well. "Just the two of us. All you'll have to suffer through is seeing the pictures in my wallet. Besides, it would be unjust to subject you to Milton. If he heard how well your business is doing, he'd hit you up for a large donation."

Meinhardt promised to send an unsolicited contribution. "My atonement for insulting his mother."

Chapter 45

After reminiscing about *Oz* with Margaret and hearing about Milton, Meinhardt wondered what the Becker children were up to. When he and Charles last spoke, Robert was an automotive engineer and money from the auction was putting Bella through college. Meinhardt had sent Hazel a check to open her dance school. He was curious whether Charles had heard from her.

"It's been a while. She was full of plans for the school right after the auction, but when she stopped talking about it a couple of years back, I was afraid to ask.”

“Maybe Joey drank up the money.”

“Poor Hazel.” Charles sighed. “She’s a story with a sad ending.”

Meinhardt wondered if he should have done more. Sending the check was like buying her off. Margaret was right. Guilt was harder to get rid of than anger. “Tell me more about Bella.”

Charles brightened. “She’s thriving. Too busy to make the one-hour bus ride from Ann Arbor to Detroit more than once a month. You know how social she is.”

“Like her parents.” Meinhardt was grateful Charles and Jessie had continued to reach out over the years. Left to him, the friendship would have unraveled like an old forgotten sweater.

“She’s thinking of going into the ministry. You heard the Lutheran Church now ordains women?”

Meinhardt had. His Oma would have made a good clergywoman. That is, until the Nazis’ barbarity shook her faith. “A woman is one thing, but is the Church ready to ordain a midget?”

“Her big brother will see to that. Robert’s fighting for every institution to open its doors to little people.”

“I thought he was busy improving car doors. What other doors is he opening?”

“Ask him yourself. He’s here helping me and Jessie clean out the upper cabinets. Even climbing up on a step stool is getting hard with our arthritis.” Charles called his son to the phone.

“Your father says you’re a real gentleman, Robert. You’re opening doors for Bella.”

“Not only Bella, Uncle Meinhardt. I started a local chapter of Little People of America in Southeast Michigan. Is there an LPA branch in Los Angeles?”

Meinhardt had never heard of the organization. Robert said it began thirteen years ago when a man named Billy Barty called on those 4'10" and under to meet in Reno. Twenty-one little people showed up. A *San Francisco News* reporter had written that the event turned small people from oddities into humans. Robert sighed. "Unfortunately, since then, LPA has barely grown. Other civil rights movements grab all the media attention these days."

It didn't sound like an organization Meinhardt wanted to join, although he'd make a note to add their membership roster to his mailing list. He asked why Robert had gotten involved.

"I used to be so ashamed of my parents, I couldn't wait to escape them. But Bella grew up smart, smarter than me, and it made me angry to see her picked on and treated like a child."

Meinhardt understood. It was easier to stick up for a sister who brought out his protective instincts than it was to defend his parents. But Robert added that watching Bella's struggle also made him see his parents in a new light. "I appreciated what they went through to have a decent life. It was hard for them to speak up for themselves. I have a better chance of being listened to."

In Meinhardt's view, midgets didn't need to be spoken for at all. Actions, not words, succeeded in the end. Nevertheless, he knew what it must mean to Charles and Jessie that Robert had grown closer to them. He was like Milton, a member of the younger generation working to improve the world. "I'm sure your parents and sister are proud of you."

"LPA is holding its national convention in Anaheim next month. I'm flying into Los Angeles see to my old college roommate, then driving down to the meeting. Come with me?"

Meinhardt, recalling the drunk and rowdy Munchkins at the Culver Hotel, wanted no part of the midget conventioneers. All the same, he was touched that Robert was trying to recruit him and curious to see for himself the adult his godson had become. All he'd ever seen were photos. If nothing else, the LPA meeting might result in some business connections.

"I'll only go if you let me feed you breakfast first."

Robert accepted, then whispered. "I'm sure your breakfast will be better than my mom's. The cupboard I'm cleaning out is a shrine to Frosted Pop Tarts."

Meinhardt remembered the awful meals Jessie had served when he'd stayed with them during the war. Nevertheless, he felt an urge to defend her. "She makes excellent coffee. Besides, I think packaged foods are your mother's way of asserting that she's a typical American."

"Gee, I never thought of it that way, Uncle Meinhardt. Good thing you're coming to the convention with me. You can bring me down to your level when I get above my raising."

Robert tripped walking up Meinhardt's front steps. Narrow, with low risers, they were one of the house's many customized features. "Are you okay?" Meinhardt caught the elbow of his six-foot-plus guest.

"The steps caught me off-guard. My parents adapt their apartment, but the building's owner could care less about making accommodations outside. I wish my folks had been able to afford their own home." Robert looked around. "The place suits you. Dad always admired your attention to detail, like the tailoring of the clothes you sell. Everything simple but high quality."

"The house is made of adobe. I wanted a warm material to stand for everything Germany wasn't." Meinhardt rested his hand on the sun-heated brick before leading them down the cool hallway to the tiled kitchen. They sat at a low table where sections of false flooring could be removed to hold chairs for people of normal height. "I'm not much more of a cook than your mother, but I make a good omelet." Meinhardt served generous helpings, along with the donuts he'd bought at Du-Pars yesterday when he met Margaret for lunch. He hoped the visit with Robert would go as well. He'd spent the afternoon berating himself for letting guilt deprive him of Maggie's company for five years.

She'd told him not to lose heart about getting back into show business and joked that she was fortunate witches and spinsters were eternal characters. Meinhardt was as eager to hear about Milton and his family as Margaret was to talk about them. He pored over their photos. Milton was tall and still almost gaunt, with the same piercing light eyes. His tiny wife Nadia and their children were dark and round, their playful smiles an antidote to his seriousness. However, when he looked at them, instead of the camera, Milton's joy was clear. He'd made a good match, a feat Margaret hadn't managed and Meinhardt hadn't tried. He never told Margaret about Celia, remembering how forgiving she'd been toward Judy Garland. He was afraid she'd scold him for being too hard on another young woman doing her best to make it in a tough industry.

Meinhardt compared the young man sitting at his table now with the photos he'd seen the day before. Robert was five years younger and taller than Milton, as square-bodied as a midget. Whereas Milton tensed his muscles, Robert was relaxed and expansive. Meinhardt could see how he'd be a good organizer for LPA. His height wouldn't be intimidating because he was so unassuming. Maybe his naturalness came from growing up in a loving family. Charles and Jessie were as made for each other as Milton and Nadia. Meinhardt wondered if

Robert would find the same happiness and whether a prospective wife would risk marrying into a family of midgets.

It was time to leave for the convention. "I'll bring the car around front," said Meinhardt, "so you don't trip on the steps leading down to the garage."

"I thought we'd take my rental car," said Robert. "I didn't know you had one."

Meinhardt described its custom features, the extended gas pedals and handbrakes. "The passenger seat is fully adjustable for a normal person, so I'm sure you'll be comfortable."

Robert reached into his pocket for the rental keys. "The thing is, I'm not normal either. I got an oversized sedan to make sure there was room for my legs and head." He chuckled. "Very tall people have problems comparable to very short ones."

Meinhardt didn't believe that for one minute.

It was Robert's first trip to California. He exclaimed over the waving palm trees and mellow air until they approached Anaheim. The city's outskirts were a tawdry version of the Disneyland theme park, complete with a Snow White Motel of bungalows named for the seven dwarfs. His spirits didn't revive until the convention center's glass-walled dome loomed ahead. Meinhardt, by contrast, grew queasier. He wasn't looking forward to mingling with his own kind.

Both were awestruck, however, entering the arena's main lobby, whose atrium soared 190 feet. Meinhardt joked to hide his nerves. "Couldn't the Little People of America find a more proportional space to meet? This ceiling dwarfs us!"

Robert grinned and pointed to the enormous "Think Big" banner behind the registration area. "The whole point is for midgets to set their sights higher."

239

Meinhardt looked at the full-size tables and chairs where short people stretched to sign in and get name tags. He thought of how Jenny Grossinger went out of her way to preserve their dignity. "Too bad the staff couldn't adjust the furniture lower to accommodate their guests."

Registration for the national conference was barely 50. Seeing Robert's disappointment, Meinhardt told him, "If there's a market, the world will pay attention. People care more about cash than causes. Follow me." He led Robert into the exhibit hall to see if manufacturers were beginning to take notice of a lucrative opportunity, as he had nearly twenty years ago.

Two dozen vendors occupied a space designed for a thousand. Most sold predictable products — heel lifts and shoe inserts, step ladders with extra rungs, clamp-on shelves that fit under cabinets. A portable folding step stool would be handy to take to take to the supermarket, providing a stock boy didn't confiscate it. He was also impressed by "Instant Alterations," a no-sew press-on nylon tape to shorten cuffs and hems. He'd add it to his accessories catalog. No competing clothing companies, thank goodness, although many people wore things made by his.

The medical quackery was all-too familiar: pills that promised to lengthen bones, and inhalers that claimed to lower voices and boost lung capacity. Fortunately none of the convention goers were buying such trash; they recognized the insult to their intelligence. The vendors, all normal size, didn't have a clue what midgets needed or the respect to discover and deliver it.

What Meinhardt hadn't anticipated were the ersatz Munchkin items, including knock-offs of the costumes they'd auctioned off. He looked toward the exit and tugged Robert's elbow. "Let's get out of here before I'm recognized."

"No disrespect, but thirty years later, minus the outfit and red goatee, that's not likely."

Meinhardt wouldn't take the risk. In this setting, his *Oz* association could be a liability. What the general public viewed with affection might be seen by LPA members as demeaning. Robert saw it differently. "Suppose you intentionally reminded people of your role? And played up your business success at the same time? Exploit your fame to become a spokesperson for little people. The public listens to me more than my parents, but they'd really listen to a star who is also midget." Robert's voice rose with excitement.

"Calm down. If you talk any higher, you'll start squealing like your father."

"Not a chance. I didn't inherit any of his traits. Or his willingness to accept things. I'm a go-getter. Like you." His eyes dared Meinhardt to contradict him.

Meinhardt scanned the exhibit hall. Amassing in this vast public space made them look smaller than ever. They deserved better and there was a chance he could help raise their status. On the other hand, he risked lowering his own. "I'll think about," he told Robert.

They were subdued on the drive home. Darkness hid the landscape and Robert was in no mood to exclaim over anything. He was disappointed at LPA's failure to swell its numbers or address discrimination in a meaningful way. "They need to lobby members of Congress, get legislation passed, and pressure big corporations. You could really help them, Uncle Meinhardt."

"You keep saying that, but I don't see how."

"*Oz* gets more popular every year. Use that. Testify before House and Senate committees to include midgets in laws for the handicapped. Pose for photos with their kids and constituents. If your acting career revives, start a Hollywood LPA chapter and get other stars to support our cause. Advocate for the rights of children like Bella to get a good education and good jobs."

Meinhardt thought of the midgets wandering around like lost souls. Throughout the convention, they'd never ventured beyond the center's walls, instead huddling together in mutual complaint sessions. Meinhardt turned to his godson. "They're a miserable lot, Robert. I can't work for people who wallow in self-pity and won't stand up for themselves. How can you?"

Robert stared out the windshield at a lone star in the hazy sky. "You only had to deal with your own struggle. I saw three family members suffer. It may sound odd, but I think I'm more aware of bigotry than you. Compassion toward others is easier than kindness toward yourself."

"If I speak on behalf of midgets, I could be perceived as being kind to myself. Suppose it backfires and I'm seen as just another aggrieved handicapped person asking for favors?"

"You won't be. You're better off than most." His eyes turned from the empty highway toward Meinhardt. "According to my logic, you should be more compassionate too."

Meinhardt shrank further into the big car's seat with each remaining mile. Wasn't it enough that he gave midgets jobs and decent clothes? Or did he swap money for commitment? He longed to be home, soaking in the tub, letting the troublesome questions float down the drain.

Robert walked him to the front door. This time he didn't trip. Meinhardt raised his hand to shake goodbye, but Robert swooped down to hug him. "What do you say, Uncle Meinhardt? Should I ask the national office to send you the forms to start a Hollywood LPA chapter?"

Meinhardt pulled back so his voice wouldn't

be muffled inside Robert's embrace. In the deepest baritone he could muster, he answered, "I'll call you. First I need to resurrect my acting career." He knew he'd let Robert down. Maybe tall people were at a disadvantage after all. When they fell, they had farther to go. Living close to the ground was safer.

This time the call came from his agent, not the casting director. "Penn cut your character to focus on the plight of Indians. He's afraid adding another downtrodden group will dilute the message."

"The more varied the victims, the more people will identify with being an underdog."

"Penn's not interested in the universal. His movies are specific."

"Okay, here's another take. I portray a strong and independent midget and the audience roots for the Indian to achieve the same self-sufficiency."

"Stop wasting your breath on me. It's Penn's decision." His agent softened her voice. "He liked your performance, maybe too much. I'll let you know if something else comes up."

Meinhardt snapped that the only roles he could expect were more victims. He was wrong to think he could play Little Little Man, whichever way Penn chose. It wasn't his nature to be downtrodden or taken advantage of. He couldn't act a part he didn't believe in.

The rejection gave him an excuse to turn down Robert. He might be correct that being an outsider allowed him to feel compassion, but he'd never understand how being an insider made Meinhardt want to get out. They ran in opposite directions. Robert's commitment was tenacious and straightforward. Meinhardt zigzagged. As a child, his Oma's faith let him deny his disability. When that later proved impossible, he accepted his difference and used it for financial gain. Now Robert was urging him to embrace his identity with pride and

243

fight for the rights of others.

Meinhardt drove comfortably in his Gremlin to Safeway. The sale on Milky Way and Three Musketeers would be over, so he could reach the Baby Ruth Bars easily. With his screen prospects most sincerely dead, he no longer cared about gaining a few pounds.

PART NINE

Looking For My Heart's Desire

Dornum, Germany, 1980

Chapter 46

Meinhardt read the inscription above his Oma's grave, *Näh und Aussaat für den Herrn*. Nearly thirty years ago, Sadie had written for his permission to have the words "Sewing and Sowing for the Lord" carved on the simple headstone. She asked if he'd prefer a standard phrase, such as "In Loving Memory" or "Resting with the Angels," but he told his grandmother's friend to choose the words that would comfort her and whoever else in Dornum visited his Oma's place of rest.

On top of her monument was a mysterious row of small stones, the same slate gray as the craggy bluffs above the North Sea which the rustic cemetery overlooked. His grandmother Gretel had asked to be buried here, rather than in the graveyard behind the historic St. Bartholomaeus Church where her funeral service was held. She wanted to lie beside the ancestors who'd lived in this tiny fishing village for centuries. The sand along the shore was almost black, as though it too mourned the dead, its smooth surface pierced by shards of frost-covered grass. Seagulls swooped in the chilly mist and fishing boats swirled like bobbins on the wind-rattled waters.

The bleak cemetery was far from Berlin, where Meinhardt's Oma had sewn a web of tiny stitches over the big scars of his childhood. He tried to recapture the warmth of their home now, but while images came easily to mind, the icy air numbed his heart. If only he had a bowl of his grandmother's potato soup with riffles to thaw his blood and untangle his seaweed of troubles.

Perhaps he'd feel better by the end of the week, when he'd meet Sadie's granddaughter, Rachel Stein, but that was a chilly prospect too. When he'd called to tell Rachel he was coming, her response had been "It's about time!" He already berated himself for procrastinating; he dreaded a scolding from her as well. So he was relieved when a prolonged trip to London delayed her homecoming. Rather than postpone his own flight to Germany, Meinhardt decided to come early and get to know the town. The less foreign he felt, the less defensive he'd be.

He walked along the tree-lined Dornumer Tief Canal that wound through the village and connected it to the seacoast. Compared to the rest of the world, especially East Germany, West Germany was prosperous. Little Dornum was no exception. Its red- and white-washed brick buildings with their steep tiled roofs were in good condition. Tourists came to see the old church and hear about the place where Minnie Schönberg, the Marx Brothers' mother, had grown up before moving to America as a teenager.

Meinhardt was surprised Sadie had survived the war. She and his grandmother had been best friends for eighty years by the time Gretel died. Though Meinhardt had known Rodge nearly half as long, they'd never developed that same closeness. Maybe men, especially men like them, didn't. Rodge lavished his friendship on everyone while Meinhardt doled out feelings sparingly. They protected themselves against intimacy the way the stone lions Meinhardt was passing guarded Dornum's old city hall.

Sunshine had parted the clouds by the time he reached the village center. Snow melting on the roofs glistened like boiled frosting sliding down the sides of a streusel cake. The sight whet his appetite for pastry. He was glad he was meeting Inge at the coffeehouse in an hour.

Inge Shultze was the granddaughter of Tilde König, a childhood friend of Gretel and Sadie. Then in her twenties, Inge had played the organ in St.

247

Bartholomaeus Church at his Oma's funeral. She hadn't known the elderly women well, but Meinhardt hoped she would remember the stories they told about village life when they were growing up.

Café Schneckenhaus was a white-washed stone building in the middle of the town square. Outside the entrance stood a stout woman of average height, wearing a brown woolen coat with an orange scarf. Her dark hair, graying at the temples, was sprayed in a short bouffant that held its shape in the east-blowing breeze. She glanced at Meinhardt, frowned, then looked over his head in the direction he'd come from.

"Frau Schulze?" he asked, extending his hand.

Alarmed, she withdrew inside the recessed doorway before touching his fingertips with her leather gloves. "Herr Raabe? I didn't know ..." He should have warned her ahead of time to avert the nervous chatter he'd come to expect whenever people were unsure how to react to their first sight of him. Her words tumbled forth. "Shall we dine inside or on the terrace? It's cold, but the sun will heat up the metal chairs. I'm sure we'll be comfortable outside."

Meinhardt let Inge lead them to a table near the wrought iron railing overlooking the canal. It would give her a chance to regain her composure.

"I recommend the breaded fried white fish," she pattered on, "with mayonnaise sauce and potato salad. It's the house specialty. My husband and I order it whenever we dine here."

"My treat," Meinhardt said, glad the table was wide enough that his legs, sticking out, wouldn't poke her. "Please save room for coffee and dessert, as well. The pastry here is good?"

The muscles in Inge's neck relaxed as she described half a dozen tortes. Meinhardt hoped eating would calm her, together with the fact that he looked almost normal sitting down. The verbal stream continued, however. Either she was still flustered or prattling was her habit.

After the meal, Inge gave him a tour of the town's landmarks. She pointed out the red brick Dornumer Fischecke, which had supplied their fresh fish at lunch. Opposite was the school where their grandmothers and mothers, and even Inge and her children had gone. The school had operated continuously for 150 years, except for a brief period during the war when teachers were serving at the front or manufacturing munitions. Inge was a teenager then, and she her classmates were proud to do their patriotic duty by sending care packages to Germany's brave soldiers.

"Of course, we didn't know what the Nazis were doing to those people in the cities."

"Those people?" Meinhardt could not resist asking.

"You know. The Jews, the camps. Those supposed experiments with the mongoloids and cripples and deformed." Inge looked down and continued hastily. "I mean, we're a small village. We've always caught fish, raised our families. Defended the motherland. The way everyone was made to suffer after the war, it wasn't right. So much deprivation when we did nothing wrong."

"And your children?"

"*Gott sei Dank!* By the time my daughter and sons were born, Germany was prosperous again." Inge paused. "So I don't understand when my own children say the whole country must share in the guilt. The men responsible are dead by now or dying. Why should the rest of us be punished for their offenses? *Lassen Sie es sein.*" Inge swept her arm toward the shimmering canal and the storekeepers putting up holiday decorations. "Life is too good. Let it be, already."

249

Entering the hushed darkness of St. Bartholomaeus Lutheran Church, Inge finally grew quiet. Meinhardt read the illuminated plaque telling visitors that the organ, built in 1710 by Gerhard Van Holy, was a national treasure. He pictured the sanctuary filled with mourners as a younger and perhaps less talkative Inge played *Amazing Grace* at his Oma's funeral. She directed him to a pew near the front and sat at the keyboard, where the swelling notes of *Go My Children, With My Blessing* soared up past the windows and echoed back down from the vaulted ceiling. Sadie had written him that it was his grandmother's favorite hymn. Meinhardt hadn't known. His Oma wasn't observant when she'd raised him, and had only returned to her faith when she returned to Dornum. It was kind of Inge to remember thirty years on and play it for him.

Inge's tongue loosened again as they left the sanctuary, joking that Minnie Marx, born in 1880, was more famous than the organ, built 170 years earlier. Near the door, a sunbeam, stained red by the glass, lit up a gospel quote carved high in the stone wall. Meinhardt, unable to see so far above his head, listened as Inge read the words aloud. "Whatsoever you do to the least of my brothers, that you do unto me --- Matthew 25:40." He was struck by the reverence in her voice.

"That's what people said about your grandmother at her funeral, how she treated the least of them like the best. She must have done the same when she brought you up."

The least? Meinhardt bridled, but chose to credit Inge with admiring his grandmother, not diminishing him. He recalled Mr. Schwartz, the Jewish neighbor his Oma had healed with the same egg-white balm he'd put on Margaret's burns. The old man had received his grandmother's ministrations not only with gratitude, but with stoic grace. Maybe accepting help was itself an act of generosity whereby the receiver ennobled the giver.

Inge held the heavy door open as they emerged from the dark church into fading winter light. She told him that before leaving, he should be sure to see the windmill, Beninga Castle, and the fortresses just outside the city. He thanked her for showing him around. "Now I know the place that made my grandmother who she was."

"You might also be interested in seeing the Jewish cemetery. There's a synagogue too, although it's used as a museum now. Ask Sadie's granddaughter Rachel about it."

A fish-tasting backwash rose in Meinhardt's throat at the mention of Rachel.

"Hers was one of the few Jewish families to return after the war. She once invited me to dinner on the anniversary of your grandmother's death and they lit a special candle in her honor. Rachel said all the local Jews and their descendants do the same for Gretel."

Sadie had written him about saying Kaddish and lighting yahrzeit candles. This custom of marking the anniversary of a loved one's death had inspired his own annual ritual of the cloth.

"Those people are good at remembering their dead," Inge said.

"They've had thousands of years and millions of deceased for practice."

Meinhardt slept well that night, a combination of the fresh air and good German food. He was staying at the Dornumer Wappen, an old family-run hotel with large windows that looked onto the street. He missed the amenities that Jennie Grossinger used to provide, like step stools for climbing into the high beds. However, Europeans built things on a scale closer to his proportions than the oversized Americans. With only a little stretching, he was able to reach the sink taps.

251

The next morning, Meinhardt turned on the small bedside radio for a weather report. " ... outside his apartment at the Dakota Hotel in New York City. Lennon was hit five times in the back and cried 'I'm shot, I'm shot' before collapsing on the sidewalk and scattering the cassette tapes he was carrying." As the announcement replayed, he pieced together that a deranged young man named Mark David Chapman had shot and killed John Lennon last night. Distraught fans, waking up to the news, were trying to make sense of a violent act committed against a man who preached peace. Meinhardt wondered how Ringo Starr was taking the news.

In hindsight, he'd been right to worry about Ringo after the Beatles broke up. Tabloids had reported that his marriage fell apart, he drank heavily, and he lost custody of his children. Also lost was his sense of humor. But he was doing better now. He had a solo career, was engaged to an American actress, and renting a place on Sunset Strip, not far from Meinhardt's house. He often fantasized calling Ringo to apologize for disappointing him long ago. An older Ringo, having experienced life's ups and downs, might better understand Meinhardt's lack of idealism.

He thought of calling him now, but didn't know what reaction he'd provoke. Suppose he was met with scorn. Worse, what if their meeting was too trivial for Ringo to even remember? Meinhardt didn't want to reopen another old wound, yet facing the past to decide his future was the reason he was in Dornum. He had a long list of failed relationships to come to terms with.

Chapter 47

The idea for the trip began when Meinhardt went to see his doctor. He'd been feeling off lately, although it was nothing he could put his finger on. His energy wasn't what it used to be and now and then his heart seemed to stop for a fraction of a second. The doctor had ordered blood work, a test of lung capacity, and an EKG. Meinhardt hoped nothing serious was wrong, just normal aging, or at least what passed for normal in midgets. Heart and lung problems hit them early.

He was running late for his appointment at the hospital clinic, despite allowing extra time for freeway traffic. By the time he got there, the only empty parking places were so far from the building that taking one would make him even later. The only option was a handicapped spot. He avoided them on principle, but today he had no choice. He hadn't even wanted a handicapped sticker. The Department of Motor Vehicles clerk had automatically checked the box on his application and was incredulous when he scratched it out. "People complain because I *don't* give them handicapped stickers. You qualify for one and want to waive your right?" She shrugged and said he could change his status when he renewed his license, but that was five years away.

"Your lungs are fine, Mr. Raabe and there's no obvious heart abnormality, but we'll keep an eye on it in case you're a candidate for a pacemaker. I'm more concerned about your blood pressure. If it goes any higher, I'll have to put you on medication." The doctor frowned at his chart. "I see you're still working full time. Don't you think you ought to slow down?"

Meinhardt had no such intention but knew that saying so would provoke a lecture.

"Also, you're triglycerides are too high. There's a minor blockage in your arteries, which may explain the fatigue. If you ignore everything else I tell you, at least cut down on sweets."

Even the Nazis hadn't thought of that form of torture. Again, Meinhardt said nothing.

"An extra pound, some stress. With someone

your height, these things can't be spread across your body. They concentrate on a few organs and wear them down. Play golf, go on a vacation. You may find retirement isn't so bad. Patients who are twice your size swear by it."

"My arms are too short to swing a golf club. My legs won't stretch out in a hammock."

"You're sixty-five, Mr. Raabe. You've accomplished more than most people your age and more than others born with your handicap. What do you have left to prove?"

After his appointment, Meinhardt's eyes adjusted quickly to the glare of the hospital cafeteria's fluorescent lights. The cashier and the other patrons regarded at him with mild curiosity, then retreated into their own sad thoughts. In medical settings he was less of an oddity and more easily blended in. The coffee looked watery, so he bought a cup of tea, limiting himself to one packet of sugar. It was harder to pass by the dessert case.

Cutting back at work was out of the question. He needed to ramp up. Big People Clothes for Little People wasn't immune from the latest economic downturn. Even with his unique market, he could no longer count on business from midgets. Children's clothes were so adult-like these days they could shop in husky boys or large girls departments, without paying his higher prices or shipping costs. He'd pondered a new sales slogan, "Midgets Are Different." The phrase was meant to imply they weren't built like large children, but it could also be interpreted negatively. Meinhardt waffled. When he was younger, he would have resolved the dilemma quickly. Maybe a break would be good after all. Not to slow down, but to recharge.

The problem was there was nowhere Meinhardt wanted to go. Trade shows had taken him all over North America. Travel abroad held little appeal. He'd bounced from country to country in his youth, drawn by possibilities, driven out by prejudice. The only pull was Dornum, where he'd yet to visit his Oma's grave. He knew little about where she began and ended her life, while she'd known every detail of his. Again he waffled, until the tea was lukewarm sugar water. His desire to go back to Germany was equally lukewarm, and bittersweet. Meinhardt averted his eyes from the pastries as he dumped his paper cup in the trash and returned to the parking lot.

A tall woman with feather-cut blonde hair pushed a walker away from the car in the handicapped space next to his. Her long fingers, gripping the handlebar as she slowly crossed the pavement, tapered to bright red nails. The prominent cheekbones in her pale thin face were also red with the effort. Despite her frailty and shuffling gait, she radiated beauty.

It was more than a decade since Meinhardt had seen Celia's photo in a fashion magazine. When he dared think about how she might look as disease ravaged her bones, he pictured gnarled limbs curled in on themselves, a Dorian Gray of the body instead of the face. He was unprepared for a woman who held herself erect despite a weakening skeleton. He certainly never expected to see Celia still dressed in the sleek athletic clothes that had been her trademark as a model.

He was frozen in place when she paused to take a breath and saw him. The delight on her face faltered when she saw the look on his. What did she see --- alarm, pity, pain? Meinhardt was too overcome to do his usual self-analysis and get control of his feelings. He rushed up to Celia and put his hands over hers. The handlebars were higher than on a standard model.

"Customized for a tall person," she said.

He pointed to his car. "Customized for a

short one."

They gazed at each other until Celia broke the silence. "My physical therapy session isn't for an hour. Come have coffee with me."

Meinhardt matched his pace to hers. People stared when they entered the cafeteria. He didn't know whether it was because he'd just left or was now with Celia. A woman pushing a walker was a common sight in that setting, but they were typically old and hunched over. Celia was as eye-catching as ever. Just as during those days in New York, she took being stared at in stride. He focused on her so he'd feel less self-conscious about the looks directed at him.

Celia wheeled to an espresso bar Meinhardt hadn't noticed, then the dessert case. "Their lemon bars are the best and the brownies remind me of my mother's. The raspberry Danish are okay, but not as good as Demel's." She ordered one of each for them to share and greeted the counter staff. "I'm here twice a week. You get to know the people as well as the pastry."

They overcame their awkwardness by eating and filling in the last twenty-five years. Meinhardt told her about his company. "My doctor thinks I'm too old to worry about work."

"What do you think?"

"The business has been my life. I can't let it go downhill."

"Pity you're too independent to take on a partner." Celia took a deep breath. "You've never been one to trust others."

Meinhardt flinched, but it was true. In the decade since Robert had taken him to the Little People of America convention, he'd endowed a college scholarship and hired two interns every year. Although he taught them the skills to go off on their own, he never asked them to join the company or sought their ideas. They wore the same unflattering

256

clothes as the general public.

"They just don't think the way I do. It's not a question of my trusting them personally."

She raised an eyebrow and told Meinhardt about the small modeling agency she ran with a partner, a former clothing manufacturer whose skills complemented hers. They met when she moved to California in the 1960s, after launching a successful career in New York. The West Coast had become the hub for sportswear designers and her athletic looks were in high demand. After her health began to deteriorate and modeling work fell off, she'd stayed on and opened the agency. The warm weather was kinder to her bones than icy East Coast winters.

"For twenty years, I was reluctant to go to New York because I was afraid of running into you. Now I find out you've been in LA all along."

"I thought about calling when I got here, but I was afraid of your anger."

"I was hurt, afraid you'd betray me for your career. By the time the hurt lessened, I was used to being alone and focusing on work." Meinhardt gestured toward the people she'd greeted. "We're different. You like people. They like you. Even illness hasn't soured you." He licked cake crumbs off his fingertips. "I'm glad your hair is still the color of sunshine. It suits you."

"I have my cloudy days too," she said. "You just have to break through them."

Rodge had also confessed how hard it was to get up some mornings, but he'd dressed nattily and come to the pub nevertheless. "Clouds roll away, the sun simply waits for you to circle back," he used to say. Meinhardt admired him, and now Celia, for having the strength to keep going. It occurred to Meinhardt that in his own way, he was just as persistent.

"I'm grateful for every day I can still get around on my own," Celia said. Her condition had worsened slowly the last ten years, but it was deteriorating more rapidly now. She was still able to drive because sitting took enough pressure off her legs to be able to press the pedals, but soon she'd lose that ability too. When Meinhardt suggested she get hand controls like his car, she explained that the bones in her arms were also weakening. In five years at most, she would be dependent on a motorized wheelchair. It was doubtful she'd be able to continue living alone.

"Not even sleeping with my doctor will improve my chances." Celia batted her eyelashes.

"How can you joke like that?"

"If I didn't laugh, I'd cry. My mother used to say a joke is a well-told tragedy. Her life on the farm with my dad was full of jokes, or tragedies. Take your pick. It got her through."

"How are your parents?"

"My dad's gone. My mom divides her time between my brothers. They're still working the farm, but they had to sell it to a big corporation. Thankfully, that was after my dad died." Celia slumped before tossing her hair, squaring her shoulders, and sitting up straight again.

"I didn't mean to make you talk about something painful."

"I live with pain. Talking helps. So does remembering. It keeps happier times alive."

"Memory only brings back sorrow. The past means something is over." Meinhardt had packed away thoughts of their love affair like last year's fashions.

"Memories can be sweet as well as bitter." Celia's fork scraped up the last dab of lemon bar. "Licking Cheerio chains to the center of the table until our tongues met, walking through the red and gold leaves in Central Park, making an entire meal of my mother's gingerbread cookies. The memory is almost as satisfying as the sun and sugar themselves."

Meinhardt found himself looking ahead. He imagined sunny mornings sitting opposite Celia at the breakfast table. His house, customized for a short person, would be perfect after she was confined to a wheelchair. He'd add minor adjustments: a ramp, push buttons instead of pulls on the cabinets. The kinds of changes he'd need himself as he aged. Their needs would converge.

He steadied Celia's walker as they stood up to leave. They navigated past tables cluttered with crumpled napkins and the remains of half-eaten sandwiches and desserts. "Did you ever notice," she said, "that neither of us leaves any pastry crumbs on our plates?"

A few days later, on the twenty-eighth anniversary of his Oma's death, Meinhardt performed the ritual of the cloth. First he stroked it. Although his hands were wrinkled now and spotted with age, they remained nimble. Just touching the red silk revived them. He rolled the fabric between his fingers, hoping the gentle swish would tell him what to do about work and love. There was only silence. Then he heard his heartbeat, as steady as the treadle of his Oma's sewing machine.

Next Meinhardt carried the fabric to the window where Pacific sunlight turned the red silk into shimmering gold. He pictured Celia's hair. Seeing it glow in the parking lot, he'd longed to reach up and touch it. He pretended the cloth was her hair now, and caressed its folds.

Finally, he sucked gently on a corner. The color reminded him of *Zimt würzen Kuchen*, the cinnamon spice cake his grandmother baked each year at harvest time. He recalled the taste of Celia's skin the first time they made love, lapping buttery popcorn off each other's backs. She'd said the other day that the two of them always licked up every crumb. Would he leave behind uneaten crumbs when he died or live the rest of his life the way he ate pastry?

The annual commemoration of his Oma's yahrzeit had remained unchanged for nearly three decades. Now it was time to reconnect with his grandmother in person. She held the key to his past; she would have the answer to his future. Meinhardt would go to Dornum.

Chapter 48

The morning after his meeting with Inge, Meinhardt entered a modest red brick building with a steep tiled roof and arched windows. Dornum Synagogue looked like many other structures in the village, except for the Star of David over the entrance. It was the only surviving synagogue in East Frisia, but with so few Jews returning after the war, it was now a Holocaust museum.

"Can I help you?" A tiny but spry old man with a wide smile and the rosy cheeks of a ten-year-old boy danced up to Meinhardt. He extended a warm hand. "Menachem Aaronsohn."

Meinhardt wasn't sure why he'd come or what he expected to see. He was relieved there were no pictures of death camps or other atrocities on the walls. Instead he saw pre-war photos of children racing on the beach, women talking with shopkeepers, and men laughing in the marketplace. The Jews in these scenes of daily life looked just like the ordinary Germans he grew up with in Berlin, except that they lived in a quiet village, not a busy city.

"You expected maybe huddled families boarding cattle cars and piles of naked bodies?"

Meinhardt looked at a photo of a dress shop. In the rear were bolts of cloth and a sewing machine. A sign in the shop window said *Schneiderei in*

Rääumen, "Tailoring on premises."

"This isn't a typical Holocaust shrine," Menachem explained. "It celebrates the thriving Jewish community that existed in Dornum for hundreds of years. People came here to escape the pogroms elsewhere. We were trusting. Foolish of us." He'd grown up in Dornum and recently turned 90. Born twenty years after Gretel and Sadie, he hadn't known them. His family left for England when the Nazis came to power and escaped being wiped out, unlike those who stayed.

"Why did you come back?" Meinhardt didn't see the point. Except for Rachel Stein and a handful of other families, there was no longer a Jewish community here.

"I lived in England until I was 75. My wife Sarah, bless her memory, was gone. The children and grandchildren had their own lives. They didn't want to hear about the Holocaust. So when I got a call to help set up the museum, I came. Then I stayed on as the caretaker."

"You're still working at your age?"

Menachem shrugged. "Nu, what's to work? The janitor and a handyman keep the place running. Me, I show people pictures and mementos of a disappeared life."

"That's all?"

"I smile. I act normal. That's the point. To make visitors see that Jews are like them. Our neighbors turned on us when all we wanted was to raise children, plant gardens, and catch fish."

They went outside to start the official tour, beginning with a small metal box, called a mezuzzah, nailed to the doorpost. Inside the box was a scroll with the holiest prayer, the Sh'ma, which Jews recite upon waking up and going to sleep, and at the moment of death. "The words are simple," Menachem explained. "They proclaim the oneness of God. It's a call to Jews, dispersed and exiled for

261

millennia, to remember their oneness as a people."

Back inside, Meinhardt leafed through family photo albums celebrating birthdays, walks in the park, a new puppy. A velvet-lined tray held medals won by Jewish World War I heroes. He saw a colorful board game and stepped closer to see the title: *Juden Raus*, Jews Out! It was like a sinister version of Monopoly. Players went around the board, rounding up Jews and throwing them in jail. The first to capture six was declared the winner. Meinhardt recoiled.

"It's the only item in the museum you wouldn't find in a Jewish house, but I insisted we include it. To think that while Jewish families played other games, German children and their parents were playing this one. In some ways, it's more chilling than images of the death camps."

Meinhardt wondered if there'd been a comparable game to eliminate so-called defectives. Shaken, he turned away from the family section to images of village life. There was a poster for *A Night at the Opera*, just like the ones in Berlin in 1935. The Marx brothers' great-grandfather had been a founding member of this synagogue, another reminder of how long Jews had lived there.

"Our roots were centuries deep." Menachem unlocked a display case with a prayer shawl, called a tallit. It had belonged to the last rabbi, passed down to him on his bar mitzvah as it had for four generations before that. Menachem gestured for Meinhardt to put it on.

He hesitated. The yellowed silk was threadbare in places and the fringe badly shorn. With trembling hands, he wrapped himself in the fragile cloth, lifting the ends so they wouldn't drag on the floor. He closed his eyes and inhaled the ancient smell.

Forty years ago, when Meinhardt donned the coroner's robe, he understood Margaret's remark that putting on a costume was the last step in becoming a character. When a Jew wore a tallit, the change must go deeper. It wouldn't just alter his appearance or mannerisms, it would transform him inside. He'd connect to an identity four thousand years old. Menachem knew who he was and what he should be in the days he had remaining. Meinhardt was envious. He was no longer sure who he'd been for the last sixty-five years or what to become in the time he had left.

The rough-hewn grave markers in the Jewish cemetery dated back 200 years. Most were carved in Hebrew, but many also bore the German words for beloved family members. Some had small stones on top, like those Meinhardt had seen yesterday on his grandmother's grave. He looked through the wrought-iron star over the cemetery gate to the cloudless sky above and thought of the skies of Germany, Poland, and Austria, thick with the ashes of burning Jews.

There was no memorial for disabled people. What did their families do when they were taken away? Did they mourn or were they relieved to be free of the burden and shame? His parents hadn't waited for the Nazis to get rid of him, but what of his brother and sister?   Sadie had told him Ada's married name and said she and Karl were both still living in Bonn, where they were born. But fear that his parents had turned his siblings against him, or kept his existence a secret, prevented him from reaching out. Confident his mother and father were dead by now, he'd finally taken the risk of writing Karl and Ada before he came to Germany. Neither wrote back.

His anxiety mounting with nothing else to do until Rachel's return to Dornum, Meinhardt impulsively decided to take a side trip to Bonn, 325 kilometers south. He'd simply show up and present

263

himself to his brother and sister. If they turned him away, he'd only be out the cost of the train ticket. A last look at the headstone's inscriptions told him otherwise. There was more to lose, the last hope of having what Margaret and Charles cherished, a connection to family.

Meinhardt's resolve to appear unannounced on his brother's or sister's doorstep wavered when he reached Bonn. He treated himself to a day of sightseeing to salvage something if they weren't welcoming. The city was small to be the seat of West Germany's government, but it was quite beautiful. He visited Beethoven's birthplace and the Rococo town hall in the nearby marketplace. There were still traces of the Nazi regime, faded swastikas and spray-painted signs forbidding Jews. Meinhardt wondered if Karl and Ada were neo-Nazis or sympathizers. He needed to find a calm place to review his lines before knocking on either's door.

The path along the Rhine was deserted this time of year. Meinhardt stared at the icy water and thought of his Oma's grave overlooking the wind-whipped North Sea. He recalled what she said to him as a child, that just because his body was small didn't mean his ambitions couldn't be big. He'd believed her then, but today he couldn't summon up that confidence. Unable to evoke the words, he'd have to play this part unrehearsed. Instinct told him to try his sister's house first.

The cab drove through a neighborhood of three-story homes with sloping lawns and old trees whose leafy canopies would shade the wide boulevards come summer. It deposited him in front of a red brick house festooned with balloons proclaiming *Herzlichen Glüückwunsch zum Geburtstag*, Happy Birthday Lisle. BMWs and Mercedes lined the driveway and were parked along the street. The evidence of a large family gathering tempted Meinhardt to ask the taxi to turn around.

He tipped the driver generously, hoping it might bring him good luck.

He rang the door chimes twice before someone answered. The noise of children shrieking and grownups yelling at them to stop running assaulted his ears. He inhaled the aroma of fresh-baked cake and felt a blast of warm air drive away the December chill. Then everything but his sense of sight failed. Standing in front of Meinhardt was his Oma. It hadn't occurred to him that his sister Ada would be the same age his grandmother was when he left Berlin.

A small girl ran from the living room and flung her arms around Ada's knees. "I love you, Oma!" She peeked around Ada's skirt and asked Meinhardt, "Did you bring me a present?"

"I didn't know it was your birthday, Lisle. I will send you a gift tomorrow."

She scampered away, knocking into a large, silver-haired man who put his hands firmly on the child's shoulders to slow her down.

"Who's there?" the man called to Ada.

"Our brother," she answered.

"*Vertuschen!* Do you want the others to hear? I told you not to write him back."

"I didn't." Ada wrung her hands.

"Then why is he here?" Karl stood with legs spread and arms akimbo to block the view between the hallway and the rooms beyond.

Meinhardt repeated what he'd said in the letter. He'd come from America to visit his – their – grandmother's grave in Dornum and hoped to meet the brother and sister he never knew.

"We were never told of a brother." Karl's voice was cold and suspicious. "If you're looking for money ..."

Meinhardt assured him he wasn't. He should have brought one of his catalogs to prove he too was a successful businessman. Germans liked documentation.

"Dornum?" Ada's brow wrinkled. "Our mother told us our grandmother was buried in Berlin. She died before we were born. Our parents moved to Bonn not long afterwards."

His Oma had told Meinhardt that when others asked where his parents were, he should say they were dead. Meanwhile, her daughter was telling her children that their grandmother was no longer alive. They'd killed each other with silence. His was not a family of reconciliation.

When Meinhardt told his siblings when and where Gretel had died, Ada turned pale and sat on an ornately carved oak bench beside the door. He apologized for having upset her.

"I wish I'd known her," Ada said. "I try so hard to be a good grandmother, not having had one myself." She peered around Karl's impassive body to the lively party in the next room.

"We don't need to hear of family members long dead, or those we never knew were alive. It will only make the others worry that they carry a genetic taint." Karl moved to open the door.

Meinhardt asked if there were any other midgets in the family. Ada shook her head no.

A small boy scooted into the hallway and tugged Meinhardt's sleeve. "We need another soldier," he said. "Come play!"

"The man is leaving. He came to the wrong house." Karl turned the child around.

"He must have a piece of birthday cake before he goes." Ada stood up.

"Ada!" Karl scowled at his sister.

"I will stay with him in the hallway while he eats it," she said softly. A moment later she handed Meinhardt a china plate, and motioned him to sit beside her on the bench.

He took a bite of *Bienenstich*, the bee sting cake his Oma used to make.

"Tell me about her." Ada turned her back on Karl and watched Meinhardt eat.

He told her about their grandmother's hair flying in the wind as she chased a football with him in the park on Sunday afternoons, and how cloth became magical in her hands.

"I always wondered where my interest in sewing came from. My, I mean our, mother wasn't domestic, save for baking. This cake recipe she taught me must have come from Gretel."

"Yours is as good as hers." Meinhardt scraped up the last bit of honey with his fork. "You look just like her. Know yourself and you will know her after all."

He stood up. It would have been polite to carry the empty plate to the kitchen but Karl blocked his path. Ada took the plate and patted his hand. "I was widowed two years ago. My brother does his best to protect me and our families. Don't judge him harshly. He means well."

"Ada, enough. Lisle is waiting for you so she can open her presents."

"What shall I send her?" Meinhardt asked his sister.

"Perhaps a little embroidery ..."

"Nothing." Karl moved again toward the entryway.

Ada closed her mouth. Karl closed the door swiftly and firmly behind Meinhardt.

He told the taxi driver to take him to Der Rodderberg, a volcano south of Bonn that last erupted 250,000 years ago. Now it was only a small hill with a shallow crater filled with dust and soil. Meinhardt tried to feel angry --- at his parents for abandoning him, at Karl for throwing him out, even at Ada for not standing up to her brother. He felt only mild disappointment. His anger was as extinct as the volcano. It was like closing the script on a role he was never meant to play.

Chapter 49

Rachel Stein, Sadie's granddaughter, was short and round, with wiry gray curls and a wide smile. She clasped Meinhardt to her bosom, stood back to look at him, and hugged him again. His fears of being reprimanded like a naughty child evaporated instantly. When Rachel proclaimed, "It's about time!" it wasn't intended to make him feel guilty. She was just happy they were finally meeting. He felt more connected to his grandmother through her than he had with his siblings.

Rachel settled them both on the couch with footstools, and sank back into the cushions. "It's good to be home. Everyone in London was in mourning over John Lennon's death. People sobbed in the streets and handed out flowers in the tube stations. So much for British reserve."

Meinhardt remembered the city as cold and bleak at this time of year and tried to picture it full of hot tears and foliage. His mind drew a blank.

"Usually a hugger like me feels like an outsider there," Rachel continued, "but on this trip, I was the outsider for not beating my chest and rending my clothes." She repeated how glad she was to be home, where she belonged.

Meinhardt looked at a silver menorah on the mantel. "Aren't you an outsider, living in Dornum? There's no Jewish community to speak of, save one or two old souls."

Rachel confirmed that few Jews had returned after the war. Survivors emigrated to Israel or the United States. Sadie came back because her father's family, which was Catholic, still lived here. "Before the war, my grandmother practiced both religions, but afterwards she identified solely as a Jew. That's how it's been ever since in our family, including my own grandchildren."

"My Oma moved back during the war, yours returned after it ended. Rekindling their childhood friendship must have been bittersweet."

"They both drew solace from their respective faiths. It was central to who they were."

Meinhardt was surprised. His Oma had never been particularly religious when she was raising him, and certainly not in the years before he left home.

"Your grandmother returned to her Lutheran faith when she returned to Dornum. Living in Berlin under the Nazis disillusioned her, but being here and doing God's work brought her back to the church stronger than when she'd left it."

Sadie and Inge had also mentioned Gretel's return to her faith, but Rachel was the first to say how important it had become to her. He asked, "Doesn't every observant person do God's work or did my Oma do something special?"

"You don't know?"

Meinhardt shook his head. Now it was Rachel's turn to be surprised. She brought them each an extra cushion, and took a deep breath. "When my Bubbe Sadie prayed, she would ask, 'So God, what's the story?' We're all looking for the story. Here's your Oma Gretel's."

Rachel told Meinhardt how Gretel had helped save Dornum's Jews. She and other sympathetic gentiles hid Jewish families in their homes and snuck them aboard private fishing boats, which traveled through the night to Denmark. From there, hundreds of small boats took them and other Jews to nearby Sweden, a neutral country. Some members of the underground network forged papers. Gretel used her skills as a seamstress to disguise humble Jews as prosperous Christians. With her expensive fabrics from Berlin, she trimmed their old coats and repaired frayed hems. Inside the

269

linings, she stitched the escape routes that took them from one safe house to another on their silent journey to the harbor. She also sewed false pockets to hide their family treasures — not jewels, which few owned, but keepsakes such as photos, mezuzzahs, and Sabbath candlesticks.

Rachel brought out a dark woolen coat with a narrow fur collar and gold cuffs. "I'd model it, but I was much thinner when I was girl." Pinned to the underside of the lapel was a dried and pressed daffodil. She explained. In silent sympathy, a few brave Germans wore yellow flowers, the same color as the Stars of David that Jews were forced to sew on their sleeves. Gretel couldn't wear one in public for fear of attracting attention to her work, so she hid a tiny flower in each coat as a blessing. Finally, Rachel undid a piece of tissue paper and handed Meinhardt a shimmering green and gold paisley scarf. "Gretel also made us each a silk muffler to put over our noses because the fish smell was so strong when we crouched down in the boats."

Meinhardt looked at the intricate stitching, stroked the scarf, and inhaled deeply. "To this day, you must hate the smell of fish."

"No. To Dornum's Jews, fish is the smell of freedom. The North Sea was our Red Sea and Gretel was our Miriam. Like Moses's sister, her courage and love saved our people."

Sadie had written Meinhardt after his grandmother's funeral that the only thing that could induce Jews to creep back to Dornum was their love and gratitude toward her. They'd whispered among themselves about how Gretel helped them, and the pastor said her good deeds earned her a place of honor among Jews in this life and among Lutherans in the eternal one. Now Sadie's words, which he'd taken for general praise of his Oma's goodness, took on a specific meaning.

"Inge told me you light candles on her

yahrzeit."

"We also put stones on her grave. Flowers are for life, they wither and die. Jews use stones because they represent permanence. The souls of the deceased live within us forever."

For years after sailing to America, Meinhardt felt guilty about leaving his Oma alone. He knew now that she wasn't alone. Her life in Dornum was filled with love for and from the people she helped. He was absolved of his guilt, but sadness, even resentment, took its place. Meinhardt had always been secure in the belief that he alone was the center of his grandmother's world. He worried that his leaving had deprived her of a reason to work, cook, and awaken each day, but in fact, he was not irreplaceable. He thought he'd abandoned her; now he felt abandoned.

Rachel let Meinhardt absorb the story while she went to fetch tea and cookies. She apologized that they weren't homemade since she'd just gotten back, but told him that a couple of years after the war, when food was no longer as scarce, their grandmothers had traded cookie recipes. Sadie claimed that baking redeemed the oven from being a chamber of death. "I loved being in the kitchen with them. The only thing warmer than the oven was their friendship."

Meinhardt waited for another wave of jealousy to rise in his throat. None came, only a swell of gratitude for the woman who'd been like a sister to his Oma. Rachel felt like his cousin.

"Friday night, when I was in London, I went to Shabbos services and heard this midrash. A story is told of two men, a rabbi and a tailor, who befriended each other during the Shoah. One day the SS officers made them dig a large pit. They knew the plan was to line them up in front of the pit and shoot them. The rabbi suggested that he and the tailor join hands, run, and jump over the pit to safety. The

271

tailor hesitated. 'If we don't try,' the rabbi urged, 'we will surely die. What have we got to lose?' And so the men ran, hand in hand, and jumped to safety. When the rabbi asked the tailor how he made it, the tailor said, 'I thought about what God did for my ancestors in times of slavery and inquisitions. I put my body in God's hands and trusted that God would see us through. How did you make it?' 'My friend," the rabbi answered, 'I put my trust in you.'"

Meinhardt wondered what opportunities for freedom he'd lost by not putting more faith and trust in others. What if he'd accepted Rodge's invitation to go to the movies? Why had he again let his friendship with Margaret lapse? Jessie had died five years ago, and Meinhardt didn't call Charles as often as he should because he assumed his life was wrapped up with Robert and Bella. The midrash, and the story of Gretel and Sadie, told him that people needed friends too.

"Germans may never understand where they failed in their moral obligation," Rachel said. "Many will deny knowledge of the Holocaust; others will say they were not responsible. Some, like Gretel, acted out of love. Others did the right thing out of a sense of duty."

"Perhaps my grandmother's love for yours sparked a sense of duty to help those like her."

"Something we take on as an obligation can become an act of love. Like prayer. I used to make myself pray because I thought it was good for me. Now I look forward to the daily ritual because it comforts and inspires me. What I once forced myself to do is now a free choice."

Before Meinhardt left, Rachel gave him a suitcase that held a photo album and the weekly letters he'd written his Oma from age 20 to 36. There were over 800, wrapped in an embroidered cloth. "I considered the letters private, but I hope you don't mind that I looked at the pictures."

He himself was curious to see what he'd looked like as a child and as a young man.

"You were quite handsome," Rachel teased. "You're still good-looking. Sixty-five isn't too old for romance." She said her children were urging her to date again, since it was three years since her husband had died. The problem was finding someone Jewish who lived nearby.

Meinhardt thanked her for keeping the pictures and letters for so many years. He should have returned sooner to claim them.

"You came when you were ready. If you're still in town next Friday, come for Shabbos dinner and meet my family. I promise to remember more stories and tell you another midrash."

Meinhardt would be gone; he was leaving in two days. "You've given me enough stories to ponder. Now it's time for me to read these old letters and write my own midrash."

Chapter 50

Meinhardt carried the suitcase to his third floor room. The old hotel had never installed elevators. By the time he hoisted himself up the last flight, he was breathing heavily. This was not what the doctor had in mind when he'd told him to replace desk work with light exercise. If Meinhardt wanted to avoid a pacemaker, he had better take more brisk walks and eat fewer Baby Ruth Bars after all.

Silk ribbons were wrapped around the letters, one bundle for each of the seventeen years between his leaving and his Oma dying. The last bundle was thinner than the others, since Gretel had died in the fall. Meinhardt read, beginning with his year in London.

Dearest Oma,

Tonight there was a scuffle at the pub. Some veterans, not our regulars, called the young men chicken for not volunteering against the Gerries. The lads said if there was another fight, they didn't plan on getting as messed up as the shell-shocked loonies from the Great War. An old guy brandished a Luger. The publican pleaded for everyone to calm down. I hid behind the bar.

Rodge arrived and asked what the shouting was about. The vets were speechless. They'd never seen one of their own like him. The lads, who see Rodge as a father, said the vets were talking as if Great Britain was already at war. Rodge faced his compatriots. "It's the young men who risk their lives. They're a brave lot and will honor our country if called, but I hope to God they're not." Then, to make peace, he told the barman to order a round on him. Of course, Rodge never paid a tab in his life, but the publican was happy to oblige. The lads hoisted Rodge up on the piano stool and soon young and old were singing like fine old pals. I got the week's best tips.

I wish I were as brave as Rodge, but I haven't been battle-tested enough to earn that kind of respect. You say I showed courage by leaving, but sometimes I think going was a retreat. Still, the gentlemen at the Arts Club and my landlady test my dignity every day. Perhaps I'll become more courageous with time but never, I fear, with the wit and good cheer of a man like Rodge.

Your loving Enkel,
Meinhardt

It was surprising how many letters that year mentioned Rodge. Meinhardt had tried to protect his independence by remaining distant outside the pub. He'd been fooling himself. Looking back at his words proved how much he'd counted on Rodge to restore his spirits with the perfect quip.

"Today I was so *traurig* selling ruffled blouses at Gertie's Dress Emporium," he'd written midyear, "that I was ready to try my luck again on Savile Row. Rodge saved me from humiliation by warning, 'Rowing upstream won't get you the prize. It's already been carried off.' He said I'd find good prizes downstream if I let myself float along and look for them."

To this day, he quoted Rodge's lines and felt a gratitude he hadn't acknowledged when his friend was alive. He read the next year's letters that began by describing how Harpo's kindness had enabled him to earn more as a busker. Months later, he was furious when Harpo volunteered his name to the midget troupe, but now he questioned if he'd been too harsh. His funny friend, a descendent of a once-honored Dornum family, had only meant to help.

The following year, Meinhardt had rejected Margaret's offer to put in a good word during his tryout for the role of coroner. He winced when he read, "I showed her I didn't need anyone's assistance. I got the part on my own!" Not a single letter credited her helpful advice when he'd prepared to audition in the first place. Even Charles, he now realized, by backing off Meinhardt's favorite street corners, steering clear of the part he was interested in, and even choosing not to pursue Hazel when he sensed his interest, had always put Meinhardt's needs above his own.

Friends had given him more than he appreciated. How much had he given back? Pete, the boy who'd written after Rodge died, said Rodge was grateful Meinhardt never turned his back on his old pal when he got rich. Rodge felt proud to advise and cheer his famous friend decades into their relationship. Leave it to Rodge to thank Meinhardt for the opportunity to serve him.

Reading through the next ten years, Meinhardt looked for signs he'd done enough to help others. He measured himself against friends with his limitations or worse. In addition to Rodge, there was Margaret, saddled with spinsterish looks in an industry that valued beauty. She taught Sunday school and raised a son devoted to eradicating poverty. Charles, stuck with being even shorter than Meinhardt, also produced two admirable children. Robert overcame shame, and Bella rose above her own handicap, to inspire those who were less fortunate.

"Dearest Oma," he'd written, traveling home from Detroit. "I've seen American injustice toward minorities and women nearly as bad as any directed at my kind. When I open my business, *Ich schwöre* I'll go out of my way to hire those others reject." In keeping this pledge, he'd honored his Oma's legacy, but he failed to do more on a personal level. Had he extended to Hazel a tiny fraction of the care Gretel had given to her neighbors in Dornum, he might have rescued her too. He wondered if Joey was still alive and if it was it too late to save her now.

Rachel had debated whether duty or love came first. If Meinhardt forced himself to help others out of obligation, could he eventually be someone who acted with kindness by choice?

Gray daylight seeped under and around the brocade curtains when Meinhardt held the last letter. Gretel had died before it arrived, so Sadie had put it, unopened, at the end of that year's bundle. He washed his hands, slit the envelope with a nail file, and read the words his Oma never saw.

". . . wheat, barley, and sugar beets are being brought in from the fields around Dornum. Alas, here in California, the fruits of my labor are still not yielding a harvest. No banker wants to hear the

276

business ideas of a midget. After a day selling clothes to self-satisfied customers, I'm ready to give up. I wish you could mail me the aroma of your spice cake to revive my spirits."

Rachel had said that when Jews were ready to abandon hope, Gretel's determination made them brave. In the same way, Meinhardt had turned to her to ward off despair. He'd never thought that when he poured out his doubts, it might upset her. Was that selfish of him? Or was he merely allowing his Oma to be the healing source of strength that everyone cherished?

". . . invited me to Detroit for Thanksgiving. They are good parents. Charles is raising Bella to believe that being a midget needn't hold her back, just like you told me. I have decided not to visit them, however, as it will only make me sadder. Having a family isn't for me, yet I regret not passing along the goodness you showed. Perhaps I'd be less frustrated about work if I were busy taking care of someone else. Then again, the responsibility might make me worry more. Ach, I am only 37 and talking like an old man. *Was für ein Unsinn!*"

Meinhardt never had a chance to write about Celia, who he met three years after his Oma died. He'd never written or talked with his grandmother about love at all. She rarely mentioned her own husband, who died young, and Meinhardt was abandoned by his parents long before he could witness whatever love existed in their marriage. Did Gretel hope he would meet someone to share his life with, or did she fear love was unattainable and he'd only be hurt trying to find it?

Reading the letters brought forth as many memories about the decades since his Oma's death as they did about those when she was alive. Remembering helped him understand what was happening at the time, but his reactions had shifted with the years. His anger had lessened, his regrets increased. As his insights changed, so did his memories. Rodge was more nurturing, Harpo kinder, Charles more noble, and Hazel less confident than he perceived on the set of *Oz*. Celia was no longer so untrustworthy. Thinking that her illness destined her to a life without love and family, she'd done what she needed to succeed in her work. Just like he had.

Along with the past, Meinhardt churned over the future. If he could change what was to admit his shortcomings, could he revise what lay ahead? Forgiving Celia might render yesterday less painful and store more good times for tomorrow. Accepting his need to give could open the door to letting her back in his life. At 65, it was now okay for him to sound like an old man, taking stock of the years he had left and honoring his Oma's legacy in his choices going forward.

The sea below the cemetery was calm. Sun sliced through the early morning clouds and warmed Meinhardt's fingers. Sitting beside his grandmother's grave, he wrote to her on hotel stationery.

Dearest Oma,

This letter will catch you up on my life. You used to love hearing about famous people, so I will tell you about the others I met, good and bad. Jenny Grossinger was as kindhearted as you, and as great a cook. Unlike what most people fear, the more she gave away, the more she became herself. Andy Warhol was a shrewd artist who proved the Wizard's dictum that a brain is a very mediocre commodity. He cast me in a movie so boring that I never even watched it. I also met the drummer of the most famous band in history. Its leader was killed last week. I want to reach out to the drummer but I don't know if he'll welcome my condolences. Millions of fans are writing him, so what does my note matter? And yet, it would make a difference to me to send it.

I finally started a clothing business. People admire my success, but is it enough to honor your legacy? Sadie's granddaughter Rachel said you earned both respect and love. The Wizard claims a heart is not judged by how much you love, but by how much you are loved by others.

When I heard how you saved Dornum's Jews, I'm ashamed to say I was jealous that your life no longer revolved around me. Now I see that after getting me out, you helped others escape the Nazis too. You honored *my* memory by expanding rather than replacing your love for me.

Once I thought being a midget gave me three choices: denial, acceptance, and embrace. I trapped myself in the very identity that I sought to flee. Those were my options as a midget, but I can simply be a man. I don't have to embrace a cause, I can simply embrace the people I love.

Recently I had a health scare. My doctor told me to slow down at work. At the same time, the market is changing and my business is under threat. I read that after a crisis, we either change or go back to being what we were, only more so. I must decide what direction to go. I can try to mentor an "heir," but then I must trust that person's integrity and capability. The Cowardly Lion was so lacking in courage that he scared himself. Perhaps courage is allowing others to be brave.

"There's no place like home" is the famous last line from *The Wizard of Oz*. I understand it differently now. Going home doesn't mean returning to the security of before. The home you made gave me the courage leave it. When you returned to Dornum, your life took a new direction. Soon I will go back to California, to my home for one. I must decide if there is room for more.

Your loving Enkel,
Meinhardt

The wind had picked up again, but now it was blowing toward the west. The first time Meinhardt had traveled in that direction, he was a small man crossing a huge ocean with big dreams. This time his dreams were smaller. Perhaps he would grow into them.

Acknowledgments

A Brain. A Heart. The Nerve. originated with a short story, "The Munchkins at Grossinger's," in which I envisioned a little people's twenty-fifth cast reunion in the Catskills. When, a few years later, I was encouraged to write a novel, the story's protagonist, Meinhardt Raabe, beckoned. Hence, this fictional biography was born. And I do mean fictional. The only aspects of his life that are true are his name, year of birth, and movie role. The same holds for the book's other historical characters. Names, dates, and roles are "real," the rest is pure invention.

My first thank you goes to Nelson Lowhim and Alternative Book Press for appreciating the novel's quirkiness and recognizing the genuine cry for justice beneath imaginary encounters. We share a conviction that unconventional tales can reveal conventional and universal truths.

I'm indebted to my critique groups from whom I continually learn the art of storytelling and the craft of converting a narrative jewel into a book-length saga. My Saturday writers group provided feedback on the catalyst short story and the novel's original drafts. Special thanks to members Brandon Marshall, Lawrence Coates, Lori Eaton, Amy Gustine, Marni Hoffman, Keith Hood, Danielle Lavaque-Manti, Paul Many, Cathy Mellett, Polly Rosenwaike, Deepak Singh, and Sonja Srinivasan. My Sunday writers group entered the picture after the book was done, but the lessons they imparted allowed me to kill my darlings during the development edits once it was accepted for publication. For their unflagging encouragement and advice, I thank Janet Gilsdorf, Marty Calvert, Danielle Lavaque-Manti (again), Cynthia Jalynski, and Jane Johnson.

I've also had the good fortune to attend story- and novel-writing workshops with Dan

Mueller, Margo Rabb, and Antonya Nelson. From them I learned, respectively, how to find the sweet spot between what an author and reader each bring to the literary effort, why to put conflict (inner or outer) on every page, and how to use the whole stage — dancing forward, gliding backward, and sometimes lingering in place. Thus are the mind's rhythms transferred to the page.

Every writer needs a guaranteed audience, regardless of whether the work is published. For that reassurance I thank Gerald Gardner, Lynn Liben, Benedette Palazzola, Jennifer Burd, Sue Terdan, and the late Terry Alexander, among others. I'm further blessed with supportive relatives, notably my brother Joel Savishinsky and cousins Pam Alson and Joy Bader. My son-in-law Milton Dixon lends an interested ear when I wax enthusiastic about the latest gem of history, science, or human behavior that I've uncovered while researching my stories and books. Daily play dates with my grandsons, Oscar and Emmett Dixon-Epstein, always include time to read books. Every writer also needs a guarantee that the next generation will boast readers too.

Like generations of fans, I have always been fascinated by *The Wizard of Oz*. Rebecca Epstein, my daughter, was nicknamed The Munchkin as an infant. I decorated her first birthday cake with the words "The Munchkin is #1." She is still, and always will be, #1 in my book. Her brain is sharp, her heart is big, and she has more nerve than I do. She's a parent's heart's desire.

These acknowledgments wouldn't be complete without kudos to L. Frank Baum and the cast, crew, and creative team that gave us the Land of Oz and a host of memorable characters.

Finally, my appreciation and admiration go out to all the little people in this world. Like Meinhardt, they seek the rights and respect accorded others, regardless of size. Today they have

283

to fight for it. Tomorrow I hope it's a given. Truth, as well as fantasy, can be an inspiration.

Ann S. Epstein

June 2018